Ryan Oliver Brandt

October Sign

ISBN: 978-1-68510-178-7 (trade paper)
ISBN: 978-1-68510-179-4 (ebook: ePub)
The Library of Congress Catalog Number has been applied for.

First printing edition: March 27, 2026
Published by JournalStone Publishing in the United States of America.
Cover Design: Alyssa Brandt
Edited by Sean Leonard
Proofreading and Cover/Interior Layout by Scarlett R. Algee

JournalStone Publishing
1400 North Wood Rd.
Murphysboro, IL 62966

JournalStone books may be ordered through booksellers or by contacting:

JournalStone | www.journalstone.com

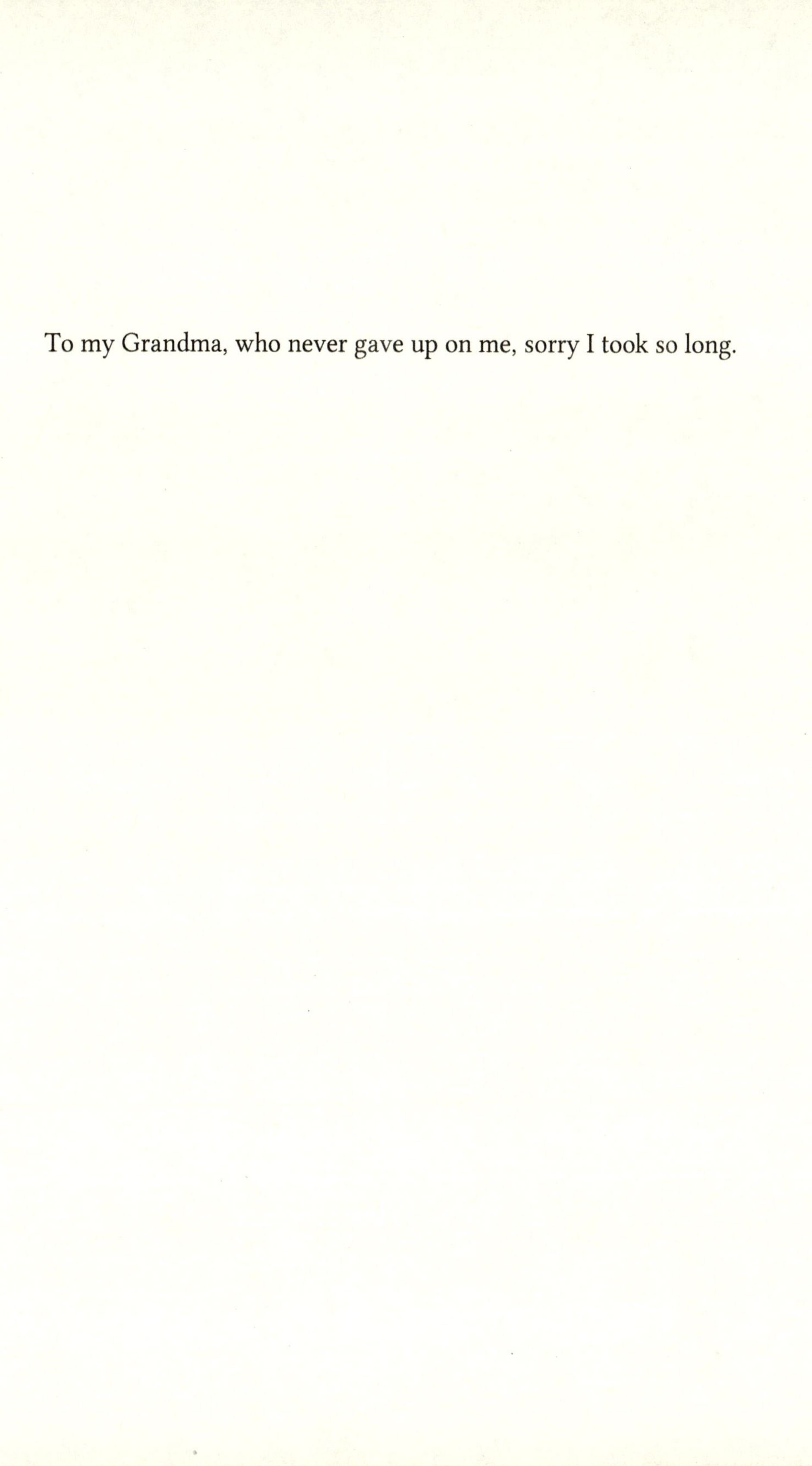

To my Grandma, who never gave up on me, sorry I took so long.

OCTOBER SIGN '22

Chapter 1

"Inside my mind is a black place. Not a dark place. It's like a script covered in marker. A second skin covering an eye lens." The words fell from Conan's mouth like an object slipping out of shaking hands. A growing heat behind his closed eyes simmered.

After demanding to stay in school, he left the principal's office and drifted like a ghost to his spot at the outdoor lunch table. Brandi-Lynn had her head resting on his shoulder. She sat up and, with heavily mascaraed eyes, glanced down at his dingy lyric book.

"New song idea?" she asked.

"What're you talking about?" Conan grunted, biting the inside of his cheek.

"Ew. You're being extra creepy today."

Brandi pushed herself away from him, glaring down at the mess of scribbles that graffitied every inch of his wide-ruled notebook.

"Do you want to talk about something?"

Her words were too distant. He instead lost himself in the portal of his written musings. He tried to replay drafting the words, to make sense of scrunched together syllables that swelled from his pages, ebbing and flowing, on tempo with the volume of Peralta High School students laughing, screaming, droning.

I think I'm going to die soon, the last line read.

He shut his notebook.

A visiting girl from Preston High Song Club approached from across the busy quad. She wore her mandatory uniform of skirt, tie, and coat. Her skin was pale as a phantom's; her hair, dusty black, and her eyes, deep-sea cobalt.

Brandi sat up, rigid at his side, glancing from him to this complete stranger.

Jackie stirred on the bench across from them and clattered his skateboard on the ground. He flipped his maroon baseball cap backward, leaning toward the opposing song girl.

The ghost stood before Conan and placed her hand over her heart.

"Do you remember me?" she asked.

Conan's eyes stayed glued to her lips. A lump grew in his throat. Somehow, gazing at her cooled his aching retinas. Had he fallen in love? No, more like her existence made nothing cruel in the world matter.

"No," he said with a stiff shake of his head.

"And where would he know you from?" Brandi asked, forcing a laugh.

"Nowhere," the dark-haired girl said and shook her head. "It doesn't matter."

She crawls beneath my eyes, a pulse, like rain.

More words from a song he couldn't remember writing. Why couldn't he? They were in his lyric book. He clenched his fist as a sharp pain settled in the center of his skull. It was like a shovel stabbing into his brain, trying to dig up something that wasn't there.

"I'm sorry about your father," she said, then turned away and disappeared into the crowd.

"What's your deal?" Brandi shoved him. "Stop staring. You shoulda just taken a picture. Dickhead."

"I didn't tell anyone." He stood so quickly that a spell of dizziness hit him. "Where'd she go?"

"What? Gonna go chase her?" Brandi asked, rolling her eyes.

"Yes."

"If you do, I'm not driving you home, Conan. I'm serious. You're acting like an asshole, and it's not funny."

"Fine," he whispered.

"You're seriously doing this in a breakup sort of way right now," Brandi said, raising her voice loud enough to gather unwanted attention.

"Fine!" Conan threw his hands in the air and shouted. "It's over, done. Is that what you wanted to hear?"

Brandi's full lips opened and her eyes turned glassy.

"Daaaaaaaaaammn!" someone shouted as Conan walked away.

"Not cool, bro," Jackie said, hurrying to his side. "What the hell was that about, dude?"

"She knows my dad died. I didn't tell anyone."

"Shit, dude. Wait, today? And you still came to school? Totally brutal."

"I know I shouldn't have. My head's killing me. It's like *déjà vu*, but not. I'm sorry. I just— That girl, I have to find her."

"I'm the one who's sorry, man. Seriously? Today? That's—that's fucked up."

"I'm— Yeah. Everything's like being flipped on its head."

"You're going through it, man. Whatever, let's find this chick. Song girls were supposed to stay in the auditorium, right?"

Dad, you're trying to reach me, aren't you? That's what this is, right? Don't worry. I'll figure this out.

"God dammit," Conan barked and kicked the closest trash can. It fell over and the odor of stagnant pizza and hot dogs made him gag. "I need a cigarette," he said, and cleared his throat.

"Me too." Jackie shrugged. "Well, which is it?"

Conan paused and, just like his father had taught him, gazed upward and closed his eyes. He didn't have time to count backward from a hundred. So he started at ten.

Three...

Two...

One...

"Auditorium," he said. "I have to talk to her, Jack. It's killing me. I have to."

"All right, man, all right. Let's go."

As they walked through the hallway, a pair of Preston song girls walked directly opposite them. Stranger than that was that they both shared the pale skin and cobalt eyes of the ghost he was chasing.

"I'm always impressed with the minor talent found in these public schools," the slender one with a Caesar haircut said. "Why they send us on these trips is beyond me. They're so hopelessly novice."

"Seriously, what a shithole," the thicker girl with calico, black, blonde, and red hair replied. "I've only seen, like, maybe two hot guys all day," she said in passing, and winked at Jackie.

Jackie grinned.

"Hey, do you—"

Conan placed a stiff hand on Jackie's shoulder and squeezed.

Insatiable mouth of hell

Swarm of demon entities

They're haunting. They haunt me.

"What's that about?" Jackie asked.

"They gave me bad vibes," Conan said, and turned down the hallway.

She was waiting for him, leaning against the pale-green wall and gazing at him. As she approached, a heartache radiated in Conan's chest and sank into his stomach. He couldn't find his words and lost himself in the cold metal of her eyes.

"Did you say anything to my sisters?" she asked, hiding her hands behind her back.

Conan gave his head a stiff shake.

"I've seen you just once, and it's worse than an addiction. I had to find you."

She smiled and tucked a strand of hair behind her ear.

"I'm sorry, Conan. It's my fault."

"Something about being with you, if I can be?" Jackie gave him a light elbow in the ribs, but the pain didn't affect his lovesickness. "It's strange, maybe a little selfish, but if we can be together, I'll never be sad again."

She nodded, sending fire into his cheeks and tasteless sand to the back of his throat.

"I wish that were true, but no matter what I do, what I try, I'm the one who needs you."

I was a shadow walking beside you

A broken clock shuddering.

The more he tried to remember writing these lyrics, the sicker he became. The heartache churning his stomach twisted into nausea.

It doesn't matter, it's true magic. It has to be you, Dad. Right? It has to be you from the afterlife. I won't screw it up.

"I'll do anything you say."

"Shit, dude, I gotta grow a thin-ass mustache and straighten my hair or something. You're making this look too easy."

"Not now, Jackie," he said, but laughed. "I can't put it together. None of this. These feelings, you know my name and I can't remember yours at all. But it's like we've been together for a long time, and you need help. I know you need help. I know that, and I'd fight a T-Rex with my bare hands for you. I know that and I know I love you, and that you love me, and—"

And the avalanche rolls beneath an iceberg.

"My name is Snow," she said. "And you're right. However, don't think too much about it now. It'll make itself clear in time."

"Snow," Conan repeated. Her name washed the sand from his throat, like fresh water after a bender.

Crystalline tears frozen

Descending feathers atop an ebony coffin.

"Man," Jackie said, rubbing his forehead. "My head hurts. This is freaky. It's like, familiar? Dude, Rufus is gonna trip out when we tell him. He's gonna have, like, six conspiracies locked and loaded."

"At least he'll listen," Conan said, and glanced at his phone. He had missed three calls from Brandi, and it looked like six minutes before lunch ended.

"Wait, you said that I was right? Does that mean I'm gonna have to fight a T-Rex with my bare hands?"

Snow covered her mouth with her hand and snickered.

"Something like that."

"In that case," Conan said, "we should ditch, like, now."

Jackie grimaced at his phone and swiped *ignore* on a call from Brandi. "Yeah, totally. You know I'm always down. Where to?"

When Snow said nothing, Conan crossed his arms.

"Let's go see what Rufus thinks. He'll at least make something up."

"Early band practice? I'm game," Jackie said, grinning ear-to-ear.

***

The musky sweetness of fallen leaves filled the neighborhood roads. They shined golden atop the blacktop, illuminated by a low-hanging October sun. Intruding thoughts of Snow being taken away had Conan on his toes, rubbing the back of his neck and gazing over his shoulder. They avoided the main street just in case they were unlucky enough to cross a police officer or a concerned parent.

If anything happens to her, you have no one to blame but yourself. You can't screw this up.

Although he'd switched his phone over to silent, Brandi still called an indiscernible amount. He stared at the screen and rolled his shoulders. As soon as he put his phone away, Jackie's vibrated.

"Go ahead, answer it," Snow said, letting her gaze wander.

"I don't think that's a good idea." Jackie chuckled, followed only by the sound of dead leaves crunching beneath their feet.

"She's just upset," Conan said, shoving his hands in his jeans' tight pockets.

"Of course she is," Snow said, and kicked a patch of leaves up into the air. "Answer it. She might say something important."

Conan shrugged half-heartedly and Jackie swiped the answer button.

"Hey."

"What were you two idiots thinking?" Jackie's phone wasn't on speaker, but Brandi's static voice came through clear enough. *"They shut the entire school down to look for that girl you clowns ran off with. You're lucky I didn't snitch, but I should. Tell Conan that I fucking should."*

"He, uh, *yeah,* he caught it."

"Good, and I hope she can hear me too. Hear me when I say he's a total piece of shit."

"Yup, loud and clear."

"You guys fucked up. That girl's like royalty over at Preston. You idiots have to come clean. She needs to call her parents. I don't know what that heartless piece of shit is thinking. Rumors are already going around school. They're saying she disappeared like Kylie. Peralta High is gonna be so screwed over by this. Put Conan on."

Jackie pinched the skin on his throat. Conan took the phone from his clammy hand.

"Yeah."

"After everything I've done for you, every fucking little thing I did for you, I should want you dead. One more chance, Conan. I love you, and you better fucking love me too. I'll help you get out of this if you say it. Okay?" Her voice cracked.

"Sorry," he said, gazing at his sneakers.

Click! He hung up.

"That's fucked up," Jackie said.

"It's whatever," Conan replied, a scratch swelling in the back of his throat.

"What she said about Kylie? Janna last year too. She's got a point. We should tell somebody, I dunno, so it doesn't mess with any missing persons' police stuff?"

They both turned to Snow. She'd been holding a golden sycamore leaf up to the sun.

"None of that matters really. We can keep it a secret, or tell whoever you want. Something really big is going to happen in a few days. I'm sure you can remember it if you try. Let's ignore it today though. Really, it doesn't matter." She let the leaf sail down to the blacktop. "Honestly, I think nothing we do matters. There are lots of ways to get us there and I think it all ends the same."

"Bro, she's right. This atmosphere is totally serious." Jackie rubbed his temples. "I'm standing right here, but it feels like I'm falling. What's going on?"

"In the coming days," Snow laughed, "it gets worse."

Conan gritted his teeth.

"You're wrong," he said, and gripped Snow's soft hand in his. "I don't care what it costs or what I have to do. I want to spend every moment of every day I can with you. This is the first time in my life I've felt this way. Whatever is coming, whatever I have to face, I'll do it. I promise."

"Your track record with soulmates is kinda skewed, bro."

"Shut up, Jackie," Conan snapped.

"He's right," Snow said, a somber frown creasing her features. "Peel back my deepest scar, and see that without you, I am not alive."

She squeezed his hand harder, and he grew lightheaded. What she had said were words torn right from his lyric book.

"Never give up. Rufus taught me that, and he'll come up with a plan for us. Come on, we're almost there."

Conan tugged her along until she picked up speed. Their footsteps crunched in the leaves and echoed down the empty streets.

Rufus's venue wasn't some hipster masterpiece. Club Depression was a theater that could hold a few hundred kids. Rufus had spent four years renovating, and Cassandra, the booking lady, loved him for it. For good reason too; some big-time acts had come through town because of him. That, and if their band landed this major contract, then she'd be on the map. Just thinking about it pricked Conan's skin with goosebumps.

Jackie shot up the steps two at a time, fearless, despite almost breaking his neck gapping them with his skateboard earlier that year. Snow pulled Conan aside and a fresh wave of dizziness washed over him as he lost himself in her stare.

"There's something I have to tell you," she said. "Anyone and everyone who gets involved, their lives will be endangered, but it's most important that I do not go back to my mothers. That would put *everyone* at risk."

I grieve you, though you're at my side.

If I had wings, they'd be yours to fly on.

"All right," Conan said, and brushed a lock of her hair behind her ear. He kissed her. She wrapped her hand around his neck and kissed him deeper. She tasted like honey and lilies, a taste he could see himself becoming dependent on.

"Today," she breathed into him, "we don't have to worry. Come on."

Stepping into the club was like walking onto a hardwood basketball court. The floors were so polished, their sneakers squeaked, and as Jackie stomped to its center, the acoustics boomed like bass drums.

The aroma of grilled meat leaked inside from the back patio. Rufus stood on the porch wearing a black apron, his bleached mohawk smashed down and his onyx skin glistening with sweat.

"Took your asses long enough," he said with half a glance backward. "Did you idiots walk or something?"

Rufus turned completely around and raised an eyebrow at Conan, then glared down at his and Snow's clasped hands.

"Oh, no shit, you did? *Haaa.*" He put his hands on his hips and his spatula dripped red juices onto the concrete below. "Nah, no way you're that stupid."

"What's with the spread?"

"Young Jack shot me a text and told me about your pops and you needing to ditch school to have some fun. No clue it was supposed to be a code for man-whoring though."

Conan met Rufus's sober eyes and didn't look away.

"I, *uh,* I wasn't kidding," Jackie said, a twirling drumstick appearing in his hand. "I just left out some details that weren't any of my business."

"You're a dumbass," Rufus said, and frowned. "And you're lucky I feel sorry for you. Come here." He opened his muscular arms for a hug and Conan's stomach sank.

"No way, dude, you're all sweaty." But it was too late; Rufus engulfed him with his embrace, reeking of body odor, cigarettes, meat, and propane.

"Sorry, man, no matter what, I got you."

Rufus squeezed him tight enough for the breath to catch in his lungs. "I know, of course, man." Conan patted his mentor on the back and cleared his throat. "Might need some more help here pretty soon actually."

Rufus raised his eyebrow and glanced over at Snow.

"October sign," he exclaimed. "You're from that bougie-ass school up on the hill, right?"

"October sign?" she asked with a tilt of her head.

"Random thought," Rufus shrugged matter-of-factly. "Prolly a past life trying to tell me something."

"Rufus is out of his mind, but, like, in the best possible way," Jackie said, untwisting a bag of hamburger buns.

"Right." Snow nodded and gave a half curtsy. "My mom owns Preston."

"Owns it?" Rufus asked, stacking a tower of sizzling burgers.

"No—not tonight. Not tonight, right? Tonight's for fun, and band practice. Right?" Conan said, glancing at Snow and then back to Rufus.

Rufus shrugged. "Ight then, fuck 'em up, Marc!" he yelled out to the patio.

"Marc's here already?" Jackie asked just as a pink water balloon shot past Rufus's head and exploded on Conan's face. The stink of rubber clung to him and icy water soaked his shirt.

"Go, go, go!" Rufus shouted and kicked over an ice chest full of Super Soakers.

"Don't worry 'bout the floors. I gotta mop this bitch up tomorrow anyway!"

Jackie ran out onto the patio so quickly he almost slipped. Before Conan and Snow could make it out, Rufus blocked their way.

"Yeah, there's gonna be a lot of cleaning up tomorrow. All because of you two, huh?"

She crawls behind my eyes, a pulse, like rain
Downpour in a barren desert sky
If there's no place here for you
Then how can I survive?

Chapter 2

Brandi's phone sneered up at her, taunting her, calling her the biggest moron that ever lived. Her lock screen was a picture of Conan, and she watched it until it turned dark.

Sorry, he had said, then ripped her heart out and spat on it.

She wanted to hurt him so badly it made her stomach sick. Worse than that, she wanted to hurt herself. They were supposed to be together forever.

She wouldn't let her phone be right.

Mr. Stephend opened the door to his classroom. He had his long coat on and a book-pack slung over his shoulder. He carried himself with unnatural stillness, like he'd been waiting outside.

"Sorry. I know I promised you could stay here as long as you wanted," he said.

Brandi hurriedly picked her things up and stood from her seat.

"Hey, that doesn't mean I'm kicking you out. I overheard you mentioning Kylie. It's not fair, I get it."

"What's there to talk about?" Brandi waved him off. "Conan will come around, and Kylie ran away. She always hated it here, you know that."

Brandi kept her head low and scuttled past her favorite English teacher. The occasional stinging tear leaked out from the corners of her eyes. She absolutely refused to let herself cry.

Maybe I'm a ghost? Already dead and haunting this place. A local legend.

She scratched her face until she knew her makeup was ruined. Her stomach tightened into a rope of knots.

Everyone's worried about that pale bitch. It's got them all talking about Kylie again.

The two of them hadn't been spending nearly as much time together before she disappeared. Brandi had been too wrapped up in devoting herself to Conan and his band. Remembering Kylie's freckled smile was like yanking at the stitches of a freshly sutured wound.

Wherever you are, I hope it's better now.

The parking lot was deserted, aside from a handful of police cars. Brandi stomped toward Scrambo, her 1998 navy-blue Chevy Suburban. Her shaking hands fumbled with her keys and accidentally dropped them to the ground.

Should you really be driving? she imagined Scrambo asking.

"No," she growled and stabbed the key in his ignition.

Drive home and eat a stack of waffles—wait for Conan to come around? Or drive to Rufus's and make him?

"Fucking fuck!" she snapped, as Scrambo's engine coughed to life.

I'll get him. One way or another, he's still mine.

The yellow trees lining the way to Rufus's that afternoon blurred. Conan was all she thought about. She wouldn't even own Scrambo if not for his band needing a truck to haul their stupid equipment around in.

You really shouldn't be driving.

Her brain played Conan yelling at her on repeat. How little had he really cared about her over the past four years? Her skin turned gross. Returning to the air he'd breathed on their way to school that morning coated her skin with an imaginary film. Everything smelled like him, cigarettes and cinnamon.

She parked outside and forced a laugh at the name written in black and white cursive: *Club Depression.* Ironically, it was always a kind building to her. She imagined the door and staircase like a welcoming grin, and if it talked, it would speak like one of those big friendly bears from kids' cartoons.

"But in real life, the bear's hungry, and he eats you," she said and glanced down at her lock screen. "Who would text you anyway? Your only real friend's gone. Forgot all about you, huh, dummy?"

She remembered how Kylie used to do the Mickey Mouse hot dog dance when she wanted to cheer her up. It never worked.

She got out of town. She met a cute boy and shacked up with him. That's that.

Brandi slammed Scrambo's door shut. He said he didn't mind if she smoked inside, but she knew he really preferred she didn't.

Her thoughts slowed as she inhaled her sweet and woody American Spirit, another terrible habit she blamed on Conan and the crowd he hung out with. Blowing out a stream of smoke, she glared up from the club and toward the glassy horizon.

"What are you doing here?" asked the sky, speaking slowly.

"I need to get him back, or hurt him. That's what Kylie would have said."

"No, she wouldn't have," the sky said in a condescending tone. *"You really can't accept that you're all alone? You're so desperate."*

"Of course I'm desperate. I *love* him. He'll see that and come back. We'll work something out."

"Sad," yawned the sky, and he had nothing left to say.

Brandi tossed her cigarette to the ground, threw her middle finger into the air, and drove away.

***

Brandi was only halfway through her double-bacon-cheeseburger and chocolate shake combo before her chest started breaking out. She swallowed one more mouthful of savory, salty, crispy bliss, wrapped her dinner up in its yellow paper, and thudded it onto Scrambo's dashboard.

She reached for the bong she'd made out of a water bottle and hollowed-out pen. The erupting smoke filled the cab with a strong pine and reefer aroma. As long as it wasn't some backyard boogie, Scrambo didn't mind. After coughing a significant amount, she scrolled through her phone to find some emo instrumentals and started wiping her makeup off.

When she'd finished, she stepped out into the abandoned K-Mart parking lot and sparked up a cigarette. She didn't mind the K-Mart at night. It didn't talk much, usually just warned her if a bum was posted up inside.

She pulled out her mirror and gazed at her dull features. Not much personality without makeup. Forehead, cheekbones, dirt-brown eyes; she was plain. Not at all like that girl he ran away with, Snow Devereux. That girl didn't even need eyeliner.

"So what?" Brandi spat and dropped her half-smoked cigarette down into the growing pile of butts. She hopped back inside and pulled out her makeup bag. "He can't stay with her. Not after all I've done for him. He needs me."

Brandi wanted to make herself into a living doll, like ghastly perfection. With her brush skills, she'd do it better than Snow's natural beauty. She'd beat her at her own game. Rich girls might be book smart, but they can't figure anything out themselves.

"Conan's trash at it too. He won't last, *they* won't last," she explained to Scrambo. "I give it three more days before he crawls back to me."

She tied an ashen ribbon in her hair and gave herself a wink.

"Stupid slut," she grumbled. It wasn't easy to talk trash without a friend.

She punched Snow's name into Google and Adria Devereux appeared, current president of Preston Academy and winner of the Corvid Award. Kylie used to call Preston "the witch's abode," and looking at the online pictures, she could see why. Blindfolded chairperson, gargoyles, black cats, vegan menus, you name it.

"Conan, I swear, if you're only doing this for recording money, I'm going to kick your teeth in."

From social media she found the link about their field trip to Peralta. The entire thing put River Devereux on a pedestal. She was definitely the skinny girl asking about Snow earlier, her sister. She was the president of the math and science clubs, lead soprano, and first-chair violin.

"*Pfff,* never stood a chance. Community college versus Harvard over here. I hate rich kids."

She found a group picture of the Preston High Song Girls, scanned their faces, and frowned when she didn't find Snow. There was a Misty Devereux who shared the same eye color, but she definitely wasn't Snow.

Brandi backtracked through her history and found Adria's page.

Stinking rich, blind, two daughters, River and Misty. Their father's deceased.

"She didn't make it up. They said that was her name. Those are her sisters, but—"

A distant chattering interrupted her, followed by a stray cat's yowl. She glanced around the empty parking lot and over her shoulders. A brief shiver crossed through her.

"This is so obnoxious. I should tell them where she is. That would end this whole stupid thing." She paused and rapped her fingers on the dashboard. "Yeah, why not, Scrambo? I get rid of her and he comes back to me, right?"

Scrambo did not protest, but was on edge from whatever creature they'd just heard.

Brandi leaned back in the driver's seat and blew a lock of her hair up, keeping it levitating in place for a moment before letting it drop.

The Preston song girls were worried *and* frightened. They had searched for Snow like their academic lives depended on it. Even when the police came, they had to be forced off the campus.

"What do you think, Scrambo? It's the right move, yeah?"

Scrambo didn't reply, but the blown-out K-Mart gave her a judgmental glare. Possibly trying to guilt her. After all, it's not like she tore the town apart when Kylie disappeared. She didn't even visit her parents.

A faint scratching made her jump in her seat. She surveyed the area for a culprit, but heard nothing else besides her drumming heartbeat.

"I should really wait until I'm sober to kick this stuff around, damn." She rubbed her head. "It's not *snitching.* Even if it was, why should I care if they get in trouble? Might actually learn a lesson for once in their lives."

Scrambo remained aloof. She almost fired him up and drove off to anywhere else, thinking whatever was around, imagined or not, was a sign to get moving. She blamed the weed, but even so, everything seemed off.

The sisters... She saw them together when she was heading to Mr. Stephend's classroom. They didn't look concerned at all. River was impatient to leave more than anything.

"Yeah, Scrambo, the K-Mart's right. Something is fishy."

Brandi scrolled through her phone's contact list and found Rufus. He always gave the best advice.

"If Conan really kicked me to the curb, do you think that means none of them will talk to me anymore?" she asked Scrambo. "No, you're right. Rufus isn't like that. He's probably mad at Conan's dumbass too."

She swallowed a lump in her throat and called, but after the fifth empty ring, the call went to voicemail and she hung up. She buried a high-pitched scream deep in her chest.

"I guess it's just me and you now," she sighed.

She grabbed her burger and took the biggest bite she could. Her mouth was so full of cheesy meat, tangy mustard, and extra pickles that it was almost impossible to chew.

Her phone rang.

She worked hard to get through the ridiculous mouthful. Whatever she had heard scratching before must have tipped over a trash can. There was a *bang!* by the K-Mart and she nearly choked. She picked up the call on the last ring and coughed.

"Hey," she said, clearing her throat and peering out her windshield.

"Was worried 'bout you, longhair," Rufus said, loudly biting his nails. "I'm honestly surprised I didn't see you pull up with a drum of gasoline and try burning this place to the ground. How you holding up?"

She saw light movement in the distance. It could've been a plastic bag, a cat, or anything.

"Dunno. I think I might be schizophrenic, but whatever. So they're still there?"

"Yeah. Honestly, they're making me sick with their puppy-love bullshit. I don't get it. I tried warning these clowns, and I've told Conan he was the luckiest fool in the world to nab you. Apparently, nobody listens to me anymore. Sorry about this, Brandi. It's fucked up, but I still got your back."

"Maybe I'm a ghost? I'm already dead and gone, like in Conan's song. That would explain why none of it matters to him. Drama, drama, drama. Whatever. What about her? How does she seem to you?"

"Her?" He paused for a minute. "I dunno, she's nice enough, polite, but I can't help but think something is being held over her head. She says something big is going down in three days. By the sounds of things, I think she's in a lot of trouble."

More scratching, more movement.

Brandi sat up straighter, but couldn't make anything past the K-Mart out. Probably just a small dog or a cat digging through trash and chucking it into the breeze.

"It's weird. I was looking into some stuff. The song girls were worried, but her sister wasn't. She was, like, irritated. That, and get this. I looked her family up. They have pages and pages on her sister River, but there isn't a word on Snow. Not a picture, nothing, like she doesn't exist. Oh, and I'm pretty stoned, but hearing some weird shit out here. So if I get murdered, tell the cops I was near the abandoned K-Mart."

Whatever movement was across the parking lot had stopped. She stepped out of Scrambo and lit the half of a cigarette she'd been smoking earlier, grimacing at the first rancid puff.

"Smoking alone will do that to you, fool." He paused. "But what you were saying? That changes things. Honestly creepy, like some hostage shit. I'll try to talk to Snow. Things are starting to point toward her disappearing, right?"

"Why would anyone go through the trouble?" Brandi asked.

She snapped alert. Even through her cigarette smoke, the air was wrong. She caught a whiff of something like wet-dog, strong enough to carry.

"I dunno. My first thoughts are for something evil. If that's the case, we should burn their whole damn mansion to the ground."

"Why do you always want to burn shit to the ground?" She chuckled and put her cigarette out. An enormous rat scurried out from behind K-Mart and she rolled her eyes.

"I dunno, really weird dreams lately. Keeps happening, those and ones where I'm trapped."

"That's scary," she said. "You wanna talk about it?"

"Nah, don't worry 'bout me. I think we should help her though."

"Yeah, well, we can't assume, not yet. Anything she says could be a lie. I got a bad feeling in my gut, and not from the chocolate shake I got at Benny's. People are worried sick about that girl."

The stench had become frightfully overpowering. Brandi leaned over Scrambo and peered in the K-Mart's direction.

The parking lot asphalt had come alive.

"I'll talk to her and fill you in on—"

"Holy shit!" Brandi screamed and leapt inside Scrambo.

The parking lot turned black with stampeding rats. The repulsive odor had her choking on the acidic burger settling in her stomach. She covered her mouth and whimpered as rats climbed up her windshield and scratched the roof of her truck.

"What the fuck?!"

"What? What's going on?"

"Rats, thousands. They're running, they're all running away, like when fucking Godzilla came to New York."

She checked to see if there were rats squirming into Scrambo's back seat and reached for her baseball bat. She held it tight and closed her eyes.

"Did you get shrooms or something?"

"I'm not kidding!"

The rats' scrabbling was like pouring rain atop her roof. Like a plague, chaos, judgment day. Then gone, save for a few stragglers.

"Whoa," Rufus said. "I see them here too."

"It's gotta be an earthquake or something, right? Animals sense that stuff."

"Yeah, an omen, for sure. This ain't right."

The phone line went silent and Brandi let her heartbeat slow before speaking again.

"Hey, what if she casted, like, a love spell on Conan?" she said and burped into her fist. "That entire school looks like nothing but witches. Then there's Mr. Murphy's car crash. She knew. She already knew before Conan told anyone."

"Damn, they're moving. Those rats don't give a shit about nothing. They outta here. And don't be crazy. I dunno about Conan's old man, but ain't nobody casting no love spells."

"It's not crazy. Those rats, *that's* fucking crazy, and we just watched them. Whatever."

"Yeah, this is wild, you're right 'bout that, but hey, Brandi, while I got you on the line, I gotta say it. What you did for us, driving, taking care of business. I know it's because of Conan and I appreciate you... Consider cutting your losses. You and Kylie were, like, the only kids I thought could go to college and, you know, make it out of here."

Brandi was squeezing her phone so hard that it hurt her hand. Her dinner was bubbling inside her and her grinding teeth made her ears twitch.

"Fuck you. Ever consider that I thought it was fun myself? Does it matter? Kylie *did* get out. Tell him I hope these rats bite his balls off."

She hung up and tossed her phone into the passenger seat. She took a heavy breath, then screamed and hit Scrambo's steering wheel with the palms of her hands until they throbbed.

Scrambo shook, subtly at first, then violently. It felt as if the earth beneath was swelling atop an ocean's wake. Rising and falling, she propped her palms against the roof and clenched her eyes tightly shut.

This is it. This is the end.

She opened her door and vomited violently, coating her mouth with burning bile. The stench was almost enough to make her empty her entire stomach. She picked up her phone and selected Conan's name, but then tossed it back onto her passenger seat.

"Maybe we're all ghosts, cursed to stay here forever." She seethed. "Because I'm *hoping* they're gonna hurt you, rich doll-faced bitch."

Chapter 3

You are everything
Beating against my heart
Let me become the memory
That can't be forgotten.

"You'll have that book filled soon," Snow commented, resting her head on his shoulder.

"The words won't stop coming. But they're like shooting stars. If I don't catch them right away, they're gone. I think they might help us."

Frantic squeaks chorused from the mass exodus of rats outside. A grown man howled at the gas station across the street.

"Hey, Conan, get your ass out here," Rufus barked from the patio. "I can't believe you're not watching this."

"Like you said before, it doesn't matter, does it?" Conan asked, and placed his hand atop Snow's. She intertwined their fingers, pressing their palms together. Her radiating warmth soundproofed existence.

Rufus's brother, Marc, Marc's girlfriend, Kimberly, and Jackie walked back into the theater. Jackie jumped behind his black and gold drum kit.

"Should we run through the set one more time?" he asked with a glow on his cheeks. The way they all grinned made Conan think they were hiding something.

"Conan, come here," Rufus barked. "Alone. I got a gift for you."

His brain scrambled for an excuse, but Snow pulled away. His stomach tightened at the prospect of leaving her alone. Stepping outside, the faint aroma of liquor spotted the patio. He knew they broke out the Grey Goose before he even saw Rufus pouring shots.

I can't be conscious
Knowing you will leave
Knowing you will leave me hollow.

Conan rubbed the center of his skull and took the shot glass. They threw them back, and the smooth, tasteless alcohol burned warmth into his gut. Rufus took the glass and wiped his lips with the sleeve of his crimson hoodie.

"So, you still got any respect for the shit I gotta say?" he asked.

"What kinda question is that?"

"You tell me. A sea of rats just rolled through here and you couldn't be bothered." He handed Conan another shot, but left his own on the table. "I was on the phone with Brandi. She was there when they first started coming."

Rufus leaned against the railing and crossed his arms.

"Aren't you gonna ask if she's okay?"

"I'm sorry we won't have her truck anymore, but Snow means more to me—"

"You're not getting it." Rufus met Conan's stare with eyes of flint. He came off the railing. "You know, all this shit going on. We have to be dumb as hell to not see the signs."

Rufus reached for his spirits and threw it back without cheers.

The vodka bottle jingled against the flat glass table, then fell and rattled violently. The concrete rumbled to life, like a slumbering beast stirred below them. Conan rose and fell with the earth, grabbing the railing for stability. He stared back into the theater. The bottle tumbled and Rufus caught it before it could break.

"Everyone, get outside!" Rufus shouted.

Jackie was already moving with Marc and Kim, each of them holding a unique piece of his drum kit. They wobbled and slowly placed the cymbal stands and toms down, as if on a rocking boat.

"Leave your shit, dumbass."

"No way," Jackie protested. "If the club sinks, it's not taking my baby."

Everyone was out but Snow. The earth turned violent, as if trying to split itself in half. Conan sprinted inside the club and saw Snow staring out the window.

"We have to get out of here," he said, taking her hand. As soon as his skin touched hers, the tremors subsided. Conan still wobbled, his equilibrium resetting. Snow hadn't moved, nor did she meet his stare. She was a statue, the brilliant shine in her eyes gone, darkness taking its place.

Spirit me away
If it means you've found peace.

"Snow?" he asked, and her eyes lit up like storm clouds.

"What is it, Conan?" she asked, craning her neck.

Conan hugged her close to his chest, clenching her as tight as he could without hurting her. He buried his nose into the top of her head and inhaled her clean smell.

Dad, I know you're watching out for us. I'm sorry you couldn't meet her.

"Hey, Snow," Rufus hollered, stepping back into the club, Jackie and Marc close behind. He had a guitar pick in his hand and tapped it against the wall. The club's acoustics made it click like two rocks banging together.

"No offense, but I gotta ask. See, I've got responsibilities to these idiots and can't afford a kidnapping charge. There's a lot of weird shit going on. You included. Feel me? I'm just asking if there's anything we should know?"

Remembered like a blister's irritation

Hollow like the crater left behind.

"My family is dangerous," she said without hesitating. "Keeping me here is a risk. That earthquake was most likely their doing. It's going to get worse until Sunday's over."

Jackie ticked his high-hat, testing his spacing and re-positioning his throne. Kimberly whispered to Marc, and all three quietly chattered like mice in the corner.

"You're scary as hell," Rufus said, scratching his chin. "Got a little rat in me too. I might head for the hills myself."

Jackie tested his bass drum with a pair of booming triplets.

"Dude, shut up for a sec," Conan said and splayed his palms up at Rufus. "I'll handle it. Okay?"

"I could leave," Snow said. "I don't want anyone to get hurt because of me."

"She's not going anywhere!" Conan shouted.

Rufus slapped his own face, dragging his hand down to his chin.

"Calm your perfect-pitched ass down. I didn't say she had to go anywhere. But you're a straight dumbass. Three nights, she says, and what, you're magically home free? Where you gonna stay? I shower with a hose, yo."

"I feel it," Jackie said, tapping a steady *pssh, pssh, pssh* from behind his kit. "I feel it in my balls."

"Jackie, shut the fuck up. She'll stay with me, all right?" Conan said.

"*Pfff,* your momma was never cool with Brandi staying over. You think she's gonna be cool with her?"

"I'll be lucky if my mom can get out of bed tomorrow," Conan said. "Besides, it's different with Snow. She'll understand."

"All the way down to the bottom," Jackie snickered to Marc. "To the bottom of the balls."

"Fine." Rufus walked to the patio and grabbed his keys. He pointed at Marc and Jackie. "Y'all mothafuckas stay put. We gonna have a lot to smoke about when I get back. Y'know, discuss finding a new drummer."

"Don't even joke like that, man," Jackie whined. "Saturday and we're on, right?"

"It's like a dream, but the contracts are real," Rufus said, then glanced at Conan. "We just gotta show up, play, sign some papers, and hit the road. Already talking about us hopping on a tour with Harbinger."

Conan took Snow's hand and followed behind Rufus. The air had a taint to it. Rat piss and shit covered most of the street. To Conan, the reek was extra potent. He realized he hadn't smoked a cigarette all night.

***

Their journey from the club to his place took forever. Something to do with the silence in Rufus's Honda Accord. Halfway home, Rufus rolled the windows down and the air turned cool and autumn-spiced.

"Thank you for not making me leave, Rufus," Snow said at a red light.

"Why would I do that? You ain't never did nothing wrong to me?"

"In a different life, you would have. If you thought it would protect your friends."

Rufus's eyes flashed in the rearview mirror, but he kept to himself. The city slumbered that evening. Even the McDonald's drive-thru was empty, and they only saw a couple of cars on the street. They pulled into Conan's driveway, and Rufus shook his finger at him.

"No babies and no missing practice, you hear me?" he said to Conan. "Hey, promise me?"

"Fine, dude, I promise."

"For whatever that's worth," Rufus said and peeled out.

Conan's mom's car was in the driveway. All the lights in the house were off. He pressed his finger to his lips and led Snow inside. He was never home, but still worried that his room would stink like old socks. When they stepped inside, he breathed relief after seeing that his mom had cleaned up. She'd even washed his sheets. The only odor was a linen air freshener plugged into the hallway outlet.

"I'm going to take a quick shower," Conan said. "I'll get some pajamas out and leave the water running if you wanted one after me?"

Snow nodded, and Conan dug out extra towels. He wasted no time getting into the shower, but after he soaked his hair and splashed his face, he turned the temperature down, saving Snow the hot water.

One hundred...

ninety-nine...

ninety-eight...

He closed his eyes and counted all the way to zero and then hopped out and quickly got dressed. While Snow showered, he fixed them a couple of frozen pizzas, and his mind drifted away.

Beep! Beep! Beep!

The microwave blared, and he hurriedly silenced it, worried he'd wake his mother. After a moment of panic, he plated the pizzas. Snow didn't take long, and met him in his cave a few minutes later. She'd wrapped her head in a towel and wore one of his Peralta High School gym shirts.

Conan scratched behind his ear. He added habanero hot sauce to his pizza and took a bite. Synapses fired off in his brain. The liquid fire was exactly what he needed to become alert.

"Tell me everything," he said.

"It's mostly a blur." She smiled and took a bite of pizza. "It ends the same way every time. I will die in three days, and this will continue."

All the hurt buried inside

Still searching for your missing goodbyes.

"You'll say how you'd do anything for me, and you have. You've killed for me." Her hand brushed his cheek. "You've died for me. I've used you and gotten sick of you, but here we are, trying again."

He took her hand and squeezed.

But I've got you on my side, right, Dad?

"None of the past matters. If it's destiny, I can change it. I've got magic of my own. I promise, this time will be different."

"Relax," she said, pushing him down and kissing him. "Don't be scared." She traced his jawline with her fingertip. He was worried that pepperoni and hot sauce breath would put her off, but she only kissed him deeper, pressing herself onto him.

He wished the night would never end and prayed he kept his promise to Rufus. When she fell asleep with her head on his chest, he wanted to stay there forever, but couldn't keep his eyes open.

Three more days.

Conan awoke to the rumination, like a nightmare had crawled into bed with them. Snow stretched. The sunlight illuminated her pale skin. His fingers glided over her shoulder. She gazed up at him and he grinned like a fool.

Knock knock knock!

"Are you going to school or am I calling them for you?" his mom asked.

Conan's heartbeat raced. He hesitated.

"Call out sick—" he started, but his mom was already opening the door.

Her eyes were puffy and red. She gazed straight through him and at Snow. She turned around and slammed the door. A moment passed and a ruckus of slamming cabinets and crashing dishes came from the kitchen.

"Go to her," Snow said.

"Don't worry," Conan said, grabbing his jeans off the floor. "She'll be fine. Just wait here for a sec."

He scrambled into the kitchen, where his mom was pounding coffee and shoveling down Advil. She glanced at him from the corner of her eye and mule-kicked the refrigerator door closed.

"Sit," she snapped.

He didn't.

His mom looked like she was going to throw her cup of coffee at him. She inhaled a monstrous breath.

"Does Brandi know?"

Gripping onto everything you've said
Until your texts were strangled and blue.

"She does. We broke up."

"Because of her?" She gestured toward his bedroom. Conan leaned against the wall and crossed his arms.

"Yeah."

Strangled and blue

Strangled and blue because of you.

"Fucking pig." She laughed and took a sip of coffee. "That girl gave everything she had to you. After all your promises to her? You're disgusting."

He came off the wall. His mother's amber hair had lost its shine and frizzed at the sides. She looked like a bag of knives, more frightening than he'd ever seen her.

"Nobody understands what it's like," he pleaded. "I'm sick of people saying I needed Brandi. Snow is the one who needs me. You have no idea, and you have *no idea* what Dad would say about this."

She poured her coffee down the drain. "Get out of my house." The venom in her words made his pulse hammer in his throat.

"You're losing it," he said. "Dad would have understood. I never loved her."

His mom didn't even look at him. She glared down the drain.

"Whatever," he said, lowering his voice. "He's the one that left you behind."

Conan turned his back on her and walked to his room. Snow had helped herself to his wardrobe. She was holding his leather jacket and already slipped into a pair of skinny-jeans and a black long-sleeve with a man's rib cage splattered open on the front.

"Kinda smelly, but they'll do."

He dropped onto his bed.

"Just give me one minute," he said, and closed his eyes.

He tried to count backward, but there was too much noise in his head. He sat up and kissed her.

"We're going to have to be extra careful. My sisters, they'll start hurting people now."

"Three more days, right?" He got up and grabbed his black hoodie.

Snow's eyes were pure crystal. "Did you remember something?"

He shook his head.

"No. What if we run away together?"

"You'd have to take your mom's car, but we wouldn't get far and she'd hate you forever."

"She already might."

"No, she doesn't. You've got a wonderful mother."

"Yeah."

Sorry, Dad.

"All right, so that's off the table. Well, my band's got our gig coming up. After, Rufus said we'll be going on tour with Harbinger. We can take you along."

Snow slipped his leather jacket on and sorted through his closet.

"If we last that long. What time is it?"

"7:40, why?"

"You should check on Brandi-Lynn, see if she went to school today."

Her mentioning Brandi's name made him aware of his mouth's dryness.

"That's not a good idea. I'd rather never talk to her again, honestly."

"I'm worried. Sometimes, by now, she's disappeared."

Strangled and blue

Strangled and blue, because of you

Collapsing, but I will never, ever let you go.

"It would probably make things a lot easier for me if she *was* gone."

Snow dropped a graphic t-shirt and stomped to his side. She slapped him hard on the cheek.

"Never wish that on anybody. I'm the one who took you from her. She deserves better. That's more than I can say about myself."

"Okay. I'm sorry, my head's a mess right now." He sucked on his cheek, tasting blood. "Is it because we're selfish?"

She hesitated, then nodded.

"I'm sorry. It's not gonna get easier, Conan, but I think you're right. Your writing might help us. I won't bother you. You said it's the only part you liked about singing in your band, right?"

"I told you that?"

His notebook was open on his desk—he searched for a pen.

"You did." She nodded. "I asked you why your songs were short. You said you write for yourself more than your band. You won't use the majority, but it's for you and no one else."

"Well, yeah, that's because it's mostly garbage." He laughed. "Well, I shouldn't take long. Twenty-two minutes tops."

Gripping onto everything you've said
Until your texts were strangled and blue
Strangled and blue, because of you.
Collapsing, but I will never, ever let you go.

Knowing I cannot rest
My head on your chest
Again.

Chapter 4

An ivory Rolls Royce SUV roared into Preston High's parking lot. Its tires screeched as it came to a stop, crowding into the spot beside Scrambo. Eyes bored into Brandi through the limo-tinted windows. She sipped her discounted coffee, bought with change dug up from her back seat, and watched two girls step out of the luxury vehicle. Every car she'd seen had cost as much or more than her parents' trailer.

"Don't be self-conscious, Scrambo, you're beautiful," she said, melting in her chair. "We figure out how to get Conan back and *boom!* We never have to see these spoiled whores again. Easy."

The words trailed off her lips as a skeleton of a sophomore huffed up to her truck. She'd seen his kind while working shifts at the cake shop. A rich kid, irritated because he was told to do something. After a glance at his pointy dress shoes, Brandi wanted to grab him by his Scissorhands hairdo and force him at gunpoint to scrub dishes for six hours. Wanting to sell her case, she rolled her eyes and started Scrambo's engine.

"What are you doing here?" he asked, giving the window a *tap, tap, tap* with his bony knuckles.

"Oh, I was—"

"Get out, I don't care," he said and pulled on her door handle. "River wants to speak with you."

"Okay. Where is River?" Her breath snagged in her throat.

No, Scrambo, that wasn't too easy. She gave his steering wheel a reassuring tap. *Don't be scared. What would shading me get? They need help, remember?*

"Just come," the boy said and kicked Scrambo's tire.

Brandi took a sip of her oat-milk mocha and swished it around until the inside of her mouth tasted chocolatey. She gazed beyond the young man and over the crowd. Out of the Preston murk, the Devereux sisters manifested.

A freshman girl with black hair held a paper bag of donuts for Misty. She paid Brandi no attention, busy swigging her latte and jawing off to her slave. Although the sisters appeared to be triplets, Misty's pearly Cheshire smile was gargantuan in comparison. River's reptile glare was nearly as distinguishable. If eyes could dig beneath your skin and peel back the layers, Brandi would be nothing. River's blue eyes had crawled under her neck and moved like spectral fingers down the length of her back.

Brandi looked away.

Bad vibes, yup, real bad vibes. She glanced up and saw that River had crossed her arms, appearing far more approachable. *This is ridiculous. She looks like Snow, just shorter hair, skinnier, and tired. She isn't dangerous, she's worried.*

"She *doesn't* wait," snapped the skeleton.

"Tell her to come here then," Brandi said, raising her eyebrow and killing the engine.

The boy's lips curled. "Stupid bitch," he said, and recoiled from Scrambo.

"Hey," Brandi snapped, and hopped out. Her fingers reflexively curled into fists. "Excuse you? Wanna run that by me one more time?"

The Johnny Depp wannabe didn't have the balls to turn around, but every kid in the parking lot stopped to stare at her. Brandi remembered that Scrambo couldn't actually watch her back, and as the cult of uniformed teens glared at her, she hugged herself tightly.

Misty Devereux finished her latte, grabbed another from the tray behind her, and snatched the bag of donuts from her servant. Her sudden movement toward Brandi triggered the students to go back to their business. Her tight slacks, studded belt, and cat-fur hair made Brandi somewhat comfortable in the sea of black uniforms. The obvious ignoring of the dress code was otherworldly in the crowd of stinking-rich Preston sleaze. She carried her curves well too, one foot in front of the other, like a dancer.

"Hey, cutie," she said. "I'm Misty. *Love* your makeup and your truck. Want some?" she asked enthusiastically. With impressive athleticism, she leapt up and *thudded* loudly onto Scrambo's hood. His suspension creaked in protest.

Brandi took a beignet and chuckled at herself for thinking the rich girls would've had glazed donut holes. The pastry had an aroma like fresh baked bread, covered in cinnamon, with a light airy texture; piping hot too. She dunked it into her coffee and tried not to shed a tear when it melted on her tongue.

"Let's go talk to my sister, yeah? She's the scary bitch over there." She hopped down from the hood. "Only reason you're here, right? Come on."

Brandi really liked Misty, which made her even more unsettled. Everything about this said she was getting strong-armed, and normally she'd be on her toes. Misty made it seem like it was just the two of them.

Exactly like what that witch did to my Conan.

"You coming or what?" Misty laughed.

Brandi glanced at Scrambo. He seemed worried.

"Yeah, I get it. She sat on you, red flag," Brandi whispered. "Magic's not real, though. They're a couple of weird-ass rich girls worried about their sister. It's why I'm here. You really think they'd hurt her? No way. I'll bring Rengifo if it makes you feel better."

Brandi popped open her glove box and laughed as the powerful reefer stink blasted her face. She dug out her tiny platypus plushie and gave him a kiss before burying him in her pocket.

Rengifo told her to leave and never come back.

River's glare was a camera, or like an ancient reptile frozen in time. Preston High was alive and flowing. Kids laughed and shouted. Pop music played from a nearby speaker. If River was the school's heart, then Preston was alive without a pulse. Brandi squeezed her platypus friend tight and rooted herself before the queen.

"Where is my sister?" River asked. When she spoke, the music went silent.

"What are you talking about?" Brandi asked, pulling her hands from her pockets and shuffling her feet. "Who even are you?"

"Tell me what you know."

"What's in it for me then?"

River smiled. Her high cheekbones showed like blades.

"You're right, Misty, she is cute."

"Yeah, huh," Misty agreed, dumping the remnants of cinnamon and sugar down her gullet. "She's better at doing her makeup than Kat, and her truck smells like weed. We should hang out."

"And lend her some products? Imagine her in Louis Vuitton? She drives too? How about we get a new car?" River pulled out her phone and explored Brandi with her iguana eyes.

No way she's serious. I don't need any expensive shit, right? I just need Conan back.

"I think we may arrange something," Brandi agreed, and tried wiping the sweat from her hands on the legs of her pants.

River swiped her phone, and before the words *black limousine* popped into Brandi's mind, a blacked-out limousine rode up next to them. The absolute perfect car for a mobster to torture somebody in; scream-proofed, bullet-proofed, and definitely Brandi-proofed. She glanced at the sisters. Their blue eyes were the same, but completely unique. Despite having just tanked a dozen beignets, Misty's gaze still appeared hungry. River's were an alien's, a predator to humankind.

And what's wrong with that? Brandi thought, shaking her head. *Helping doesn't make me selfish, especially if Snow is anything like Conan.*

"No way. That thing creeps me out." She jammed her hands into her armpits. "I drive."

"Shotgun!" Misty shouted. She downed her coffee and skipped toward Scrambo. It wasn't until River wordlessly started toward her truck that Brandi replayed events in her head.

This is the right choice. I can get Conan back. Maybe something for my troubles. Yeah, now we're talking. Hey, Scrambo, we might even get your a/c fixed.

***

"I absolutely love your truck," Misty said as they hopped onto the freeway. "Fits a lot of boys, huh? Or girls, anyone you wanted. Has to be great for going to the movies. Could fit dogs in here too, or cats. Cats like me more than dogs."

She hadn't shut up since they started driving, but Brandi didn't mind. Misty hadn't been impolite and was actually kinda fun. She felt like an old friend. If it wasn't for the explosive peach-scented Hugo Boss perfume, she may have forgotten who she was dealing with.

Brandi bit her lip and turned up her music; the atmospheric dirge of black metal guitar tremolo paired with a ride bell and double bass brought her back to reality.

I have to back off smoking so much weed. Misty's cool and River's weird, but they're not dangerous. I'm the outsider here.

"What'd you get such a big truck for?" Misty raised her voice over the music, always smiling.

"It's my first car. A big truck like this is a lot safer. I mean—don't worry, I'm a great driver."

River chuckled from the back seat, the first noise she had made since leaving. Brandi glanced in her mirror and saw her staring out the window, her knuckles resting under her chin. Brandi tightened her hands around the steering wheel until her knuckles turned white.

"That's a good call. We've got lots of cars. I like driving the bigger ones too. I don't get to drive as much as I'd like, but I got my license because Mom said I had to. Still, she has us picked up and driven everywhere; kinda a pain when you just wanna go to Benny's for a burger. Big truck like this, though, would be great to haul a lot of stuff around, go somewhere. Camping or road tripping. Like an actual bandwagon, right? There are a few good local bands around here. Know any?"

Brandi opened her mouth but held her tongue. Scrambo and Rengifo both shot psychic warnings right into the worried part of her brain. Her stomach did a handstand.

She's digging? Wait, she knows? Shit. They're smarter than me. She's been putting it together the whole time. One slip and the guys are gonna be so screwed. Well, there's no going back now.

By the time they arrived at the Devereuxs' mansion, a panicked monkey bounced around in Brandi's chest. And as she followed the sisters up the driveway, the monkey started writing its last will and testament. She wished she could ask Scrambo, talk with Rengifo, or call Rufus. Anything but march through the massive gate guarded by ugly gargoyles.

Next up, double-doors and a long crimson hallway—decorated with suits of armor, gripping swords and strange jeweled knives. In the gaping center were statues of women with dog heads, brandishing wicked tree branch scepters. Most unsettling of all were the portraits of creepy old white people gazing down from the ceiling.

You've got this. Be brave. She clenched her jaw tight and quickened her pace.

"This place really is just for show. Bunch of old expensive shit Grandpa wasted money on. Mom won't get rid of none of it. I told her she should sell it, make it look less gaudy, but no one ever listens to me. I dunno. I kinda like the dogs, but—"

"What the hell is that?" Brandi asked, interrupting Misty's string of syllables.

A baritone chanting reverberated through the corridors, followed by a high soprano, repeating the same foreign phrase. A mantra sung before Cthulhu crawls up from out of his dark chasm.

"Human sacrifice." Misty laughed. "Nah, just extra choir practice. Wait here, I'll grab Mom."

Misty trounced off and Brandi nodded her head to her back, too scared to speak. Her fingers found Rengifo in her pocket and gave the plush a squeeze. She wasn't the smartest girl in the world, but she'd listened to enough death metal to know Latin when she heard it. The only word she understood from the drawn-out chant was:

San-gui-ne-us!

San-gui-ne-us!

"Would you want to come back on Sunday?" River asked, turning away.

"What's Sunday?" Brandi blurted, a little more urgent than she meant.

River glanced up. She inhaled a deep breath; the skin surrounding her cheek bones turned a strawberry shade.

"Our eighteenth birthdays," she said.

"I, uh..." Brandi needed to regroup. "Yeah, sure. "

She dismissed River as she would any other awkward social situation and pulled her compact and makeup bag out of her backpack. Rengifo was telling her she needed to decide. Brandi hurriedly touched herself up. She darkened her eyeliner with cool tones, and the choir's chant ended as she matched her blush. She had a plan; it could absolutely backfire, but she had a plan.

I'm here, but none of this is my fault.

River had been watching her the entire time, pretending to adjust her collar. Brandi got her attention by fluttering her eyelashes and slapping her mirror shut.

"You're very talented," River said. She'd gotten her blushing under control and stood rigid as granite.

"You don't gotta act like that," Brandi said and feigned a yawn. "I like girls. It's cool. Don't worry about it. Wanna go on a date before Sunday?"

River's cheeks turned nuclear red. She fidgeted, cleared her throat, turned around, and then turned back.

"Say nothing to my mother," she whispered. "It's rare for— Yes, I would—I would like that."

Misty appeared just as the awkward silence became unbearable. She'd brought two other women tailing behind her. An assistant with the accouterments of a sexy librarian. Petite, dressed in black slacks and a business coat, glasses, and mousy brown hair tied back in a long braid.

The other woman was Adria Devereux. She wore a black gown and dark jewels on her neck and fingers. Her hair looked teased to a professional hairdresser's standard. A black blindfold covered her eyes.

One glance at the matriarch and the tiny hairs on Brandi's arms stood on edge. She held her breath, scared that any slip and the witch would steal it from her lips.

"Where is my daughter?" Adria asked. A woman without time to talk.

"I—" Before Brandi could get the syllables out, Misty grabbed her wrist and twisted her hand backward. Brandi let out a squeak as Misty pulled out a leaf-shaped blade knife and pressed it into her thumb. A drop of scarlet blood fell onto the maroon carpet below. Misty tilted her knife and let the red fill the leaf and vine designs. She cleaned it with her tongue and exhaled an exasperated sigh.

Brandi hissed. A thread of searing pain shot up her wrist, stemming from the ruby wound. She reflexively put her thumb in her mouth, tasting copper, unable to hide her grimace.

Don't freak out. Do not. Fuck! Rengifo, don't freak out. We're not getting murdered and we're not leaving empty-handed.

"Oh, she's nice," Misty said. "Nope, we shouldn't have to hurt her anymore. There's a bit of malice, and she isn't happy with her situation. Yup, she's totally one of yours, Mom."

"Right when we needed her," Adria said with a stiff nod. "What is your full name, darling?"

Brandi still clenched her thumb. Nothing she did mattered. She was in a horror movie, surrounded by the *Texas Chainsaw Massacre* family. Her thoughts and her body were separate things. She was part of the audience, gazing at herself on a screen. She was always going to confess. Conan was all that mattered. Nothing had changed.

"Brandi-Lynn Elena Taylor."

"Brandi-Lynn?" Adria laughed, shaking her head. "Undoubtedly from one of those trailer parks?"

"My parents own a house," she lied, lowering her chin to her chest.

"You've piqued my interest, Miss Taylor." She waved dismissively. "Be honored, not confused. Comply, and you'll not need to see Misty's gift further exercised. Do not cooperate and she will eat you alive."

Brandi glared at Misty, who shrugged and loudly closed her knife.

"Miss Taylor, where is my daughter?"

"What about the other missing girls?" Brandi grunted, hiding her hand in her jacket pocket and squeezing Rengifo. "Kylie and Janna, I know there are others too. Are you doing something to them? Is that why she ran away?"

Brandi glimpsed Misty nodding matter-of-factly and absolutely believed that she would have no issues eating her.

"I do not know anything about any missing girls. I am sorry," Adria said. "All I care about is my Snow. If you help me find her, I'd gladly use my resources to help you find your friends. I would, however, call it a waste of your potential."

Brandi pulled her hand from her pocket. The wound still stung and the metal stink found her nostrils. She glanced at River, who slowly turned a shade of pink.

Maybe I'm a ghost and I don't need to worry about Conan, Kylie, or Snow? It's their fault I'm even here. Whatever, I'm just a shitty person.

"Why not show her your gift, Riv?" Misty chuckled.

River took Brandi's hand. A heartbeat passed between them and the cut glued itself shut like two lips pressing together. Relief shot from the wound and her shoulders slumped. Brandi couldn't shut her mouth, staring at her sutured flesh like a beautiful sunrise.

"What gift—" Brandi said, and cleared her throat. "What gift would you give someone like me?"

The blind witch beamed. Her black lipstick stayed smooth as satin. She spread her gloved arms outward like a massive crow preparing to take flight.

"Darling, you tell me."

Brandi stepped around in a circle, imagining the dream would end any minute. Is this really what she wanted? She came here for Conan, because it was the right thing to do.

Sorry, Rengifo. Kylie wasn't the first lost girl and Snow's not gonna be the last. It's not my problem.

Misty nodded vigorously. They'd be best friends. She'd taste all the delicacies life offered. River would not meet her gaze. She kept her hands clasped firmly behind her back.

"I'm so tired of worrying about my future, about money, having my heart broken. I want to take care of myself. I don't want to be scared ever again."

Please, please, please.

Her feelings for Conan had not changed. She loved him more than anyone, and just thinking about Kylie ripped a hole in her heart. Adria was going to hurt Snow, but she was offering Brandi a way out. A way to fill the hole. Not just a gift.

"Then you will have a place here by my side." Adria twisted her wrist, holding her hand to her assistant. "Help me make your dreams come true, Brandi-Lynn."

"I don't know where Snow is," Brandi said, and clenched her fist. "But I know who she's with."

Chapter 5

"Do you find all these kids watching you practice strange?" Snow asked, flipping her hood over her ears. Conan held the door open for her and the icy wind snagged in his lungs. He slap-packed his Camels against his palm and shook his head.

It'll be the first cold night of the year.

"Not really. It's only weird that they know my name, but I don't know theirs. It's Rufus, really. He did the same for us when we were younger. He's a middle child of seven and knows a ton. Not like school. Time signatures, music theory, useful stuff. Nobody's been through as much as him. That's why I'm not scared of touring. He'll watch out for us."

"Watch out for us?" Snow chuckled, accepting one of Conan's cigarettes. He dropped eye contact when she bore into him.

"That's never gonna happen, Conan."

"You keep acting like that, but you're wrong." He shuffled away from her and snapped his fingers. "Wait until you see that I really am your knight in shining armor."

"Don't say that. It's sad. People will get hurt trying to help me, Conan."

Ocean waves cover tracks in the sand
The sea itself
Waters of our memories.

"I don't care."

Conan waved her off and lit his cigarette, taking a double inhale of the spicy Turkish tobacco. He puffed and smoked until his mouth tasted like fireworks. "I don't care if we tour, or if people get hurt. All I care about is you. Shit happens. It's not our fault."

He turned to Rufus and Marc—playing long-catch in the street. The cherry sunset became murky behind them. Auburn leaves speckled the asphalt and crunched beneath their running feet.

"You freshmen gotta stop with that furry shit!" Jackie shouted from inside the club. "Nobody should want to bang a turtle. It just ain't right."

"You're actually kind of sweet," Snow said, accepting his lighter.

On her exhale, Conan breathed in her secondhand smoke and lost himself in the aroma of fire and autumn. He didn't even need her honey kiss anymore, entirely intoxicated by her presence.

"Yeah," Conan said and stroked his sleeve. "And if we *can't* go on tour, or you don't want to, then we'll run away. These guys will be fine without me."

What do you think, Dad? We can get out of town. I can learn to drive a semi like you did.

"Hey," Jackie said, coming onto the patio. "If we're gonna be playing a forty-minute set, we need to draw it out."

"You heard the boss," Rufus barked and took his baseball glove off. "Let me get a puff of that." He walked up to Conan and took a massive drag of the cigarette.

"Let's play 'Ghost Steps,'" Jackie said. "It's been awhile."

"You're just making songs up now?" Conan laughed, shrugging. "How about '99 Feet'?"

"Why are you being so wack, dude?" Jackie said and rolled his eyes. His gaze landed on Snow, resting with disdain.

"I seriously don't know it." Conan crossed his arms over his chest.

"Yeah, you do. We played it a few days ago. It goes *bah-bah-bahhhhh* and I go all Mike Portnoy and shit with the fill."

"Whatever, let's just play."

"Let's just play with these nuts," Jackie laughed, grabbed his crotch, and moonwalked into the light of the club.

"Give me a sec," Snow said. "I want to meditate."

Conan kissed her. One more dose before following the others inside.

Thanks to Rufus, they always played for a crowd. Almost two-dozen kids showed up just for their practice. He made it a point to invite the hoodlums; to keep them out of trouble. It's how Conan met Brandi.

Sorry, Dad.

He cringed as guilt shot into him and hurriedly pushed Brandi to the back of his mind. He snatched his Shure SM58 microphone from its stand, but didn't have time to count backward, not even from ten. Instead, Jackie did it with his drumsticks.

One...

Two...

Three...

Rufus's guitar and Marc's bass exploded into heavy down-tuned chords. Jackie occupied the measures with one of the fastest drum solos he'd ever played. He was right, Conan remembered the song. His blood boiled with adrenaline. He didn't remember writing it, or the last time they played it, but he remembered it by heart.

Maybe I'm a fucking ghost
Lost and dying sucked to the bone
To reach you, to be with you, it's just another omen
Maybe I'm the fucking villain
Broken, swollen but not forgotten
In back of your mind, always on rewind
Just forgive me, why not forget me?

Rufus followed the verse with a melodic riff directly into a pure stop and an earth-shaking breakdown.

Regenerate
Regenerate
Born again
Regeneration

Conan roared from the deepest trench of his diaphragm, exhaling his building anxieties. His heart throttled in his chest. Feeling invincible, he gazed around the dance floor. Snow hadn't returned to him, but a stranger had wandered into Club Depression. He recognized her: Snow's sister, the short-haired one. She glared at him with the stare a teacher would give him before kicking him out of class. Her presence was like a weight pressing on his shoulders. He spat onto the stage.

Reflections that are not our own,
Making themselves at home,
A muddy place,
Buried in acid rain.

I can still hear your footsteps
Splashing on the waves

As they rounded the verse, and Conan's tenor matched the key of Rufus's soaring high notes, Snow's other sister appeared. She wore her emotions more vividly on her painted features—plucking at her clothes, crossing and uncrossing her legs, shouting over the music with a big mouth and pouty lips.

Conan did his best to watch them from the corner of his eyes. Both the girls laughed and bobbed their heads to Jackie's bouncing rhythms. Another pair of strangers appeared behind them, a couple of tall, lean types. One with long black hair and the other with a gray tattoo on the side of his neck, both strong in a ropey kind of way. They didn't seem the least bit entertained by the set.

"Hey, you totally changed the lyrics?" Jackie said as soon as the song finished. "I liked the old ones."

"Nah, dude, you're tripping." Marc laughed. "Regenerate, regenerate, that's been my favorite forever."

"No way, fuck that. Dude, I'm freaking out. Rufus, you remember that time-morphin', parallel-universe, voodoo conspiracy bullshit? The one we got stoned and watched, like a week ago? Bro, I think we're whirlpooling smack fuckin' dab right in—"

"Hey, yo, don't mean to be rude," Rufus cut him off, calling out to the strangers in the corner. "Y'all lost or something?"

Conan opened and closed his fist, flexing the muscles. The bigger sister slowly closed her eyes and then opened them, placing a hand over her chest. Her eyeliner style was somehow familiar, but he couldn't figure out why.

"I am so sorry. It surprised me when I didn't see a cover charge at the door. We were just driving by and heard you playing. I *had* to drag my friends in here and see what I was missing. I've seen you guys before, *Larry's Pizza* up north, right?"

"No way, you saw us way out there?" Jackie said, overly excited.

Conan and Rufus both shot him dirty looks. He retreated behind his kit, holding his hands up in surrender. Conan's muscles quivered. He imagined punching the tatted goon in his face.

Not a chance they can take all of us.

Marc raised an eyebrow at Rufus. He gestured by raising his lip and nodding toward the door. Kimberly led most of the kids outside, laughing and poking each other. The only kid that stayed behind was Big Ben, the 6'8" demon of the mosh pit.

"Yeah, that was us." Conan took the liberty of cracking the already broken ice. "Thanks for stopping in. We are just about done for the night. We've got a big show coming up."

If they're fans, this is gonna be easy.

"Ah, no way? We were just getting into it too." She ran a hand through her dyed hair and winked. "One more song for us? We've been stuck in Bummersville all day. Driving around town and looking for our probably dead sister. Can we show you a pic? Maybe you've seen her around?"

Calls of the haunted,
The only sounds,
In the empty home we built.

Feedback from the amp cabinets buzzed, but Rufus didn't shut them off. Sweat dripped down Conan's forehead, half from the music high, half because he was walking a tightrope inside himself. They'd gone over Snow with everyone, but Jackie might be too stupid and accidentally let something slip.

The big-mouthed girl walked up to the stage. She held up a photo of Snow dressed in her school uniform and, after gazing through it, Conan shook his head.

"No. Sorry, I haven't."

We keep cool, and nothing happens. Just breathe. He imagined himself in a box, taking a deep breath and pressing himself against it.

Rufus crossed his thick arms.

"That's a goddamn shame too," he said and shook his head. "This town's getting real shitty. She ain't the first girl gone disappearing. Getting worried for y'all. Even if you're just driving around town."

Conan risked a warning glance at Jackie and ran his teeth over his gums, tasting the tarry residue leftover from his cigarettes.

"She was taken from school," the short-haired one said, a quiet voice that could silence any theater.

"That's even worse," Rufus said. "Really, sorry for y'all, but we *do* gotta call it an early night."

Conan bit his lower lip, unsure why Rufus of all people would antagonize them. He glanced down at the sneering goons and clicked his teeth. Every part of him said to fight.

The tension turned from a tightrope to balancing on a knife tip. The chilly sister walked toward Conan. She was nothing like Snow; a robot, a skeleton. The tips of his fingers started shaking. He hid them in his pockets.

"Tell us where she is," she said.

Rufus was moving toward the back of the stage. The thicker sister pointed, as if snitching on him. The two goons behind her puffed out their chests and marched forward.

"I just said I hadn't seen her." Rufus chuckled, backing away with his hands up. "I wish it was different."

"Find her," the robot ordered, and the two wordlessly marched forward. The first headed toward backstage, the other toward the patio.

"Motherfucker." Rufus put his guitar on top of his amp and leapt at the first goon. Big Ben moved toward the second with a violent sparkle in his eye.

"I said I hadn't seen shit. You coming back here and messing with my home is a whole other thing. That'll get you fucked up."

Conan hopped off the stage and started toward the patio. Rufus hit the goon in the face with a right cross, and Big Ben had the other backing up toward the wall.

What the fuck, hey, Dad? What's going on? Okay, all right. It doesn't matter, as long as Snow's hidden and nobody panics. I should find her. You got our back still, right?

"Holy shit!" Jackie screamed from the stage.

The large sister had him by the hand, squeezing tightly enough to have Jackie on his knees.

"Dude, this bitch has a grip like a crimper. *Fuck!"* he growled and slammed his fist down against the stage.

"Don't worry, Jack, these dumb hoes ain't gonna risk a lawsuit," Rufus barked.

"Wow, that's so rude," she replied, and stifled a yawn with her free hand. "This is gonna be so sad. You're great behind the skins. Kinda cute too."

"*Fuck, fuck, fuck.* She's breaking my hand, dude, she's fucking breaking it." Jackie sounded small. His eyes spilled tears down his cheeks.

"Bitch, get off him." Rufus ran to them but stopped in his tracks.

Crunch!

A bone in Jackie's hand exploded like a popcorn kernel. Everyone froze in place and Jackie screamed bloody murder, thudding his feet against the stage, kicking and rumbling in a spasm.

"That's a goddamn shame too," the witch said. "This town's getting real shitty. His ain't the first fingers gone disappearing. Getting worried for y'all." She smiled, showing a massive mouth of teeth. "Where's Snow?" She lifted Jackie up like he was an unwanted pest.

"I told you," Rufus seethed. "I haven't seen her."

The witch looked bored. She glanced at her sister, who gave her a sharp nod. She grinned, impossibly large, showing more teeth than any human mouth could contain. Her smile grew wider and wider, the skin on her face peeled back and wrinkled like a pushed-up sleeve. Her face amalgamated into a monstrosity more teeth than skull.

Conan's heart stopped beating. He couldn't feel it.

"No, no, *NO!*" Jackie screamed as she placed his hand into her gaping maw.

Snap!

Crunch!

Crunch!

Crunch!

Conan clasped a hand over his mouth, tasting sour beer and French-fry regurgitation bubbling in his throat. He fell to his knees and vomited.

No. No fucking way this is real.

She dropped Jackie screaming to the floor and loudly gulped down his fingers. Everyone stared in horror as blood spurted from his severed digits and the witch re-adjusted the skin on her face like a loose mask.

"Miss River, Miss Misty, I couldn't find anything," a third blond-haired goon said, appearing from outside the patio. He'd been searching the entire time.

Misty was looking at herself in her compact. She stomped her foot into Jackie's bleeding nub. He didn't scream, but froze completely, staring at the wound, his eyes twitching. A puddle appeared beneath him and the powerful stink of urine filled the club.

Regenerate

Born again

Regeneration

"Fucked up my makeup doing that, asshole." She kicked Jackie aside and slapped his cymbal stand onto the ground. Jackie's favorite ride crashed loudly, a large crack splitting into its side.

Nobody moved, stricken by the violence. Conan heard something, a noise from inside himself. Guttural demonic rumblings, noises you'd only find in hell. He turned and saw River staring at him, two inches from his face, standing in his vomit.

"I love my sister more than you could ever realize. I understand what you're trying to do here, but there is no point. It will only end in others getting hurt. She needs to come back to us soon."

Misty belched loudly and exhaled a powerful stench, like iron and sulfur.

"I could always put them back, you know? With River's help, he'd be as good as new. No issue at all. Seriously. Call me." She had Jackie's phone in her hand and was punching digits. She smiled and took a selfie.

"Smarter than they look," she said, dropping the phone. "Not a single word about her, huh?"

The goons were already walking away, but River met Conan's eyes. It was as if spirits danced behind hers, phantoms drifting in an ethereal night fog.

I'm done pretending that nothing bad happened. You started this, Dad. Now Jackie? Why are you letting this happen?

"Is there something you want to say to me?" River asked.

"I'm going to kill you," Conan said, his breathing loud in his ears.

"Good luck. Figure it out soon. You've got a big show coming up. We'd hate to ruin it."

Misty hopped down from the stage.

"Let me eat him if you guys can't find a replacement and I can play for you." She laughed. "Or just tell the truth and get his fingers back, okay, *byeeeeee!*" And as simple as they came, they were gone.

Marc was the one pulling overtime. He'd got first aid from the kitchen area and the aroma of antiseptic covered the reeking plethora that consumed Club Depression. He wasted no time wrapping Jackie's fingers.

"This isn't good, man. He's turning pale. We gotta get him to the hospital."

"I'll fucking kill them," Rufus said. "You quote me in front of God, in the court of law. When they burn to death in their fucking mansion, tell them I did it and I'm not sorry. Jackie's our ace. He was gonna be a fucking god, man." He kicked the wall so hard, he put a hole into it. He punched in another, torso high. "It's war, it's fucking war."

"Help me out, guys." Marc was trying to move Jackie.

"Yeah," Conan said, gazing at Jackie's red bandages through tunnel vision.

"Dude, come on! Come the fuck on, guys!" Marc screamed and let tears free fall from his eyes. Big Ben moved to help him, and together they got Jackie to stand. As they worked toward the door, Conan stepped to Rufus.

"We can do it tonight. We get some fucking gasoline and do it tonight."

Rufus's eyes blazed with hatred. He nodded before he could even say no.

My commitment
Martyrs those around me
I'm afraid to scrape my palms
Reliant on their tears.

Then she appeared, out of thin air, a ghost. Her steps rhythm'd through the club like a beat and Rufus glared at her with pure disdain.

"Sorry," she said, and blocked Marc and Ben's path. "I warned you all that this would happen."

"Ah, I must have missed the meeting where you warned us that bitch would come through here and bite my boy's fucking hand off," Rufus growled and marched toward her.

"Please, please move," Marc said, keeping his head low. "We *have* to get him to the hospital. It's not good."

"Shut up, Marc. I can still play," Jackie said, turning a shade of green. "We can tape the stick to my hand. Don't worry, you fucking idiots. We got this."

Snow reached up and squeezed his nub in both her hands.

"*Ah, ah, ah!*" Jackie groaned, squirming in pain.

"Yo, you're hurting him," Marc said. "Stop, what's wrong with you?"

When Snow's hands came away, a bead of sweat broke on her brow. Jackie smiled like an idiot, staring at his completely restored hand.

"Bro, no wonder they're after her. She's a fuckin' angel," he said and immediately passed out. Ben and Marc both went slack-jawed and accidentally let him fall to the floor with a resonating *BOOM!*

Calls of the haunted,

The only sounds,
In the empty home we built.

Tear out my guts,
With tooth and claw, a thousand
Make the empty cavity,
A bed for you to rest in.

Chapter 6

"His name is Weasel," Misty said, wiggling her fingers through the grid of the Pallas cat's enclosure.

Brandi cleared her throat and took a step closer. She couldn't help but feel warm and fuzzy inside as the gray-furred, round-eared ball of fluff emerged from its hovel and lunged at the red meat dangling from Misty's fingers.

"Oh my god. Look how small his little legs are. Is he mean?"

Brandi refused to ask about what the sisters had done at Club Depression. She had chewed all her fingernails off while waiting outside in the limousine. Worrying about Conan had planted a seed of sharp pain in the back of her throat.

If somebody got hurt, it's because of you, Rengifo nagged from her back pocket. The stuffed platypus had developed a critical attitude since she ratted out the boys.

"Hell yeah, he is," Misty said, squirming from cuteness. "But if he eats until he can't move anymore, he'll let you pet him."

The closer Brandi got to Weasel's cage, the more she could smell his powerful odor. Like piss, musk, and lemons.

"That makes two of us." Brandi laughed and covered her nose with the sleeve of her hoodie. "I'll pass. He reeks."

River clicked away on her laptop at a rapid pace. She occasionally huffed and glanced up at Brandi, as if trying to get her attention. Finally, she closed her computer and rested her hands on it.

"Brandi-Lynn," she said. "I met your boyfriend this evening. Excuse my brashness, but I've spent considerable time on the subject. Good riddance. You'll do much better without him."

Misty snickered and dropped another piece of meat into Weasel's squawking mouth. "*Jealous,*" she sang.

"Did—did you hurt him?" Brandi asked, biting her lip.

How can you be so contradicting? Rengifo growled. *You're like a deer in the headlights. Everyone knows you still love him.*

River met Brandi's stare with a pinched expression and gave an uninterested wave of her manicured hand.

"Are you sure you want to know?"

It doesn't matter, Rengifo said. *Nothing will ever be the same.*

Brandi's stomach flipped upside down. The lobster frittata and unagi sushi they had for dinner had been too rich for her. She burped into her fist, and pungent indigestion expelled from her nostrils.

"Please," she said.

"I didn't touch him," River snapped, and hurriedly returned to her vigorous typing.

"But I ate his drummer friend's fingers." Misty giggled, letting go of another piece of meat. It hit the bottom of the cage with a wet *slap.* Weasel's cat mouth smacked loudly as he chewed the morsel.

"Wait, Jackie? Why? He didn't do anything. He—"

"He didn't," River cut her off. "But we needed to show them we were serious. If they comply, then I can return his fingers without issue."

"You mean he is there right now—with his fucking fingers torn off?"

River glared from below her brow. Her peach-colored blush returned.

"We didn't have a choice in the matter. We're not as lucky as you."

Weasel made a strange chattering noise, and Misty tried her best to imitate it.

Maybe I'm a ghost? And I never belonged here.

"You didn't say anything about hurting them."

"If they cooperated, we wouldn't have had to. Don't be upset."

A jingling bell announced the server entering Weasel's domain. The man had a gigantic hook nose and his feet didn't make a sound on the imperial rug, but the nutty aroma of fresh espresso made Brandi's eyes big. He placed the platter in front of River and wordlessly faded back into the mansion.

"You still have your choice," River said, taking a spoonful of sugar and pouring it into her espresso. She stirred the sugar into the cup and offered it to Brandi. Just because her stomach was getting upset didn't mean she'd say no to a $40 cup of coffee. Her hands shook as she brought it to her lips. Balanced, rich, and a smooth finish. The perfect cup. Despite that, her tongue only caught the bitter notes.

"You don't have to do *everything* she says," Brandi said, staring at her reflection in the dark liquid. She had to fight the urge to pull out her compact and touch up her makeup.

"Is that what you think?" River took a sip from her own cup. "I never wanted to hurt anyone; same as I never cared for the violin. She *made* us, Brandi, each for a purpose. My destiny is hers, to *be* what she wants me to be. Misty is her guard dog, and Snow is her key. Your fate is your own. An empty canvas."

She's right, you can still make things right, Rengifo said.

The pain in the back of her throat grew past a dull ache. She placed her cup and saucer down.

"Why don't you try to help? You love Snow, right?"

"No *duh*," Misty laughed. "And you still love Conan."

"I can speak for myself, thank you," River snapped.

Misty ignored her outburst and did something that made Weasel yowl. She tried to match his pitch, as if conversing with the wild animal.

"Of course I do," Brandi exhaled. Saying the words out loud was like pulling a weight off her chest. "He's the entire reason I'm here, but it doesn't matter. Not anymore. Things will never be the same."

"She's getting it, Riv," Misty said, then walked over and downed her espresso in a single gulp. She rushed back to Weasel's cage and went back to chattering.

"Am I?" Brandi asked, rubbing her brow. "I'm thinking you don't get it. I think about him—what he's done to me—I get mad. He hurt me and I want him to *know* that. But if something were to happen to him, I'd never forgive myself."

You're forgetting about your appearance. Rengifo warned.

River glanced away. Her pride usually radiated like a lioness's, cold and calculated, her movements smart and with purpose. She winced and stared down at her hands, appearing like a normal eighteen-year-old girl for once.

"You want me to tell her, Riv?" Misty asked.

"No," River smiled, her eyes glassy. "But why do you care? She took *him* from you. You should hate her."

"This town's already swallowed at least two girls that I knew, one that I loved," she said, and the pain in her throat stabbed like a knife. "I don't care if she's a total bitch. It's more important that she has a future than me being here."

River's lips curled into a snarl.

"There has to be a way for everyone," Brandi quickly added. "Don't worry. Like I said, me and him will never be the same. I haven't forgotten about our date either."

"What date?" Misty boomed, her gusto completely restored.

River turned back to her laptop and pretended like the entire conversation hadn't occurred.

"Oh, fuck both of you," Misty sighed, resting her back on the cage. "Whatever, nothing we can do anyway. Two days left."

The bells on the door rang again and Weasel hissed before retreating into his cathouse. Adria and her assistant walked into the room. The matriarch had exchanged her earlier clothes for a nightgown matching the blue of the sisters' eyes. She did not wear her blindfold, but her eyes remained closed.

There's still time for you to help her, Rengifo whispered. *Do the right thing.*

"Good evening, ladies," Adria purred. "I hope you do not mind the intrusion. I only wanted to bring Miss Taylor a gift. An accessory that us long-haired women wear so eloquently."

Her assistant hadn't changed out of her business attire. She held up a red pillow with a black pearl choker resting atop it.

"What are you going to do to Snow?" Brandi asked, walking right up to the blind matriarch. "Are you going to hurt her?"

Adria's lips turned into a tight frown.

"What does that have to do with our arrangement, Miss Taylor?"

"I don't care, tell me," Brandi demanded. Misty appeared out of the corner of her eye and shook her head, drawing a line on her neck.

"Oh," Adria said, her lips making the shape of the word before forming a grin. "In that case. Yes, I plan on hurting her. Do you think that's wrong?"

"Are you joking?" Brandi threw her hands in the air. "No wonder she ran. You're no different from Kylie's abusive *fucking* dad. You never told me you were stealing from her."

Her ears pounded, and blood rushed to her head. She didn't care that she was essentially a prisoner and would never find her way out of the mansion alone. Rengifo had been right all along.

"Stealing?" Adria said, nodded, and turned her back to them. "That's how it is then. Follow. There are things you should see that I never could."

River trailed behind her mother, completely unfazed. Misty waved goodbye to Weasel and gave Brandi a hopeless roll of her eyes. As they marched into the parlor, Brandi considered making a break for it. The only thing that kept her from running was her trust that River would protect her.

But would she?

Adria led them through the crimson hallway decorated with suits of armor, then to a room that looked like a museum, filled with various occult items in glass cases. The centerpiece display was a golden knife with a blade carved from a tooth. The name above was written in Hebrew, if she had to guess. Brandi was so enamored by the weapon that she forgot they were walking. She hurriedly snuck a phone picture before she turned her head and gazed into the recess of a dark basement.

"Children," Adria said, as she placed a hand on her assistant's shoulder and stepped down the stairs, "are all potential enemies. Whenever you have worked as hard as I have, children are the only thing that can crush those labors in an instant. If I had eyes, I would have never needed to procreate, but because of my handicap I am entirely reliant upon legacy."

The lighting into the stairway was sparse and pure crimson. It reminded Brandi of a photo development room. The deeper they marched down the stairs, the louder her heart beat. She swore she heard an occasional wailing scream. After the third time, the hairs on her neck stood up. It wasn't imagined, but coming from inside her own mind.

River walked to her side and gave her palm a quick squeeze.

"Don't be scared," she assured. "Nothing will happen to you."

The basement was lit by the same harsh red, but the darkness beyond appeared to stretch endlessly. It stank like bad fruit and open sewage, a rotting rat that had been locked in a storage closet for too long. The cries inside Brandi's head became louder and more frequent. As River stepped onto the soil floor below, a circle appeared at its center. It produced its own light, white like chalk, and made up of over a dozen pointed triangles.

Brandi's legs cemented themselves to the ground.

Having a monster help find out what happened to Kylie will not bring you closure, Rengifo confirmed what had already been going through her head.

As Adria approached the circle, Brandi became increasingly more unsettled.

"Children must be cultivated like a farmer tends to his field. Seventeen triangles for evoking seventeen unique spirits, demons, and lesser-gods. Each year, a different sacrifice, and a new life conceived. The eighteenth seal is the circle itself, to be used to evoke a god."

Adria placed her hands behind her back and laughed. Her white teeth appeared wine-colored and slick with black grease. As she spoke, the groans and screams reached a chorus. They blended together, creating a shrieking siren. Brandi focused on Adria and how much she disgusted her.

Focusing on her anger—to hold onto her sanity.

"The link between the living and the dead, god and humankind. In this circle, the devourer shall be born. Snow, my daughter, will be our last sacrifice."

Brandi imagined the butterflies she'd get from knocking out Adria's perfect teeth. She didn't care if the witch was blind.

"You're feeling betrayed? It had been expected," Adria said, already sounding bored. "I am only trying to prepare for your future. One that I will not be a part of. Give yourself to me, be my plaything. Allow me to dress you and do with you as I please. You will not regret it. In two days, humankind and beyond will both be changed forever. It's why the planet cries out to us. Worry not. You'll have your place with Misty, at River's side."

"Why would I trust you?" Brandi couldn't help but chuckle. She pulled a full sweep with both her arms and twisted around the chamber. "You're willing to sacrifice your daughter for some crazy black magic shit. Dude, seriously? Fuck this town."

Maybe I need a shower and to burn these clothes. Maybe an exorcism while I'm at it.

Adria frowned and shook her head.

"Your lack of reason is unsettling. Miss Taylor, I've already got what I needed from you. Tomorrow, your boyfriend will be left in the ashes of the fire you started. It is time for you to think about your future."

Brandi reached into her pocket and squeezed Rengifo.

It's okay to be mad at yourself, he said. *It'll help you do the right thing.*

He was right. She needed to hold onto her anger. That, or let her claustrophobia choke her unconscious.

"Snow will die," Adria said. "It is her destiny. Life isn't fair for certain souls. Do not waste an opportunity, Miss Taylor."

Adria opened her eyes, and Brandi couldn't look away. They were the same Devereux cerulean as her daughters', but bleached, and by the darkroom's scarlet light, they appeared to glow. Brandi's hand left Rengifo. Her chest crushed inward, and every strenuous breath hurt her chest.

This, this is real life. Magic. Am I mad at her, or mad at myself for wanting this? Queen Bitch is offering me a throne. If I was in her place, I'd be able to do so much better. Right?

No. Don't look at her, Rengifo pleaded.

Brandi thought she saw movement in the never-ending darkness. She credited her paranoia, but saw more and more. Strange shapes danced and jumped in the shadows. Gusts of wind fired up from the floor, one directly beneath Brandi, blowing her hair upward and passing chills through her so severely that she stepped backward. She refused to break, to show them her terror. Anything would be better than giving Adria the slightest bit of satisfaction.

"You've a lot to think about," Adria said. "I will leave you to discuss things with my daughters. But know that I love you, Miss Taylor. I'll pray that you make the right choice."

Adria walked up the steps slowly, and as she left, the chamber spun and twisted. The circle on the floor rotated and the wailing cries turned into guttural syllables. The shapes hidden in the shadows no longer danced, but stared at Brandi. Their eyes slid across her skin like insects, leaving small irritating scratches and bites.

She pulled out her American Spirits and, with an echoing click of her lighter, sparked one up. The aroma of burning was a thousand times better than the foul sweetness of the cellar.

"I get it, totally fucky, but you got this." Misty took her hand in hers and lifted. "Seriously, this shit goes all the way to the top. Not just America, you know. Mom must *really* like you. Huh, River?"

Brandi's stomach settled. Despite the basement coming alive around her, she kept her head on. She took another drag and pulled out her compact. The basement's light made her look like she was inside a volcano. She couldn't tell if her mascara had smeared.

They're in the same boat as me. This is their place and they're just trying to fit in. Adria has total control.

"I won't hurt him," River said. "She said he'd be left in the ashes. But I won't hurt him unless you want me to. He isn't your boyfriend any longer though, right? Because of what he did with Snow?"

Misty gawked at River and put her fist on her hips.

"No, he isn't," Brandi confirmed, gazing down at her feet.

Why do I hate myself for considering this? Kylie would tell me to jump on it. She fucking loved Harry Potter. This is my platform 9 and ¾. Real magic. The freaking lottery.

"I'm sorry," River confirmed. "I—I only bring it up because, what you said this afternoon. I just want you to know that Adria is evil. In the truest sense. She is illogical and unstoppable. I am not *her,* Brandi-Lynn, and—and you have a kind heart that sings to me."

River reached out for Brandi, but retreated her hand back to her side, clenching her fist.

"Thanks, River," Brandi said, and hugged her hard against her chest. She was surprisingly warm, and the longer Brandi held her, the quicker River's pulse sped. She gave her one more squeeze and rested her head on her shoulder.

Maybe she's right. How many more people can I really betray?

"Well, I've made my choice," Brandi sighed. "Guess the key now is to look ahead and don't think twice, huh?"

Maybe I'm a ghost, an outcast wherever I go.

Chapter 7

"What I'm saying is, your hand got bitten off in my dream too," Rufus said as his toaster *popped.* The sudden noise shocked Conan so badly that he nearly jumped to the ceiling.

Rufus and Jackie laughed, but Conan had put his hands over his ears. The volume of the club had him staring into space, a trance, suspending time around him. A nagging feeling started at the center of his skull. Like he had forgotten something.

I put together glass pieces
Trying to build a reflection

"After working for years, that one moment would have ended everything." Rufus flipped his eggs and waved his spatula at Jackie. "I think you're right about a time warp. I'm seeing the future or some shit, and ain't none of my dreams have us on the road."

Rufus had been talking conspiracy all morning; that paired with the nagging that drilled into Conan's skull had birthed a throbbing headache. It began at the base of his neck—making a horned moon through and to the center of his skull. He'd become rigid from sleeping on the floor and wished he'd just taken Snow and ran away.

"Why wouldn't you say anything until now?" Conan asked, twisting his fork between his fingers.

"Y'all know I got a fucked-up head. Besides, it's my own damn business. Like you'd listen anyway."

Conan let his fork drop and rattle on the table. He blew out a sigh and leaned back on the hind legs of his chair. Jackie flexed his fingers, still exuding disbelief from the night before.

Conan's eyes drifted over to Snow. Her hair was a total mess from them sleeping in so late, and her only interest that morning seemed to be the promise of bacon, eggs, and blueberries. They all had stayed the night except for Marc, who freaked out and went home. He promised he'd be back for practice.

"Have any dreams about the show tonight?" Jackie asked, snatching up a piece of bacon.

"Nah," Rufus said, and swatted his hand with the spatula. "Nothing I can think of—one's been bugging the shit outta me though. I was telling Brandi, but—"

"Enough!" Conan shouted and slammed his fist onto the table. "Don't worry about it. I'll handle it. All right? Just stay out of the way so you don't get hurt."

Rufus put his fist on his hips and shook his head. He stared at Conan with glassy, disapproving eyes.

The odor of burning bacon wafted through the air. It hit Conan like a truck, making him dizzy. If he had anything in his gut, he might've lost it. He got up and sparked a cigarette, walking toward the patio and killing the stench of burning meat inside his nostrils.

"If you ate something besides Rolling Rock and Camels, you wouldn't feel sick all the time," Rufus said, and started fixing plates. "I've kept my mouth shut, but you gotta be straight up stupid not to see the bigger picture."

"Hey, Conan's kinda right," Jackie laughed, flexing his hand again. "We got the big one tonight. That's what we should focus on. Show must go on. Yeah?"

Are you listening, Dad? The big one. You better be watching out for us.

"Yeah," Conan and Rufus agreed in unison.

Rufus rummaged through his silverware drawer and loudly clinked together plates. He slammed closed the cupboards and served over-easy eggs, blueberries, and toast with jam.

Leaning over your grave
And filling the trench
With my bleeding heart.

Conan rubbed his brow as the lyrics floated in and out of his head. He saw other images. He couldn't make them out exactly, dancing shadows in a red room. Snapping bones, like Jackie's fingers. His heartbeat shot up into his throat. He pushed the images to the back of his mind, tossing his cigarette aside and picking up his lyric book.

"My head's a mess," he said, sitting next to Snow. "It's like trying to split into three different versions of me."

Snow chewed and swallowed a mouthful of bacon. She slowly washed it down with orange juice.

"It's the same for me," she said and smiled. "But try thousands."

"Is it because of your magic?"

"I'm not sure." She wiped her lips and wrapped her fingers around the steaming mug of coffee. "But I've got a terrible feeling about tonight."

"God dammit, I wish you'd say something helpful for once," Conan said, rolling his eyes.

"I already told you—"

"Yeah, I know. There's no point."

He picked up a piece of toast, but set it back down without taking a bite. Club Depression's stage had been bathed in golden light from the morning sun. He passed a quick glance to Jackie and then to Rufus.

"We gotta play," he said. "Show them we aren't scared."

"That's what the fuck I'm talking about," Jackie said, clapping his hands together. "We ain't never been scared, even after getting my damn hand minced. Our music is ours."

Break my skin
A river to drown beneath
Here, inside of me.

Writing anything down seemed pointless. Even lyrics he didn't remember coming up with felt emotionless and stupid. Just thinking about all the time he'd spent practicing and writing made a weight press down on his shoulders. It wasn't an emotional outlet; it was exhausting.

"Now hold on for a second," Rufus said and took his apron off. "What I was telling you was serious. If I don't—"

"That doesn't matter," Conan said, and shot up from his seat. "We're here because of you, Rufus. You got your dreams, and we're just the supporting cast. Let's go."

Rufus threw his spatula into the sink so hard that it flew back out.

"Motherfucker, you're not listening."

"I don't give a shit." Conan threw down his chair, and it bounced off the hardwood flooring. "You've put us through a lot of shit. We gotta get you to be one of the greatest guitar players of all time before you're twenty-eight so you can OD, remember? Your *real* dream."

Snow didn't seem to mind the noise. She reached over and took Conan's eggs off his plate.

"Oh hell yeah," Jackie chuckled through a mouthful of bacon. "That gives us plenty of time to piss people off. Look at us, agents checking us out, hitting the big time, playing metal and hardcore music? Fuck your dreams."

Rufus roared. He picked up Conan's chair and threw it across the club. It exploded into pieces. As the *thud-crack* echoed off the walls, he took in a deep breath.

"My heart's telling me that if I don't go burn those witches' house down today, something real fucked up's gonna happen to us. Like I got no free will for it. If I don't go now, I'm toast." He rotated his arm like a windmill.

Conan glared at him, noticing how different he looked after skipping a couple days of shaving. He wasn't the Rufus that helped him grow up.

"So what, you're tapping out?" Conan asked and folded his arms.

"Fuck that," Rufus chuckled. "I'm calling Marc. We got six hours until bands check in."

***

"That crowd was absolutely insane," Bryan said as he came off the stage and gave Conan a hug. "Thanks again for letting us open, man. We owe you, seriously!" He had to shout over the crowd's chatter and the thumping hip-hop music being played over the PA.

You'd have been here tonight, huh, Dad? We finally did it, just like you said we would. You know, a little assurance would do me wonders.

"Of course, dude," Conan said, forcing a smile.

There was a dull ache right in the dead center of his brain, but he credited it to smoking over a dozen cigarettes during the last two bands' sets. His throat and chest burned. He'd picked up a consistent cough, but had talked so little that he figured he'd be fine to perform, probably.

Whatever.

It was a near sell-out, as they expected. The agent showed up, and they'd already signed contracts. Besides that, Club Depression was past max capacity and there were close to another hundred kids waiting outside. Jackie almost had his drum kit set up, and Rufus was testing the volume of his and Marc's amps. Ten minutes until they'd need him on stage. He gave Bryan a pat on the back and walked with Snow backstage.

He dropped into the couch and just like he did before every show, he closed his eyes, took in a deep breath, and started counting backward from one hundred.

Three...

Two...

One...

"You're not telling me something," he said. "Why not?"

"I'm just trying to enjoy myself," Snow said. She seemed more distant than ever. To the point where her eyes didn't see him anymore.

"You know stuff in the future, right? None of my lyrics make sense by themselves. I can't even focus."

"Conan, I've already told you everything you need to know. There's no point."

He got up without kissing her goodbye. Instead, he gave her a dirty look.

"I love you, and I'd do anything for you. But since I've met you, you've really changed me into somebody I'm not."

Then he was floating and two hundred starving faces gaped up at him from dimming pale green light. They'd waited for this day their entire lives, but Conan wanted it over. He picked the mic up and gripped it until his knuckles turned white.

Jackie counted them in.

I've made a pact with planet Earth
Beneath her toxicity and my own disappointment
I've communicated with ruin
And this is what I've learned
I am not immortal
I am not a symbol
I am not your oracle
And I am not your savior.

Club Depression exploded, becoming a living thing of raw emotion. Sweat radiated from the sea of feverish bodies like a boiling pot. Conan could barely hear himself over the sound of kids screaming his words right back at him. Their ocean took over the stage. Kids leapt into the crowd and surfed the room from front to back. Conan had to grip his mic with both hands to keep it from being pried away. His chest tightened, and each exhale coated his tongue with either blood, sweat, metal, dirt, or oil.

Big Ben lifted some poor bastard above his head and threw him over the crowd like Donkey Kong chucking a barrel. Conan followed the body with his eyes and saw a dark and unmoving silhouette in the back of the club: River Devereux, her arms crossed. Despite kids being pushed around at her sides, she remained a statue. Their eyes met and Conan lifted his middle finger and smiled.

Pry my eyelids open
And hang my fuckin' head
I cannot guarantee my next breath
I can't stop this dream within my dreaming
But when I blink again, I hope you'll still be here.

The strobe lights flickered. Rufus and Marc stomped in unison, signaling the next song and breakdown. As Jackie came in with the drums, a burst of air shot up from beneath Conan. It made his skin go ice cold and cranked his headache up to an eleven. He needed to sit down, but the show had just begun.

He gazed back into the crowd, and their red faces turned into slow motion. Like a dream—a filter over his eyes. They were ghosts with stretched mouths, laughing at him.

Misty had joined River. He watched as both of them walked toward the exit.

An ominous cloud
Fingers its throat
She purges her humanity.

They'd be on tour as soon as Monday. That would be the end. They'd be free of Snow's family. It was bullshit that they even had to go through this. His anger was eating him alive.

Dad, you were supposed to be here.

Big Ben was waving, coming toward the stage and shouting. He wanted them to stop playing.

"Holy shit!" Marc shouted. He unplugged his bass, and the cable hit the ground, causing a steady static *buzz* over the growing cries of panic.

Then Conan saw one exit was completely aflame, impassable. Thick smoke covered the ceiling. Conan caught another odor. The burning bacon from that morning? He made the connection and dropped to his knees.

Screams, young, old, men and women. Everywhere.

Cutting my fingertips
On sharded broken memories

An older punk with a pink mullet shattered a window, but all there was on the other side was black. He jumped, but fell into the abyss like he'd leapt off a mountain. Kids ran to the second exit with expressions of sheer terror, pushing each other down and trampling others. Blood gushed from the doorway as if it were attached to an electric water pump.

Dad, why'd you let me play this stupid show? If you're mad because of what I did to Brandi, just say something. Anything. You're— Are you even watching over me?

"Fuck you! You're not here because you're dead. You fucking coward," Conan said, and ground his teeth until a piece chipped away.

He couldn't look away from the bodies, so he hit himself in the head as hard as he could. The guitar feedback had become a high-pitched screech, digging into his eardrum, grinding him down. He hit himself again. Rufus and Jackie were shouting, but he didn't bother making out their words.

How about this for fucking lyrics: Magic isn't real. I hate you and I hate myself.

A flaming beam fell from the ceiling and landed atop bodies with a wet crunch. The fires spread and black fumes plumed from the sizzling corpses. River emerged from the smoke.

Bang!

The loudest sound in the world, ear shattering.

Explosive, like a thousand toasters popping at once. River frowned as fluids poured from the bullet wound in her breast, soaking her white button-up.

Bang!

Another hole opened in her stomach.

Bang!

Bang!

Bang!

Her head snapped backward, but she did not fall. Conan couldn't hear the crackling flames any longer, just a long high-frequency ringing. Behind him, Rufus held a gun in his shaking hand. His eyes bulged, a vein stood throbbing in the center of his forehead, and his lips had turned into an ugly sneer.

River moved her head back. The bullet pushed itself out of her skull and black blood streamed down her face. She took another step forward. Conan wanted to strangle her, grab her by the throat. Kill her.

"I promised not to hurt you," River said.

A voice Conan didn't recognize shrieked behind him. It was a primitive, horrible cry. Somebody was screaming for their life and their terror shot straight into Conan's stomach. It was his fault. They were here because he wanted to spite River. He'd been biting down on his lips so hard that it made him sick. He retched, but hadn't eaten, so only bitter bile came up.

"I said nothing about him." She pointed.

The scream played on repeat. No consciousness behind it trying to change the tone. Not like a movie; pure, animal fear. Conan looked backward and saw Rufus backing away, his face twisted into a mask of snot and tears. His gun made an empty clicking as he continuously pulled the trigger.

Misty had Jackie in her grip, but she had changed. Her mouth elongated into a monstrous gape. Her entire body had stretched and transformed. She'd become as long as a Nile River crocodile, sharing the same proportions, but with torn human skin in place of scales.

"No!" Conan screamed. "I'll fucking kill you! I promise, I'll kill you!"

One of Misty's eyes wept blood. She grinned and showed that one of her teeth had been shot out.

She bit Jackie's head off.

Blood gushed from the cavernous wound like a fountain. His legs and arms broke into twitching nerve-induced spasms. She put him down her throat and swallowed the rest without chewing.

Something hit Conan on the side of the head, and he collapsed. River had taken the stage and placed the heel of her foot on his throat. Her face was black with blood and illuminated by the intense flames. She applied even more pressure, choking him.

Scars like postcards
Mailed from different landmarks
That you found inside of me.

"We decide who lives and who dies. Understand? Bring Snow to us, and you'll have your pitiful, meaningless life returned to you. Anger us again and we will be certain that all of your families suffer. This is your final warning."

She said more, but the only sound he heard was a high-pitched buzzing inside of his head.

River frowned at him and held out her arm. Misty had returned to her human state. The skin tightened on her flesh, but small open wounds remained like tiger stripes all over her body. She slipped on the shirt and shorts that River held out for her.

The sisters marched through the burning exit and disappeared across the threshold of violent flames.

Conan punched the stage. "She just knows everything and I'm just fucking worthless, huh?" He groaned and punched down again. "Worthless. We'll never fucking be anything but worms for them to grind into the soil. God dammit!" He punched the stage until his knuckles turned bloody.

He laughed, noticing at some point he had pissed himself. The heat was becoming unbearable. He glanced at Rufus, or whoever had inhabited Rufus's skin. He still held his gun, but gazed around the club with a dumb, gaping expression.

The wall next to the stage caved inward and Conan had to cover his eyes from the exploding cinders. Big Ben appeared with a sledgehammer and Marc at his side. They shouted. All Conan heard was buzzing. One of them, he wasn't sure who, picked him up and dragged him out of the club. He could only focus on the bodies they left behind.

At one point, the club crumbled to the ground. A pair of blackened walls was all that was left standing. Conan's head rang the entire time. He was sitting on a curb, but the noise was all he could attach himself to. Nothing else seemed real.

"We gotta give her up, man. This isn't right, this isn't normal shit," Marc was saying to Rufus.

Conan turned to look at them and saw Rufus with his lips shut as tightly as possible. He looked like a ghost of the man he was. His eyes had dark shadows around them and his cheeks looked sucked in.

"Bro, say something. I know it's fucked, but this is like devil shit, evil shit. They took Jackie. Where? We gotta trade the girl, one for one, right?"

"She ate him," Rufus chuckled.

"What—"

"She fucking ate him!" Rufus barked in his face. Despite the cops and firefighters surrounding them, he pulled out his gun and started reloading it. Marc wrestled with him, hiding it between them.

"I don't give a fuck!" Rufus screamed. "I told you, I told you from the very start that I needed to burn them. I told you I saw it in a goddamn dream. Y'all always joking, thinking I'm crazy. I told you, I fucking told you. That was my home, everything—everything. An eye for an eye, motherfucker. I wish I hit them first. We retaliate—we fucking retaliate!"

He looked and sounded like a total madman, but Big Ben and Marc both solemnly nodded their heads in agreement.

Conan picked himself up and walked away before they involved him. He didn't know where to or why, but he was walking, heading toward the alley across the street. His arm burned, his throat ached. He didn't know if he could even talk.

Dad, where were you when I needed you most? To be a better person, I needed you to help. I needed you.

As he entered the alley, he saw Snow sitting on a blanket and staring at him with her radiant sapphire eyes. She didn't even look alive; empty, like a doll. He rubbed his throat and crumpled to the ground, resting his head on her lap.

"What can I do?" he sobbed, and finally let it all go. He cried, quietly but without restraint, letting the tears pour from his eyes and snot roll out of his nose. His breath came in a stuttered gasp and his head throbbed like a hammer was trying to smash its way out.

"What can I do?" he whimpered once more, between breaths. "Can we run away?"

Snow ran her fingers through his hair. She made him feel like a child again. Like her lap was the safest place in the world and nothing could hurt them, not while they were alone together.

"No," Snow said. "They'd find us. I think it's time for me to give up."

Conan lay completely motionless, staring down at his bloody and swollen knuckles. His tears stopped coming, but his wounds remained wet with blood.

"No. I promised I'd protect you. So, I'll kill them."

I never said goodbye
So your heaven can't accept me
I hope you're happy there

I put together the glass pieces
Trying to build a reflection
Cutting my fingertips

On sharded broken memories

Scars are left behind
Scars like postcards
Mailed from different landmarks
That you found inside of me

Chapter 8

"Want a taco?" Brandi asked, hanging halfway out of Scrambo's window. "I got an *asada, pollo,* and a *carnitas.*"

Rufus didn't look up at her until she shut off Scrambo's engine. The odor of gasoline poured inside her cab and completely engulfed her.

"Sure," he mumbled after filling one canister and starting on another.

Maybe I'm a worthless idiot who did nothing to help? Maybe I never should have come here?

Brandi handed him a foil wrapper and met his eyes. His gaze was intense, unblinking, hungry, but not for street food. Scrambo's door rattled as she slammed it shut. She took too big of a bite and had trouble swallowing, wincing as fiery *chile* coated her throat.

Don't feel guilty, Scrambo assured her. *You had to hide out today, or you'd have been part of it.*

"It's pretty late. I'm surprised you're still out and, *uh...*" She cleared her throat. "Smoking a cigarette while gassing up."

"You didn't make it to the show," he grumbled. One of his canisters grated on the ground as he scooted it away. "Good."

"I drove by," Brandi said. A howling gust of wind forced her to take a step backward. "I wanted to stop, but figured I'd only make things worse."

Because it's all my fault, huh, Rengifo? Her hand found the small platypus plush in her back pocket. *Scrambo's just being nice.*

Rufus's jaw clenched. His eyes were reflective with tears, staring down at the pouring gasoline. Brandi's breath became loud in her ears, waiting for his response.

Ker-chunk! The gas nozzle stopped itself.

"Yeah," he said, and replaced the pump. He started loading cans in the back of his dirt-covered Honda.

"I get it, I'm with you." Her chest tightened up. "We'll hit them back."

Rufus paid her no attention. He froze in place for a pair of heartbeats before punching the side of his car so hard it dented inward.

"I've got nothing, nothing left, Brandi. I'll kill them, I'll fucking—" He paused as Brandi backed away, instinctively putting space between them and stepping toward Scrambo.

He lowered his chin to his chest.

"They got Jack," he said, and continued loading gas cans. The chemical fragrance became noxious.

"They kidnapped him? Fire's not gonna—"

"He's gone. There ain't no getting him back."

You might have been able to stop them, Rengifo said from her pocket. *You should have tried instead of hiding in Mr. Stephend's classroom all day.*

She found breathing difficult. She imagined Jackie screaming as flames engulfed Club Depression, their home away from home.

He didn't deserve this.

Rufus leaned against Scrambo, took a bite of his taco, and lit another cigarette.

"Conan made the move of a lifetime when he dumped you, huh? And these dreams, I haven't been able to sleep. Saw myself get fuckin' *eaten* two days ago. Just like Jack."

It's okay if he leans against me. It might be the last time.

"Eaten?" Brandi's heart did a nosedive, plunging into her stomach. She glanced at the shredded meat inside her half-eaten taco, and sour crept up her throat. She wrapped her dinner in foil, and Rufus offered her a cigarette.

"If that girl didn't exist." He chuckled and shook his head. "Then none of this would have happened."

She stared at the Marlboro for a long time before taking it with a shaking hand. She'd been hiding all day, and the tacos were all she'd eaten. Now they coated her tongue with sand. Her head had become entirely clouded with thoughts about River and Misty. She wanted to puke.

Tell him the truth, Rengifo said impatiently. *We need to help him.*

"God dammit!" she swore and kicked Scrambo's tire so hard that pain shot through her ankle. "Rufus, I fucked up real bad. *Fuck!* Where do you think I've been? How do you think her sisters found you?"

Rufus's lips pressed into a tight grimace. He glanced down at his feet and let his shoulders drop.

"It's my fault," she said. "I'm sorry."

He raised his arms and let them fall in a hopeless shrug. Another car pulled into the gas station and a group of preppy-looking high schoolers poured out from the Sonata. They laughed and pointed fingers at each other, barreling carelessly into the gas station.

Brandi stomped to Scrambo's tailgate. She could feel her blood boiling. She pulled out her spare gas can and got into Rufus's personal space, slamming down the metal canister with both hands so hard that it rang like a bell.

"Fill me up."

Rufus ran a hand over his unkempt mohawk. The bags under his eyes looked even deeper by streetlamp light.

"I shoulda checked in with you. I shoulda done more to keep you with us."

He doesn't trust you anymore. Rengifo said, still in her pocket. *Redeem yourself, offer what he wants.*

"Revenge is all that matters. We'll kill them."

"Kill them?" He laughed. "They walked through flames like nothing. I put a bullet in that skinny one's head and she didn't even drop. I'm burning their place down cause that's all I can do."

"Fire's good," Brandi said, nodding enthusiastically. "But when I was with them, I found something better. Trust me, do what I say and I promise we'll get revenge. Deal?"

Maybe we're both ghosts? Cursed to wander this town forever.

"The others will flip out."

"They can't hear what I'm about to tell you anyway. They'll get nervous and fuck it up. I've got a plan. You'll have to go tonight, or we won't be able to pull it off tomorrow."

"*Ha,*" Rufus smiled. "You really have always been a badass. Ever since you got us home in the snow from that shitty show at that pizza joint. Tell me. Whatever you need, consider it done. Who needs sleep anyway?"

***

Brandi stopped back by the taco cart and used up her last twenty before following Rufus to the abandoned K-Mart.

"It's like you always said, Kylie, eat first, talk later," Brandi mumbled as the aroma of her peace offering made her stomach churn.

She blamed the tacos, even though she was actually worried about seeing Conan again.

Her parking brake loudly clicked into place as she shut Scrambo off in front of the guys. Conan and Snow were bundled up by a barrel-fire. Marc and Big Ben shot dice on a flat piece of cardboard.

She checked her makeup for the fourth time that day, even though she knew there was nothing to fix.

"What's she doing here?" Conan barked.

She took a deep breath and traced her eyeliner, considering what she would say and how she wanted to hurt him back. Seeing him still gave her butterflies, no matter how badly she wished them away.

"What's it matter to you?" Rufus asked. "We're gonna need all the help we can get."

Go rip it off, Scrambo said assuredly. *The band-aid.*

Yeah, it's pointless, Rengifo added. *Things will never be the same.*

She closed her mirror and stepped out into the cold.

"I brought dinner," she said with a fake grin.

Snow clinched her blanket tight and approached Brandi. It was the first time she'd seen her since Thursday morning. Her hair was a mess, and her ocean eyes screamed for a dab of charcoal mascara.

"Thank you," she said. "For coming to help."

"*Uh,* yeah."

Brandi covered her nose with the sleeve of her jacket. The stink left behind by the army of rats combined with the rotten eggs smell of the boys' trashcan fire and drilled into her nostrils.

"I met your mother. I'm sorry about everything she's put you through. It's not fair."

"So you *were* with them? But now, you're here. Interesting." Her smile reminded Brandi of a little girl who was just told a secret.

Rufus pulled Conan aside, but Conan threw his arm off his shoulder. Their feet shuffled on the ground, and they grunted at each other through light scuffling. Conan threw his lighter, skipping across the empty lot.

"Jealous slag," he spat and got between her and Snow.

His lips curved into a snarl. She'd never been on the receiving end of his rage. Seeing him like this made her feel ten times smaller.

"You snitched us out. Stupid— God dammit, I can't stand you." He turned around, scratching his head vigorously. "You know what your new pals did to Jackie? That's on you. God damn, how could you?"

She met his eyes, but refused to apologize, fighting back tears, and burying memories of when he made her the happiest person in the world.

Maybe I'm a ghost? Lost and dying, sucked to the bone.

"Fuck you," she seethed. "After everything I did for you. Four years, Conan? And you just shit-can me. You're lucky I'm here."

Snow pushed Conan aside and got close to Brandi, inspecting her. A lily-like scent emitted from her, sweet, but not strong like a perfume.

Maybe I'm a ghost? And maybe I gotta stop thinking about HIS fucking song.

"It's true, we are lucky," Snow said genuinely. "Thank you."

"Don't thank her," Conan barked. "Can't you see how jealous she is?" He pulled Snow away, but Brandi could still see her staring over his shoulder.

"No," Snow said. "We need her help."

"Fuck that," Conan growled, his voice cracking in pitch. He grabbed half a cigarette off the ground and lit it.

"She's right," Brandi said. "I'm so sick of you. You're just a fucking stupid kid. You never learned a single thing about me."

"We should stop shouting," Marc said, getting between them.

Brandi swallowed dryly, tasting spicy residue in the back of her throat mixed with bitter.

"Fine. I don't give a shit about what happens to you, Conan. I'm sorry about your dad, and I can't blame you for all of this, but fuck you."

Conan wouldn't look at her, crossing his arms and glaring at Snow.

"Why do you keep staring at her like that?" he asked like a spoiled brat.

"Because we've never met before," she replied like she'd won a prize.

"We did when you asked Conan if he remembered you."

"That's not meeting you."

"We can't trust her," Conan said as if it were a fact. "I bet you've already told your new buddies where we are."

Brandi took a step forward, raised her fist back, and let it rip like a slingshot.

She punched Conan square on the bridge of his nose. He took a step backward and his face turned tomato red. His nostrils flared, and he retaliated by shoving Brandi with both hands, sending her flying back and landing on her butt. She bit the tip of her tongue, shooting pain through her nerves and bringing tears to her eyes. She covered her mouth and let out a small whimper as Big Ben stepped between them.

"*Enuff,*" he lisped.

Brandi pointed at Conan.

"I can give a shit what happens to you. I'm here to help Snow. That's all." Her angry tears mixed with her makeup, burning her eyelids. "Janna two years ago, and Kylie last year. Girls that disappear every fucking day. That's who I'm here for. I'm willing to die for them. I need to make sure you are too."

"Brandi knows how to kill them," Rufus added. Everyone's heads snapped up like mirror cats hearing an approaching predator.

"Yeah," Brandi nodded. "Snow, your mom really trusts me, or likes me, or she's lying. Whatever. Anyway, she showed me around your mansion."

Snow nodded her head, listening to her words with so much intent that Conan threw his hands up in frustration.

Adria's influence is everywhere, Rengifo said. *Snow won't agree because she'll want to protect her sisters. You can't tell her everything.*

"Are you listening to this?" Conan laughed, checking his nose for blood. "She's fucking buddy-buddy with them. Been sucking down beef Wellingtons and shit together?"

"Conan, shut up. Your constant bitching hasn't helped anyone," Marc spat. "Come to think of it, I'm fucking sick of you, man. I honestly can't stand your ass."

"Like I care," Conan laughed.

She is hiding something, Rengifo insinuated. *We need to find everything that will help.*

Brandi nodded, as if Rengifo were there next to her. She looked at Snow and, despite her neck muscles tightening, held her chin up high.

"Adria is to blame for all of our suffering, including your sisters. Her knife, I ran it through a translator. That's the key, right?"

"So, you want to kill her?" Snow said, slowly shaking her head. "I don't think murder solves anything."

"This isn't a question of morality, Snow. She's at the heart of everything."

Brandi tasted blood from her mutilated tongue. She still couldn't believe Conan actually laid hands on her. She shot him a murderous glare and disgusted herself for still not hating him.

"Evil doesn't need a heartbeat," Snow said, and her shoulders slumped. "It's like Rufus's dreams, or the lyrics Conan remembers. If anything happens to my mother, I know it will end terribly for everyone."

Brandi trudged away, rubbing her brow. Her mind felt like a drunk trying to put together a jigsaw puzzle.

You can't get cold feet now, Rengifo assured her. *Stay with the plan.*

"We've got to strike back."

"I don't agree," Snow said.

"So you saw something?" Conan asked. "In your visions, or however you remember things?"

Brandi glanced at Rufus and started chewing her fingernails. Snow had the potential of derailing everything.

"They aren't visions," Snow said. "It's going to be hard to explain. But I'll try. The reason you remember words you didn't write, or have dreams of things that haven't happened yet, is because I've already done this, maybe thousands of times by now. I can't tell you how many."

"Done what?" Conan asked, his face distorted in pain as he rubbed his forehead.

"Jackie was right," Rufus said in disbelief. "You're fucking with time?"

Snow nodded.

The others looked at her like she was crazy. Brandi remained stoic, analyzing Snow, the way her hands moved fluidly, placing her hair behind her ear like each strand had its deliberate place. She walked over to Rufus's Honda and drew a line in the dust of his rear window, and a second line parallel to it.

"It's more like I'm hopping from one time to another, trying to find one..." she let out a sigh, "where I don't die. And I'm running out of lines to hop to. That's why your memories are blending together. A connection of subconsciousness. At least, that's how Rufus explained it to me."

"Parallel universe theory," Rufus said, blinking rapidly.

Brandi's forehead ached. She couldn't connect to what Snow was saying. Everyone else seemed in on it. She couldn't help but think of how Misty had her under her spell before, and worried Snow was doing the same here.

"So what you're saying is that you're gonna be no help. Whatever, I always have to do everything myself."

Brandi threw open Scrambo's door. She grabbed the bags of tacos and walked them to his tailgate. She opened it and loudly let it slam before dropping the tacos onto the makeshift table.

"Everyone, eat," she said. They exchanged a look, and then she slapped her hands together. "Chop-chop, hurry, the sun will be up in a few hours."

Brandi pointed at Snow as Rufus, Marc, and Big Ben made a move for the food.

"I need you to come clean, cause I'm making no sense of this."

The boys didn't wait, and seasoned meat and vinegar hot sauce blanketed the stink of the abandoned K-Mart.

"It's just fate, or destiny, I forget which is which," Snow said, not meeting Brandi's eyes. "I've died so much that I gave up hope. Until now."

"You won't again. Not this time," Conan said.

"What's changed?" Brandi asked.

Conan looked at Snow with a feverish gaze. A desperate hunger Brandi had never seen out of him. Comparing him now to who he was years ago hurt, but his desperation made it easier for her to distance herself.

Or at least you can tell yourself that.

"You," Snow said, nodding toward Brandi.

Conan turned his starving gaze on her. Brandi relaxed her shoulders, not caring what they were talking about.

"How?" Conan asked.

You're kidding yourself, Rengifo said. *If you could get him back, you'd take him in an instant.*

"She's only been in one other life, and we never met. She stayed with my mother, with River."

It would have been easy to stay. Imagine all the things you'd have earned along the way. Life would be so different.

"I don't care. I'm here to do the right thing—" Brandi paused. "Wait, you said you did this thousands of times? These four days? I was only in one other repeat?"

Snow nodded.

"What does that mean?"

"It means"—she turned to Rufus's Honda and wiped away both lines—"all those other times, you were already dead."

Chapter 9

"It should have never come to this," Conan said, glancing at his and Snow's clasped hands. No matter how hard he tried, he couldn't help but imagine her leaving him forever. He continuously flexed his free fingers until they settled into a fist. "I'm sorry. I couldn't have done it alone."

Brandi scoffed and clicked her heels against the stone walkway. Big Ben actually tried to appear determined, mumbling assurances to Marc at their side.

The manor's surrounding air had a discernible freshness, like it was being machine-filtered. Conan figured it had to do with the symmetrical brush mazes and gargoyle fountains surrounding the walkway.

River and Misty were waiting for them on the top steps. Massive double doors loomed behind them. Snow's hand left Conan's grasp, and he took her into his arms. He took a deep inhale from her scalp. The slightly pungent odor of natural oils was a thousand times better than the artificial cleanliness they forced him to breathe. He reluctantly let her go, and she stepped to her sister's side.

Brandi went next, and River ran her hand down her sleeve, exploring her with a deep and hungry gaze.

"I'm grateful for your help in rounding everyone up. I was concerned yesterday, but I knew you'd return."

Watch this one, Dad. Today your son crosses the line and becomes a murderer.

Conan held his tongue. All he wanted was to explode, but he kept his mind occupied with fantasies of revenge. They alone brought a distracting smile to his lips. He turned his focus to crossing over the threshold of no return.

Brandi brought River into a tight embrace, squeezing her with both arms. When she came away, Conan glimpsed River was actually blushing.

I still bask in feelings
Of not being good enough
For this world

To be here with you.

The water pouring from the gargoyle fountain ate away at the silence. Conan added to the ambience by cracking his knuckles and expelling an exaggerated sigh.

"Jeez, Brandi," Marc chuckled. "You two got the hots for each other? Damn, we shoulda negotiated for more." He laughed and elbowed Big Ben, who was already picking a fight with his eyes.

"There will be no negotiating," River said. "You've waited too long as is. You'll take what we offer and that's your end. Where is the loud one?"

"He wouldn't come," Conan said, rolling up his sleeves. "Marc's gonna play guitar and Ben is gonna take over on bass. It was hard coming here after...what you did."

"You had opportunities," Misty said, glaring like a viper. "No one to blame but yourself."

"That's a real fucking sick way of—"

"Shut up, Conan," Brandi said. "Do what they say and you'll be on the road in a week. By the end of the year, headlining. Trust me, keep your mouth shut and you guys will be rich."

Conan played his role well, gazing down at his feet, pounding his fist into his thighs, avoiding eye contact. His heart told him to strike out, and repressing those feelings made his muscles ache.

All right, Dad, this time I'm begging you. Let her get out of this alive.

The mansion's doors slowly creaked open, as if moaning in pain. The three sisters led them inside. Conan forced one foot in front of the other until he passed through the ebony door.

The ceiling skylight seemed an eternity away. Twin pedestals spiraled from the core and matching stairways branched upward to a second floor. A table carved of bone rested in the center, appearing like a pupil of an eye.

Conan breathed in the air and wondered how they got the fancy smell of spicy citrus all throughout the house, and how much that alone cost them.

"So, Brandi, are you and this monster actually a thing?" Conan leisurely tossed his arms behind his head. "That's gross as hell. I bet it doesn't last."

"Conan, I told you to shut up," Brandi spat behind her. She whispered something to River and reached for her hand.

I've blamed myself enough
But won't hold my breath
I think I've made us sick.

His muscles quivered, and his heartbeat pounded in his chest. He could hide the heat flushing over him, but not the sweat that broke on his brow.

"You're joking, right? It's just too much. Come on." He knew it was a mistake, but stabbed his finger toward River. "I've got to hear it from this bitch's mouth. Killing just comes naturally to you, or what? It has to. How else can you justify what you're doing to Snow? You're just like the creeps who snatch girls off the streets. Did Brandi tell you what happened to her friends? Shit, you might be worse."

"Shut up!" River screamed, so loud it echoed down the corridors.

Anxiety from walking backward
On broken crutches
A resemblance of our deadweight.

"No more," River said, with shaking shoulders. "No more talking from you."

"Bitch, I don't have to listen to you. Not like you and mommy, huh?" Conan laughed.

Misty whipped around and snatched him by the jaw. Sharp pain shot into the back of his neck. Her eyes were glossy and wild. She looked to be considering the consequences of ripping his head off.

"I told you I could take care of myself," River said, slapping her hand away. "You're exhausting, Misty. How can you act like we're not losing her?" She had raised her voice, and a cherry-red blush consumed her face.

"Oh, are you done hiding? Ready to answer for something for once in your life?" Conan smirked, rubbing his throbbing jaw. "Isn't this gonna haunt you? You love your sister, right? Why not protect her?"

"Conan, stop," Snow said after a sharp breath. "She's having a hard enough time as it is. You'll all deal with it, but now's not the time."

Snow's compliance appeared to be the last straw. Whatever emotion was dormant inside of River was trying to get out. Tears appeared in the corners of her eyes. She raked her hair with hands like claws.

"Why?" she finally said. "It's not fair."

"You want this, why do you keep pretending like you don't?" Conan said, and flinched away from Misty's approach.

"I don't care what she says, another word and I'll kill you."

"I want this?" River said, placing her hand over her heart. Her eyes darted from Misty, Brandi, and then to Snow. "You think I haven't wanted to fight her my entire life? Having her force those *things* inside of me? It doesn't matter what we do. It's destiny shaped by her perception. I hate her, I hate her for what she's done to all of us, but it doesn't matter. It will end the same no matter what. Snow knows that. It's how Adria shaped us. There's no fighting."

Brandi pulled River aside and wiped her eyes. Misty glared as Conan walked around in a circle. His eyes focused on the bone table and onyx gargoyles watching them from flint pedestals.

"If we were better, we might have found a different way."

Conan sat down and slammed his fist on the floor so hard he thought he may have broken a knuckle. Snow dropped beside him. He leaned in and kissed her. Her intoxicating sweetness seemed more potent than ever.

"You're going to meditate?" she asked.

He nodded, and she took his hands in hers. Together they closed their eyes and Conan started counting backward from one hundred. When finished, he met her sad stare.

"We're reaching the boiling point," he said. "I'm sorry."

Snow scratched her neck and gave her head a restless shake. "Don't let it ruin your future."

"My patience has grown as thin as possible!" a woman's penetrating shout cried from the hallway.

Adria Devereux and her assistant hurried into the hall. The crux of Snow's suffering wore a red gown and black lipstick with a matching blindfold and overcoat. Despite the agitation in her voice, she showed her audience a pearly white grin.

"You were supposed to meet me in the parlor. What's taken so long? Snow is here, is she not?"

The grotesque pounds in my chest
And I'm watching my fucking tongue
I wish you'd just die
God I wish you would die.

"Yes, Mother," Snow said, and helped herself up.

"Oh, well, you've worried me sick, miss," Adria said, clumsily. "See how my hair has grayed? Immature and unnecessary. You know how important today is."

"Funny," Conan said. "I thought it was *her* birthday."

Meeting Adria's sightless gaze made him want to scream. Heat flushed over his entire body and the air in his lungs constricted, as if being choked.

Adria stroked her throat, and her lips curved into a grimace.

"You speak to me?" she asked, and snapped her fingers. Her assistant began rapidly tapping against her tablet screen.

Marc gave Conan's shirt a tug and cocked his head toward the exit, but Conan found it hard to focus on him for longer than a moment.

"Hey," he said. "Cool it, man. I ain't trying to catch a bullet."

He noticed for the first time how badly Marc and Ben were sweating. He cleared his throat and, for their sake, let his anger take a back seat. Just as the thought crossed his mind, a tall, lanky man appeared from upstairs. He wore a suit and had long black hair down to his shoulders. He held up a massive semi-auto pistol and holstered it so everyone could see.

Our sanity is the enemy
And her army is not of man
Show them no empathy.

Adria's bodyguard gestured to Big Ben with a *come here* motion, then frisked him up and down. He did Marc next. Conan held his breath and sucked the nicotine flavor off his teeth as the giant palmed him up and down.

"What, gunshy?" Conan chuckled. "So you're not like River? If we shoot you, you die?"

That earned him a heavy punch to the gut.

He dropped to his knees and clenched his abdomen. His head hit the floor and sparks shot off behind his vision. The metallic tang of blood came up from his throat as he slowly regained consciousness.

When he arched upward, he expected amusement, but nobody seemed to notice him. River demanded their complete attention. She held her eyes with her hands and couldn't keep still, shaking under her skin like an addict.

"No more talking," Adria hissed. "Consider yourselves lucky I don't skin you alive this instant. Your being here is an act of goodwill and nothing further."

Conan coughed, testing the waters and seeing if that was against the rules. When he stood up, he loudly slapped his cheeks and cleared his throat. No one noticed. A vein throbbed in his forehead. He considered getting the goon back, but avoided eye contact.

Okay, all right, hey, Dad, we can't fail here, we're here for her. Help me calm down. I gotta shut up, right? Help me out, easy, right? One slip and it's all over.

"Good," Adria said with a sharp nod. "So, this is the band. Can't say you're to my liking. Regardless, you will remain as discussed. There is the matter of your drummer. As of now, Misty will fill the role. After having consumed your sacrifice, she will have his same talents. She should be able to not only play like him, but write as well."

The more she spoke, the more fiery Conan's muscles turned. He ground his teeth and traced his chipped tooth with his tongue. His anger was becoming a force of motivation, surpassing impulsive action. Tonight, it would be his strength.

"This is a favor to you, but we've our own stakes. She will remain in the band until River leaves college. By that time, you should have reached whatever miniscule aspirations you began with. Brandi-Lynn, you'll be going to college with River. However, tomorrow we will place an entity of your own within you. If you ever disappear, it will take you."

Conan's heart sped as he fantasized about driving a blade through the heart of the monster that ruined Snow's life.

"It won't make me a zombie," Brandi said, "will it?"

"N-no," River replied, giving her head a twitchy shake.

Adria clasped her hands together and craned her neck, grinning with perfect teeth.

"We have waited long enough, haven't we? Now that we are all sufficiently bonded, let's head down below."

"Hold up, do we all have to go?" Marc asked, and the bodyguard's fist plummeted into his stomach with a dull thud.

Conan met Big Ben's eyes and risked the smallest shake of his head, although his jaw ached from how tightly he clenched. There was no reason to retaliate. They had already won.

"Yes," Adria hissed. Her assistant took her hand and marched them toward a large oaken door.

The trophy room was filled with blades, skeletons, urns, and fossil displays. A handful had been hidden beneath maroon and gold blankets. There were no artificial smoke or citrus scents here. No amount of money could cover the moldy stink of ancient rot and dust. Adria and her assistant whispered together and turned to Misty.

"Where did these covers come from?" she asked.

Misty shrugged. "It wasn't me."

"You—"

A whipcrack sonic boom interrupted Adria. A sound Conan had been expecting with held breath.

We are partners, so delicate
Glass pedestal cracking
Beneath the weight of each other.

Conan didn't flinch, but the gunshot rang in his ears. Adria dropped to cover, gripping at her assistant's pant leg.

"What's happened?" she gasped.

The bullet that entered the bodyguard's head pierced through, painting a display case with his brains and collapsing him to the floor. Marc hurried to the body and took the man's gun. His skin turned a shade of green.

The pistol in Brandi's hand still smoked. She turned it onto Adria's assistant and fired three more deafening shots, dropping the woman and sending Adria crawling backward against the largest covered display.

Misty had already begun changing. Her teeth clicked as she elongated into her gator shape. Her skin stretched and tore like ripping elastic.

Brandi slid Rufus's gun to Snow. She picked it up and held it under her chin.

"Someone tell me what's happened?" Adria wailed.

River laughed maniacally. She backed toward a corner and scratched at her face, speaking to herself in a language that didn't even seem human. Conan watched her tear off and swallow one of her fingernails. Sickness swelled in his stomach.

"Gastal and Winona are dead. Brandi shot them," Misty growled. "Snow's got a gun to her head. It's triggered River. She is succumbing."

"Why?" Adria groaned. Her blindfold had tilted to the side, and her lipstick was smeared across her face. "Wretched girl, why can't you just do what I say?"

Snow grimaced, her nostrils twitched, no doubt at the sulfuric burn of gun smoke.

"I'm sorry. I shouldn't have let it come this far. This cycle of hate, suffering. It's been so long. I'm desperate."

"You thieving witch," Adria said, and began groping the display with her hands. "You've been dipping into the well? I'll kill you. I'll kill you myself."

"Mom!" Misty screamed.

The satin cover fell away, and Rufus perched inside with Adria's golden knife. He gripped Adria by her hair, and before she could groan, he ripped the blade through her neck. A curtain of red spilled from her throat and the matriarch fell to the cold floor.

A half-changed Misty stared in disbelief. Snow let the gun drop and River screeched with laughter.

I've blamed myself enough
But won't hold my breath
I think I've made us sick
Too sick to recover
Too sick for each other

You'll never be safe
Lost in deep pools
Of your own blood
Deeper
Than we ever thought possible

Chapter 10

"They're clawing from my insides!" River's scream drove nails into Brandi's ears. "It's happening. They want release. *RELEASE THEM! RELEASE THEM! RELEASE THEM!*"

River repeated herself to the point of never-ending.

A pink-haired young man with baby-bangs and bags under his eyes appeared through the crack in the door. He worriedly glanced away from River and met Misty's stunted glare.

"Bring the others," Misty ordered. "Block the exits. *Sanguinis exterminatio.*"

The young man's face twisted into a curled grimace before he skulked away. He was too far for Brandi to fire at, and Marc didn't even raise his gun.

"God dammit," Brandi said, kicking a nearby display.

Your rage got the better of you, Rengifo scolded. *You can't blame the others, you pushed them into this.*

River's wailing became severe, like a woman in labor. She flattened herself out and convulsed violently, beating the wood floor like a toddler throwing a tantrum. Rufus stood opposite her, holding his blade with a white-knuckled grip. Misty moved from the wall and stood parallel to him.

"Snow, what's River saying?" Brandi asked. "What can we do?"

Conan stroked Snow's hair and whispered into her ear. She wore a slack expression, scraping her palms on her jeans and opening her mouth, but without saying anything.

Brandi wished she could slap sense into both of them.

Another suit-wearing guard kicked open the door. He held his gun at the ready. Marc fired three shots without warning. He missed two and buried the third between the man's eyes.

"Jesus Christ," Marc added, and let loose a powerful stream of vomit that reeked like rotten parmesan.

"We're all going to jail," Brandi said. "There's not a chance in hell we don't. Snow, you didn't say there would be others. You should have warned us."

Snow shrunk in size and weakly shook her head. A wave of dizziness washed over Brandi. Her heartbeat turned rapid.

"*MOTHER, IT HURTS!*" River screamed.

Misty started toward her, but Rufus raised his blade. Despite his eyes bulging from his skull, he exuded a medicated calmness.

"I'll kill her," he threatened.

Misty tested the waters and inched forward. As soon as she was in striking distance, Rufus swung and scratched her defending hand. Misty scrambled backward, and her entire body cringed at the cut. She took a deep deliberate breath, but shook as if freezing. Her jaw elongated and sawed through her own flesh like a desperate animal. Bone snapped as she severed her arm completely.

"You stupid cow," Misty whimpered, losing her balance. "You're so fucking stupid, Brandi-Lynn."

A stink like eggs and gasoline burned Brandi's eyes. River had rolled onto her stomach and ballooned to three times her size. Every exhale of her inflated lungs was belching more than breathing. The whites of her eyes had turned flaxen and her pupils, lifeless.

You're just mad at yourself for not knowing what to do, Rengifo said. *Rage has made you forget about Kylie, your friends, and what you truly wanted.*

"Snow, do *something,*" Brandi shouted. "Pull your weight. Everyone's trying to help. What do we do?"

Brandi licked the bitterness off of her lips, suddenly incredibly thirsty. A nagging regret told her she should have listened to Snow from the start.

"We have to..." Snow said. "No. You have to make a decision."

"Fuck you. Ben, grab that guard's gun then follow—"

"There's a lot," Marc interrupted, gazing through the door crack. "W-where did they come from?"

Brandi pushed him out of the way and bent her neck to glance into the hall. Over thirty Preston students had filled the parlor, all wearing the same unsure scowl as their pink-haired leader. She swallowed loudly and noticed her hands were shaking.

It's come to this. You've made choice after choice, and for what? To save others? You'll never find the truth now. Rengifo had never sounded so patronizing. *It looks like all you've accomplished is killing your friends.*

River's bloated guts bubbled and popped like a cauldron. The stench was frightening enough to make Rufus retreat.

"Who gives a fuck?" Brandi said. "We'll cut our way out. Use Snow as a hostage again. We're getting out."

"You're so stupid," Misty said, gripping her bleeding stub. "This is the last thing River wanted. Look what you've done. You think your little pissy-fit means anything? It's nothing compared to what's next."

Marc backed away from the door and lifted his gun. Despite the Preston students' shared insecurity, they marched forward like fearless soldiers. Marc fired off a pair of shots and dropped two. The army's eyes went wide with terror, but they trampled their allies and continued their mindless advance.

Morality and human values no longer mattered. This was a fight for survival. No matter how hard Brandi tried to imagine, she couldn't see anyone leaving alive.

Marc's clip emptied in seconds. Ten students had dropped dead, and despite the remainder's profuse sweating, they marched forward as if remote controlled. The chaos had triggered Brandi's claustrophobia. River's flatulence was making her nauseated. Conan and Snow retreated toward the back of the room. Brandi followed their lead.

She fired her last four shots and threw her gun at the nearest zombie. Preston students flooded the chamber. Marc and Big Ben disappeared behind the wall of their uniforms. Fatigue enveloped Brandi's limbs, but Rufus's gunshots re-sparked her adrenaline.

"It's hopeless," she said, her words muted by the surrounding chaos. Her heartbeat, a spider crawling up her throat. There was nothing she could do to hide.

Misty passed by her, transformed into her reptilian shape. Blood poured from bullet wounds in her side, and her snapping jaws advanced on Rufus. He held her away by wildly flailing the golden knife.

"Fuck this!" Brandi said and flipped over a nearby display case.

She reached down and grabbed an ashen wooden club from the debris. The horde was upon them and she struck downward at the nearest student, caving in her skull. Blood had mixed with the stench of River's gas, permeating the room with a choking odor like burning pennies and shit.

"Brandi, Rufus, over here!" Conan's powerful lungs carried his voice above the chaos.

When Brandi looked, she saw Snow had led Conan to the basement stairwell.

Rufus changed his path and hopped backward. He dropped a pair of Preston zombies with a backhanded swipe of his knife while still managing to hold Misty at bay. Her alligator eyes showed impatience before lunging at him. Rufus bent over backward and jabbed her armpit, sending her recoiling in screaming panic. Without hesitation, she bit off her remaining extremity, but then curled up in the far corner.

You let your rage blind you, Rengifo heckled. *And failed everyone.*

"So what?" Brandi shouted back.

Despite the reluctance building inside, Brandi started toward the basement. Before she got halfway to Conan, a substantial weight gripped her ankle.

River, bloated, swollen, and leaking bodily fluids through every orifice.

"You betrayed me. You're a liar," she laughed, and a stream of blood sprayed Brandi's sneakers. Fat on River's forehead enveloped her eyes, her swollen lips dripped a flood of spittle, and her hair fell in clumps from her scalp.

"So what?" Brandi screamed, and drove the hilt of her weapon into River's face. "So what? So what?" she repeated, hitting her over and over until her nose broke inward with a sickly crunch.

River's grip became so tight that she broke the skin around Brandi's ankle.

"You could have stayed," she chortled. "We could have been together."

A shriek boomed from the heart of the chamber.

Big Ben was being clawed to pieces. The students had him pinned down under a massive dog pile. Despite their reluctant expressions, their hands invaded his throat and ripped his cheeks open into a permanent grimace. The young man with the pink hair had tears streaming down his face as he reached into Ben's mouth and tore out his tongue.

River exploded with a guttural belch, nearly strong enough to make Brandi pass out. As she wobbled upright, River climbed up her like a ladder, dragging her halfway to the ground.

"No, no, please," she begged, prying her away.

"Why did you do this? Why did you ruin everything?"

She's right, you let your anger get the best of you. You should have listened to Snow. Killing Adria only made things worse.

"Shut the fuck up, Rengifo!" she screamed.

River leaned in and oppressed her with a kiss. As her tongue tickled Brandi's, a hot, wet flood gushed down her throat, choking her. She threw River off of her shoulders and spit out the rusty vomit. The force-fed spew looked like old yellowed mayonnaise and permanently covered the roof of her mouth with rotten grease.

She coughed—coughed and ran toward the stairwell. Something hard in the back of her throat made her gag, and she let loose her own spray, spitting out blood and a handful of River's teeth along the way.

Rufus's forlorn shouts demanded her attention.

With a stare nearly blinded by tears, she glimpsed Misty had captured Rufus in her jaws. The humanoid dragon bit him in half as easily as scissors cut through paper. His torso hit the floor, and he clawed away until his fingernails bled. She leapt onto his back and deflated him with a sickly crunch of breaking bones.

"That knife! Where is that knife?" Brandi cried.

The horde retreated from the opposite corner of the cell. They gave Marc a wide berth. He had the golden blade in his hand and stabbed a path toward the exit for himself. The stink of blood and voided bowels became choking. Brandi saw Marc's arms go limp and his chest rise and fall with crushing hyperventilation. His asthma slowed him too severely. Brandi blinked and Marc was buried under the student bodies. Before he completely disappeared beneath their accumulating deadweight, he flicked his wrist and sent the blade flying toward Brandi.

Maybe I'm a ghost. Destined to die here.

Maybe I'll take these fuckers down to hell with me.

Brandi's torn ankle throbbed with every step. She punched a crying zombie in the face and limped past Misty, who'd reverted to her armless human shape. Her chest rose and collapsed like a fish suffocating on land. Brandi dove past her and clutched the knife to herself.

They're just puppets. Adria made them this way. All those that died, they're completely innocent.

When a student approached her, she did not hesitate, but saved her energy and felled them with a scratch. She wouldn't make the same mistake as poor Marc; she wouldn't exhaust herself.

"Brandi, hurry!" Conan shouted.

She reached up and brushed her lips with the tips of her fingers. Despite everything that happened between them, he came back for her. She loved him for that. She wasn't alone. Together, they did it. Snow got out.

"There's nothing down there," Brandi said. "If we're going to escape, we have to do it together."

"No!" he said. "Snow's gone. We need to find her."

A blinding crimson overtook her vision.

"You fucking worthless fuck! Fuck you, Conan, I'll kill you!"

Nothing mattered anymore. There would be no escape. She gripped the blade and marched toward Conan, striking down three more students on her way.

"I'll kill you!" she echoed.

He trembled and dropped low—scrambling on the ground. Brandi raised her knife, but fireworks exploded behind her eyes, turning everything black.

Her vision returned, but with one eye blinded by stinging blood. Conan was inches away, taking the knife from her splayed palm. He stared at her with a bulging, unblinking glare. Brandi attacked, but her equilibrium was so shaken that she barely reached his shoelaces. Conan turned his back to her and ran away without a second glance.

You're a ghost, nothing but a rumination of your own failure and disappointment.

Something had a hold of her sweatshirt. With tremendous force, it flipped her around and she was staring into River's toothless grin. She appeared nearly bald, save for a few patches of black hair on the sides of her head.

"They're shaping me in their image. I can't control them," River giggled, as if it was the funniest joke in the world.

"River, we should—"

With a flick of her wrist, River tore Brandi's arm off at the shoulder socket. Brandi stared down. Her mind couldn't process it, but she could feel her blood draining from the wound. River tossed her remaining arm off with the same haste and Brandi collapsed backward.

River threw her arms to Misty—who fell onto her side and crammed them into her gullet like a starving snake.

"Oh man," Brandi said, dizzy and fever-stricken. "My mom's gonna be so mad at me," she chuckled. "I'll have to call out of work again."

Misty erected to her full, monstrous figure. She ate the nearest slave and then slithered over the mass of bodies. Only four living Preston students remained, the pink-haired boy among them.

"I think I'll keep you," River said. "Like a doll. You'll be well again. I'll have someone do your makeup, but I haven't decided if I want you to keep your eyes."

She noticed Conan running for it, blade in hand. Misty gripped one of the dead bodies in her powerful jaws and used it as a weapon to knock him off his feet. She grabbed another corpse and slammed its skull into the back of his head, ringing like bricks cracking against each other. When the knife had left his grasp, she approached.

"Your eyes are my least favorite part of you, that's for certain. They're severely plain." Despite her tongue swelling to the size of a fist, River still projected her same voice. "Wait!" she added, and turned to Misty.

Brandi cried out as River threw her across the chamber, landing at Conan's side.

Brandi wondered about her makeup—how terrible she appeared—how it was the only thing she was ever good at. She yearned to gaze into her own reflection. To take her time and contour her face into an unrecognizable shape. Life would be so much easier in the mirror, without friends, without responsibilities. Nothing but her reflection.

"Do it slowly. I want her to watch."

"You fucking evil bitch!" Conan screamed. "What's the point? Snow's alive and your mother's dead. You're free. Why are you still doing this?" Misty hit Conan hard enough to stun him. River dropped to his side and pressed a finger to his temple, healing him with a subtle ivory glow. As soon as he came to, he shrieked as Misty bit off his feet.

"She got out," Brandi slurred. "That's all that matters. We did it."

After the sisters reduced Conan's legs to stumps, he succumbed to shock. It only lasted as long as River let it. She woke him from his stupor with another tap on the temple, then held up his hand for Misty.

"See?" River said. When she turned to Brandi, one of her eyes had fallen from the socket. It dangled on a sickly tether of dissolving flesh. "Being my doll won't be so bad."

It's all my fault, huh, Rengifo? Are you still there? Snow knew this would happen. She knew I'd make it worse. That's why she's hiding.

Brandi gazed into the corpses, focusing on their odor and trying her hardest to pass out. Anything but watching Conan. She saw movement beneath the pile of bodies.

Snow crept out from beneath the massacre.

She even waited for the knife.

Misty placed Conan's head between her teeth and slowly applied pressure until it cracked like an egg.

"No!" Brandi screamed at the top of her lungs, bringing a million needles shooting through her severed arms and into her arteries.

"How dare you! You try to help now? Run! After everything we did for you? Run away! Get away! Run!"

Brandi met Snow's eyes, and something sweet made her gag. Sweet like the fresh organic honey you get at the tea shop; not like the kind that comes in the bear, but the expensive stuff flavored with flowers and fruit.

Snow hunched herself over and shook her head.

"You bitch!" Brandi screamed. "Wipe that fucking look off your face. How dare you! You need to leave, become a ghost!"

"I'm so sick of you ignoring me," River said. "I offer you my love, and you spit in my face?"

Brandi's head was yanked back with enough force to rip a chunk from her scalp. River's decaying eye fell from its socket. Before it hit the ground, it stopped halfway in the air, completely suspended, unaffected by gravity.

Brandi gaped at her, then at Snow.

Snow held the blade out extended in her hand, as if offering it to Brandi.

"You've seen it now," she said with a bitter smile.

"Did—did you stop time?" Brandi asked, and her throbbing eyes twitched all over River's ghoulish form. "Could you always do this?"

"I wanted to show you. I wouldn't blame you if you ran away," Snow said, and let her hands drop to her sides. "You won't though. You'll get out, like everyone told you. I know you're a hero, Brandi. Start believing in yourself."

"Run away," Brandi begged. "Please, everyone's dead. They died for you. Please, if you don't get away. It won't be worth it."

"This will be the last time. It's so exhausting," Snow said, gazing up at the ceiling. "I can't even remember what the emotions feel like anymore. It's happened so many times. One more will be enough. I know it will be. For you."

Time resumed and River unleashed a scream so loud that Brandi's eardrums burst. River gripped her by the neck and pulled. Brandi's flesh stretched and tore and she watched her own decapitated body collapse. Everything turned to black. Just as Brandi's eyes shadowed, and the last thoughts of regret fired through her synapses, Snow plunged the blade into her own heart.

Chapter 11

"Do you remember me?" Snow asked.

Conan's eyes stayed glued to her lips. A hammer smashed into the back of his eyes. Gazing at her wrenched his heart. Her existence made everything cruel in the world bubble to the surface of his conscience. He slowly stood from the lunch table and his fingertips glided over her arm, barely touching her. Her honeyed scent pricked an ache in his chest; burning, choking him a little with every breath.

Do I even deserve a second chance?

"Yes," he said, and kissed her. It did nothing to relieve his affliction.

"Yo, bro? Uh, what?" Jackie laughed when he saw Brandi's serious frown.

Conan didn't meet Jackie's stare. Guilt made him want to headbutt a wall. One thing was certain: He wouldn't let him get involved again.

"Don't worry about it," Brandi said. She clicked the tip of her sneaker against the concrete and stared at the lines on her palms.

Conan shared a glance with her. An electric connection formed between their tired eyes, suspending them away from the laughter and shouts of Peralta High School. Conan saw her in the parlor, limbless and broken by his side. The phantom pain came back like a ghost's claw scratching beneath his bones.

"I remember you too," Brandi said, stretching her arms out by spinning them like windmills.

"And you're...?" Snow asked.

"Doesn't matter," Brandi said. "Clock's ticking. We gotta figure out our next move."

Preston's visiting song girls walked from the front office and into the auditorium. Conan glimpsed River and Misty at the back of the line. A basketball boomed against the concrete. Two girls with cartons of milk ran past them. Their lighthearted screams made Conan's eyes twitch.

"Let's go, now," he said.

"All right, so we're ditching?" Jackie asked, following behind.

Conan looked at Jackie's grin and thought about how young he appeared. Conan was only a year older than him, but seemed a lifetime away. He changed his attention to Snow.

"Do you always ask if I remember you?" he asked, and paused at the brown rusted school gates. "Have I ever remembered before?"

"Yes," Snow said, tugging at the hem of her skirt. "But never like this."

"And how far did we get? Have we ever gotten close?"

"All right, bro, stop ignoring me." Jackie put himself in Conan's path. "Cause I'm not gonna lie. I'm starting to freak."

Conan heard Jackie's scream play in his head, over and over. When he blinked, he was in the past, and when his eyes stayed open, life didn't seem real.

"Jackie, I think you should probably sit this one out," Brandi said, pulling out her cigarettes.

Jackie gave his head a tilt and let out an unsure chuckle.

"Bro, we got practice today. You're not ditching us, right?"

Conan's tongue wouldn't work. Nausea had sunk deep inside as he watched Misty bite Jackie's head off like a movie being played behind his eyes.

"Jack," Brandi said, her eyebrows drawing together. "It's probably better if you don't—" She paused when Conan put his hand on Jackie's shoulder.

"You can't be with us," Conan said. "I don't care if it makes you upset."

"Why're you trying so hard to piss me off?" Jackie said and quickly hid his face. "Like you've ever given a shit. I get it. Fine, I'll kick rocks. Just try to save some ladies for the rest of us. Whatever." He spat and buried his hands in his pockets, walking back into the school with his head tucked into his shoulders.

Conan sparked his own cigarette, but it tasted sharp and unpleasant, like smoking old newspapers. He rubbed his forehead and walked around to the side of Brandi's truck.

"You've got a headache too?" he asked Snow. "I swear mine carried over from last time. It's been days. It's driving me crazy."

"Last time? What *was* your last time?"

Conan watched Jackie's back as he stepped through the old gate back into Peralta.

"We failed."

"But we *can* trust her?" Snow asked, pointing at Brandi.

Brandi had wiped off her makeup and was re-doing it in her truck's mirror. Conan crossed his arms.

"Hey, Brandi, can we trust you? You're not gonna try to kill me again, right?"

Brandi rolled her eyes, but wasn't distracted from applying her foundation.

"I don't know, Conan," she said. "It depends on how much of a selfish prick you're going to be."

"So, she *was* working with my mother?"

"Yeah, but don't worry. I betrayed them and got everyone killed. You can trust me." Brandi flipped her visor shut. "The real question is, what can you do to help us deal with Adria? You told me this was our last chance. No matter what."

"That's it then," Snow said, and shook her head. "I can't help but perceive that we've already repeated a mistake, and it's only been minutes."

Conan's headache crept into the back of his neck. He wanted to contribute, but the pain was becoming too distracting.

"If you're worried about anger or violence again, don't be," he said. "We've got you to keep *us* in check."

Brandi ditched her cigarette and started her engine. Bathory's self-titled CD came on the speakers at an aggressive volume. She only turned it down slightly before closing her eyes and leaning back.

"Okay," Conan said. "Before we go anywhere, we need a plan. Snow, what's the closest we've ever gotten to winning?"

"Well..." She raised her hands and let them drop. "Last time. Or you both wouldn't remember it. What happened?"

"Seriously? Not much. We, uh, we killed Adria, but your sisters, they got us."

"I see," Snow said, disappointed. "That explains your attitude. Violence was a poor choice. I'm surprised I ever agreed."

"I made you," Brandi said. "I'm what's different. You told me one other time I worked with your mother. Every other time, I was dead."

"That's very interesting."

"Quit getting distracted," Conan said, clenching his fist. "If you've done this so many times, remember *something* that will help us. You waited until it was too late before."

"Getting angry at me won't help, Conan. None of the past matters. Only what's chosen in these final days."

Conan dropped his unfinished cigarette to the asphalt and stomped it. He rubbed his dry throat and leaned beside Snow. He racked his mind, trying to come up with a plan, but found no answer.

"Hey," a noon-duty officer shouted from inside the school. "Do you students have classes? Lunch is almost over. Doors lock in three minutes."

Conan gripped Snow's hand and led her into the back seat. Despite his rolling stomach, he couldn't help but chuckle at the strong reefer stink.

"Well, we're off to a great start," Brandi said. "Snow, no offense, but you're pretty useless. I need something to eat. Maybe then we will have some idea what the hell we're gonna do."

Conan punched his thigh. He couldn't focus and *needed* to contribute something. The back seat of Brandi's truck brought up too many distracting memories. They were running out of time.

"The knife," Conan's lips said as Bathory paused its sonic assault. "We've got to get that knife as soon as possible."

He met Brandi's glare in her rearview mirror—triggering memories of her shouting death threats as she chased him through the parlor.

"Violence will be answered with violence," Snow sighed.

"We need it as a precautionary thing. We won't use it if we don't have to."

"Conan's right," Brandi said, taking her hands off the wheel.

"I won't be able to get it alone," Snow said. "I don't know if there will be another opportunity for me—"

"You really don't listen to Conan at all, do you? Can't say I blame you. You won't be alone. You'll be inviting your new best friend over to stay the night. It's your birthday, remember?"

Snow contemplated and quickly nodded.

"An interesting concept. If you can get my sisters to like you, then a distraction won't be needed."

"Trust me. That won't be a problem."

"Wait, this is the best we can do?" Conan scoffed. "Are you kidding me? I'm just supposed to piss off somewhere?"

Brandi pulled the parking brake, killed the engine, grabbed her weed, and slammed the glove box.

"Yeppers."

"You actually expect me to sit back and do nothing?"

"It's what you're best at." Brandi shrugged impatiently.

He wouldn't be surprised if she came up with her plan solely to exclude him. That being said, she had already sacrificed everything once to help, and that life seemed like less than an hour ago.

"It's just the beginning, Conan," Snow assured him. "This is the first hope I've had in a long time. I know you want to help, and I love you even more for that. But I've finally got a real chance."

He followed Snow out of the truck and didn't say a word when she kissed him goodbye. His headache had become splitting, and as he watched the girls walk toward the front office, he confirmed what he'd been thinking his entire life.

He was worthless.

In school, he never stood a chance of going anywhere. The only reason he'd ever succeeded as a singer was because Rufus forced him to practice. He only believed in himself because his dad had told him to.

The sun warmed the back of his neck. Following the golden leaves on the sidewalk, he realized he'd been walking home. He picked up a golden sycamore leaf and stared through it.

"I know what she meant now. No matter what we do, it doesn't matter."

Arriving home, he unlocked his front door and let his backpack drop. He dug out his lyric book and sat down at the kitchen table. Staring at the blank TV screen, and at his father's La-Z-Boy, he wondered out loud.

"When it's this quiet, does everyone hear the same silence? Hey, Dad, what advice would you have, really?"

He would turn the news down and glance back at Conan with his watery brown eyes.

Have you done your writing? Don't worry about the world going by. Sit your butt down and focus on that. When it comes to yourself, never take no for an answer.

The pages, his book, everything differed from his last life. New lines he couldn't remember putting down, but nothing he read would help. He dug through the words, but no matter which past they came from, they were pointless.

Conan stood from the table, and his legs turned weak. He gripped the back of his chair and steadied himself before collecting his things and walking to his bedroom. He dropped to his desk and pulled a pen out. Without Snow nearby, all there was left was to sell his rage and pain.

Deaths gates open as the toll is paid
Your last breath fills the reaper's flask
Its worth yet to be determined
The body remains cradled in our arms
Withdrawn from life's presence
Decay is only the beginning
The soil must grow a notable harvest
In exchange for the tears we bury
Pray for sunlight
And time enough to blossom
When the light leaves your eyes
The heart stops to beat
Remain with us in blooming foliage
The tide changes as their river sails swell
I greedily fill my lungs with life's essence
Until tomorrow's morning sun arrives
Until I can pretend that the night sky never came
With a sigh of relief
We disperse our cult of heartbreak
Awaiting our next parishing
So patiently beneath God's eyes
In exchange for your martyr
Poison runs through the swelling vine
Corruption spreads throughout your garden
A rotten succor leaking into our split-open veins
The roots construe purple in suffocation
Delicate with blood that refuses to set course
We consume the pitiful flesh
For it's all we have to show
For it's all we have to show

His hand cramped, but he didn't stop. Words poured from him, and whenever a pen would give him trouble writing, he threw it at the wall and grabbed another. He no longer felt angry, but couldn't give it up either, not without trading his words for something, anything.

They'd been nothing but worthless. He hated it, how it was all he was good for. If he did anything but write, he'd be with Snow now. Worst of all was that it didn't even ease his suffering.

Knock-knock!

The door opened and a spicy *chile* aroma wafted in from the kitchen. His mom smiled shyly, her eyes puffy and red.

"I saw you were home."

"Here," he said and held out his notebook. She traded him a plate of *huevos rancheros* and glanced down.

"You're sure?"

"Mmhmm," he said, already with a mouthful of runny yolk, salsa, and refried beans. He couldn't remember the last time he'd tasted anything other than cigarettes. A tear came into the corner of his eye.

"He was so proud of you," she said, and gently put the notebook down. "You're going to do great things with your words one day."

"Words are just words. They can't help anyone."

She took a seat on his bed and placed his book down.

"They helped me. Conan, everyone has a purpose. His was to help you. Some people aren't here as long as others. That's just the world. It hurts, but know that he's still in your heart, trying his hardest."

Conan cleaned his plate. He wiped his mouth and took a long, cool drink from his water bottle.

"What if I fail? I let him down, and everyone gets hurt because I wasn't good enough? What if I do nothing with my life and I'm just worthless? He'd be disappointed. If he's here now, he already is."

"Conan," his mom said. "As long as you go through life, and you make choices you believe are right, no matter what, he will always be happy for you. It's hard, I know, but we have to accept the horrible things that happen. If we let them weigh us down, we'd never take another step again."

As she spoke, an indiscernible buzzing began. She finally sighed and held out his vibrating phone.

"Play your music, and I promise, you'll help someone who needs it as much as you do."

She ruffled his hair, picked up his plate, and then stepped into the darkness of the hallway. Conan gazed down at Rufus's name on his phone and swiped the answer button.

"Yo."

"Hey, man, what the hell's wrong with you? Choosing threesomes over practice? Fuckin' segue, we got three days left until the big one and you're seriously screwing off somewhere?"

"We got less time than that. Come get me. I'm at my place. And thank you, Rufus, for everything."

The line went quiet, except for the sound of Rufus shuffling around.

"Everything all right, dude?" Rufus asked.

"Nah. In fact, I think things are worse this time around. Like we've been dealt a really, really shitty hand and there's nothing we can do about it. It really sucks. We're gonna have to get a nice streak going, just to break even."

"Uh, all right. Jackie said you were being a dick, but I think his translation was—"

"I'm sorry. To both of you. My dad died this morning on his way to work. It's been hard to think."

He wished he could just be alone, but it was too late.

"You're—you're serious? Damn, man, yo. I'm sorry, I—"

"Lying around and feeling sorry for each other isn't gonna help. People need us. Whatever, we're wasting daylight. Come get me. Don't forget your smokes."

"Motherfu— Ight, I'll be there in twenty."

Conan hung up and fell into his bed. He closed his eyes, and felt his legs being bitten off, his hands next. Brandi's face twisted into rage as she chased him with the knife until he struck her down with the wooden club. He saw Snow and imagined how she'd died a thousand times already.

At least I've found a purpose. I'll trade anything to save you, anything but my love.

"One hundred... Ninety-nine... Ninety-eight..."

Will there ever be another
Day to understand it
I just wish your words
Could reach me here

Chapter 12

"His name is Weasel," Misty explained, twiddling her fingers into her Pallas cat's enclosure.

This episode of *déjà vu* made Brandi stumble and nearly faint. Since starting the day, she saw everything through a clouded filter. Her mind kicked into rapid-fire over rationalizing what she was doing, and despite the stakes, she cringed away from Misty. Although she had done nothing worth her resentment in *this* life, her blue eyes and stretched smile made Brandi's arms and legs writhe with the pain of amputation.

The murk became too thick for any visibility. Brandi turned to Snow to remind herself why she was there, but it was River who glanced through the fog. She hadn't changed at all in this reality, sitting with her legs crossed, reading a book with her back against the wall.

It's whatever, right, Rengifo? She had shoved her stuffed platypus into her jacket without a glance. *Just don't get upset. We do our job and nobody becomes a demon balloon.*

She covered her mouth and snickered at her own joke. Not that funny; still, it tickled.

"He's super cute," Brandi said with a forced smile, then turned to River and cleared her throat. "Is something the matter? You keep staring at me like I've stepped in shit or something?"

Brandi's grating tone brought alert to Snow's eyes, but River remained entirely stoic.

"No. My apologies. It's just a matter of—I can't help but perceive that we've met before," River said. Her hair fell across her face as she glanced down at the book in her lap.

Has it not occurred to you that she may recall pieces of the past? Rengifo's voice had become deeper, and he'd adopted a strange accent. Brandi reached into her jacket pocket and instead of a platypus, she pulled out a small black and gray, mustachioed, schnauzer plush.

The name's Charles, and now is not the time for exchanging pleasantries. The plushie's lips moved cartoonishly as it spoke. *Gaze onward now, dear.* He pointed. *Come alive.*

"Oh no," Brandi groaned.

"Are you all right?" River asked, closing her book.

"I don't think so," Brandi chuckled, and stowed Charles away. "It's strange, since walking into your home, there's a pressure, like I'm being squeezed. Maybe we *have* met?"

Brandi grinned as Charles projected into her mind.

Bravo, he exclaimed. *Good show, inside baseball. Lovely execution, Miss Brandi-Lynn.* She burst into laughter, imagining the schnauzer's mustache bobbing as he spoke.

Snow's eyes grew wide. She gave Brandi a sideways glance as River got up and approached them.

"It is truly uncanny," she said with a smile.

"Well, you are, like, totally witches," Brandi said, unable to help herself. "Did you summon me with a spell? I've wished on a couple of shooting stars myself. Have you been praying for your soulmate?"

Angry or not, method-acting River into falling in love with her and breaking her heart in one night would be a sweet revenge, although it wouldn't make them even. Her legs still ached with remissions of feverish pain.

Holy shit, I really am a ghost this time.

"Oh, totally," Misty said, pressing herself into Brandi. "But sorry, hun. If River's soulmate was at our doorstep, I'd imagine him looking like a pretty boy. Baseball stud, golden hair, blue eyes, dump-truck ass, y'know?"

"So that's what you're learning over at Preston," Brandi said and winked. "What other spells have you got for me?"

"Anything, really," Snow snapped, adding an uneasy smile.

"Anything? If I could have anything, I'd want to be strong, and be able to track down and deal with creeps myself. To be strong, you know, help girls who need it, not have to worry about myself."

Chivalrous and worthy, Charles cheered. *You may find out the truth about Kylie yet.*

River bore into Brandi. Her scorched blue eyes met hers and Brandi didn't dare look away.

"How boring," Misty said. "I thought you'd say something fun, like you wanted to fly. If you want strength, you just gotta—"

"Enough, Misty," River snapped. "I don't know why you're so compelled to entertain Snow's guest, but don't trust her unless she talks with Mother first."

"Don't trust her?" Misty repeated.

Her eyes became flint, predatorial, prepared to end things that instant. The room's temperature plummeted and Brandi's steady breaths became visible beneath her nose. Weasel let out a panicked chattering and fled into the cover of his hovel. River lowered her gaze and Misty did the same, walking to her sister's side.

Stare into the eye of your adversity, Charles blubbered. *And show no fear!*

"Hey, what's up? Did I offend you?"

Weasel burst into a yowling fit, as if he had taken Brandi's defense. The sisters traded an unsure look, and their frigidness dissipated.

"Why are you two acting so strange?" Snow asked. "I don't want to worry. I've talked with Brandi enough. You can trust her. Honestly, you're really being kind of rude."

As Snow berated her, River melted into a slouch. Weasel left his hobbit hole and Misty harmonized her alto with his chattery song.

"She's only joking," Snow added, shaking her head.

"Magic is nothing to joke about," River mumbled. "You know that better than—"

"And you think she does? It's not like she's had a spirit shoved down her throat. She probably thinks we're insane now and wants to leave as soon as possible."

She's setting you up, skipper, Charles guffawed. *Now, the kill!*

"I don't think that," Brandi said. "I'm sorry, River, I didn't mean to offend you. You're just really cool and pretty and Snow said you guys liked this occult stuff. I really didn't mean offense."

Brandi remained with steady eye contact, exploring River. She arched her back, trying to appear enticing. River squirmed away from her, nibbling her bottom lip.

"I'm sorry," she said. "We've been on edge lately. Birthdays can be a stressful time for us."

A steady piddle started behind Brandi, followed by the powerful stench of cat piss. She ignored it, keeping the drama within reach.

"I understand. I mean, I don't," she said. "Only what Snow told me."

That turned River's blush into a scowl of anger, though her clenched fist didn't seem aimed at her.

I'm just a ghost. I might hurt you. But maybe your mom's worse? Can we make you choose?

"You sure like to talk, don't you?" Misty asked, standing so close to Brandi that she smelled her cinnamon gum. Brandi stepped backward, but Misty gripped her arm.

"Our birthday should mean nothing to you. As far as you're concerned, forget about it."

Misty bared her teeth like a dog and tightened her grip, walking until Brandi's back pressed against Weasel's cage.

"Back off. I don't know what you want from River, but I have no issue killing you. We've killed girls before, and no one's ever found out. Snow likes you, and that's enough for now. But I'd have no issue ripping you to pieces."

Brandi didn't have to pretend to be afraid. A bead of sweat broke on her brow and spots appeared in her vision.

"You've killed other girls?"

"Mostly boys." She let her smile stretch. "But yeah, girls too. Family comes first, sorry."

"You're seriously doing this?" Snow said and stepped between the girls, despite Misty's narrowing glare. Snow shoved her back with both hands, wiping the smirk off her face as her feet scuffled backward.

"You do that too much, Misty, one day it'll get you in trouble. You're too stupid to be this overprotective. It really never crossed your mind why River's acting this way?"

Brandi shrunk herself. Snow and anger didn't mix. If she was acting, she should consider it a career option.

"I don't understand," Misty said. "What do you want from me? What do you want me to do?"

"You're not a dog, stupid." Snow shoved her again. "You don't need orders. Use your brain."

Misty genuinely looked hurt by the outburst. Snow threw her fist down in frustration. She leaned in and whispered into Misty's ear.

"You're gay?!" Misty exploded.

River turned her hand upward and gave Misty a disgusted look. As if to say, *Seriously?*

Snow turned on Brandi. Her eyes were like two thunderstorms.

She wishes for you to stop acting like a child, Charles said. *Put your war face on. It's time to dilly up the day.*

"Dilly up the day?" Brandi whispered aloud, unable to keep from laughing.

Snow turned back around and exchanged masks as easily as someone could breathe.

"Uh, yeah, and she and Brandi are gonna make out *tonight*," she said and threw an arm over Brandi's shoulder.

"Totally, angry and gay, but I'm into it," Brandi said, still laughing at Charles's nonsense.

River turned crimson, completely at a loss for words. Misty bunched up her fist, leapt into the air, and cheered.

They'd hardly changed. The only actual difference was how threatened Brandi felt. It was becoming hard to focus on anything else. And there was Charles. She couldn't help but wonder what else about herself had changed. What else had she left behind?

Stare into that abyss long enough, lassy. Charles said, *and, well, you'll go batty! Gwahahaha!*

The afternoon turned to dusk. Misty put on an 80s anime movie where a boy got telekinetic abilities after a motorcycle accident. They only half-watched it. Instead, they gagged down a shot of Adria's scotch, which burned like swallowing a campfire, and settled on passing around a bottle of expensive wine. It tasted sweet, sour, and with a complementing spiciness.

Although River excluded herself from drinking *and* was too cool to play *Mario Kart*, she still kept a cheery demeanor as time stretched into the evening.

This show has gone on long enough! Charles drunkenly blubbered. *You hold all the chips now, ma chérie!*

"That's not British. Are you even trying?" she furiously whispered into her jacket pocket.

"What was that?" River asked with an upturned eyebrow.

"Oh, sorry, just thinking out loud. Hey, River, want me to do your makeup?"

"What? No. No, thank you."

"Oh my god," Snow said. "River, you have to. Brandi's the best. I'm sure you can already tell."

"Lots of practice," she said with a brazen shrug.

"River, please, you have to," Misty added. "She looks like she's even better than Katrina."

"*Pleaaaase,*" Snow pleaded.

River drew it out as long as she could, holding her breath and tapping her fingers on the coffee table before gazing into her lap and grumbling.

"Fine."

Misty and Snow gripped each other's arms and danced around the couches. Their bare feet struck a steady beat against the wood floors.

"Misty, let's get pizza."

Misty stopped dancing, and the room became quiet, aside from anime civilians screaming at some giant blob monster.

"We can just order it," Misty said, wiping her palms on her leggings. "Besides, Mom won't let me take any of the cars."

Snow glanced at Brandi, and she knew what she wanted. Brandi almost slipped up and told her to shove it. There was no time. Her head was spinning in circles.

"You can take my truck."

Her heart sank. She clenched her eyes tightly shut, imagining what Scrambo would say to this. He'd only ever been good to her, and she had told him she wouldn't let anyone else behind the wheel unless it was an absolute emergency.

During war, great sacrifice must be made, Charles said. *We all must do things we don't want to. This is only the beginning.*

"But I wanted to watch," Misty said.

"That's no fun. I want it to be a surprise. Come on," Snow rebutted.

"But the wine."

"You're seriously doing this right now?" Snow asked, stroking her throat and pulling a face.

"You'll be all right?" Misty whispered.

"Seriously? Of course I will be," River said and rolled her eyes. "Just get whatever Snow wants."

"Wow, imagine that. She'll be fine. Come on, I'll order on the way there," Snow said, dragging Misty away.

As the sisters departed, an eerie music box played inside of Brandi's head. Her psyche was bending. The alcohol made her painfully aware of that. It was hard to focus on anything but the insistent melody.

Anything other than Charles.

"Do you have your own makeup?" Brandi laughed, thinking of the schnauzer's mustache.

River met her eyes, cold but shy. She really didn't even need cosmetics. The triplets all shared a complexly simple beauty. Like a refreshing breeze.

"No, but Snow does, still packaged and sealed," she said, standing. "Besides, I like her room better."

River led Brandi through the hall and up the spiraling stairs, then passed a bedroom.

"Misty's room. She doesn't like anybody in there when she's not home. If you're curious, she isn't hiding much. Lingerie, condoms, drugs, all in her sock drawer."

The second door River opened revealed a plain room with blue walls and a matching duvet. Subtle piano music played from a stereo built into the ceiling, eerily similar to the music Brandi thought was playing in her own head.

"My room, take a glance. I'm not a freak. See? The music is because I hate the quiet. I don't go out much."

The last room was a hundred thousand times more normal than anything in the Devereuxs' mansion. *La Dispute* as well as *Manchester Orchestra* posters decorated the walls. A large white and black zig-zag rug covered the floor, a matching bedspread, and a hastily set-up digital keyboard had been thrown together in the far corner. River led her inside and Brandi took a deep inhale of freshly cleaned linen.

River sat in front of the vanity that was loaded with drawers of foundation, baskets full of eyeliners, wooden racks of lipstick and nail polish. Overall, more than a couple grand worth of unopened product, *not* counting the French brands that Brandi didn't recognize. She couldn't help but grin at the loot. She'd been wanting to toy with Chanel and Pat McGrath for years, but not a chance she could afford it.

"Guess I'll get to work then."

Brandi started with moisturizer, letting her hands warm it before massaging it in with small circles. Next, she patted on primer and applied foundation, using her fingers since she hardly needed any. River had no blemishes, but she added a tidbit of concealer beneath the eyes. False eyelashes were completely unnecessary, just the unholy trinity of eyeshadow, eyeliner, and mascara. Finishing with highlights, lip liner, and lipstick. She wrapped it all up with Urban Decay setting spray and pocketed the bottle.

I'm a beautician's ghost and we're trading River's trust for a knife. Too easy.

"Now it has to set," Brandi said.

They quietly stared into each other's eyes. A minute passed. Without warning, she leaned in and pressed her lips into River's. She parted hers in reply, and greedily sucked Brandi in, starving for the affection. Brandi continued in a passionate embrace, tasting her tongue and saliva until River pushed her away and pressed her palm into her eye.

"I'm sorry, I never should have—"

"No," River hurriedly replied. "I mean yes, God, you shouldn't have. I think it's made me hate you," she said and bit down on her own fist.

"What?"

"I do. I hate you, Brandi-Lynn. It's distracting. It's only desire. I'm not a moron. We will not be together."

"Pizza and Crazy Sticks!" Misty screamed, trampling up the stairs like an elephant.

When she saw River, she flinched away, fumbling for words. She shot Brandi a quick glance before going to her sister.

You cannot think of tomorrow today! Charles warned. *You must be better than that and only face the repercussions of your actions when they come to fruition. Damn you, girl! Use your heart.*

"It's incredible," Misty managed.

"Thank you," River said, and took a cloth from the table and blotted her eyes. "I'm sorry, I've ruined it."

"You've ruined nothing. It's perfect."

"Oh," she said. "But I fear Brandi may never kiss me again."

She laughed as Misty became stiff.

"You didn't? You did."

"I dunno," Brandi said and winked. "Play your cards right, and who knows? Where's Snow? She'll want to see."

I'm a ghost? Charles is right?

"Bathroom," Misty said, looking through the used products. "She disappeared as soon as we got back. She didn't want to go at Luigi's."

***

Brandi had taken the couch in accordance to Snow telling her rigidly that's where she *should* sleep. Sleep never came, and Charles had occupied the late hours of the night with a monologue.

Continue to cut the throat around the entire neck. From the jawline to the back of the skull. Once muscle and ligament have been sliced away, the head can be cleanly removed by gripping it on either side and twisting it off. Separation occurring where the spinal cord meets the skull. This is indicative of the method to be used for dividing other bones or joints.

Brandi had to cover her mouth with the sleeve of her jacket. It did nothing to keep her from snickering though. Charles had propped himself onto his hind legs and started marching back and forth. The small lips under his mustache worked double time.

The merits of keeping the skull as a trophy are debatable for two principal reasons.

First, a human skull may call suspicious attention to the new owner.

Secondly, thorough cleaning is difficult due to the large brain mass, which is hard to remove without opening the skull.

She wasn't insane. That meant repeating things. This was a memory. Kylie brought the book up at their sleepover: *Butchering the Human Carcass for Consumption.* They'd stayed up all night reading in front of the computer screen. They had chicken tenders with barbeque sauce for dinner.

The brain is not good to eat. Removing the tongue and eyes, skinning the head, and placing it outside in a wire cage may be effective.

She caught Snow's scent as soon as she entered the room. Choking, honey and lilies. Her stomach lurched, and she burped up pizza sauce and garlic sticks.

"I've got it," Snow said. Brandi didn't even flinch, still quietly chuckling at Charles's march. "Brandi, come on."

"Maybe she's a ghost, that's why she's so quiet, huh?" Brandi said and laughed a little harder.

"Brandi? Brandi?" Snow slapped her across the face. Not too hard, but strong enough to snap Brandi out of it. She glared at Charles and saw that the plush lay on its side, unmoving.

"What's wrong with you? We have to go *now.*"

"I—I'm sorry," was all Brandi managed before collecting Charles and picking herself up.

She glanced at her phone. It was nearly three in the morning by the time they got outside. Brandi unlocked Scrambo's doors and waited for

Snow to get in before turning the key; Rufus and Conan were waiting for them. They had planned on driving a full circle around town to be sure nothing followed them. Brandi turned the key, but the battery didn't *click.*

Misty had left the headlights on.

"No, no, no, no, no." Brandi covered her mouth.

Snow was already stepping out of the truck.

"There's no time. We have to run."

Brandi looked from Snow to the dashboard and turned the key again.

You're going to leave me? Scrambo asked in a goofy voice. *I've been good. That girl will take me again.*

"I'm not leaving you, I'm not."

"Brandi, let's go. *Now.*"

Brandi didn't budge. Snow turned her back and went on her own. Brandi slowly climbed out of the cab and quietly closed Scrambo's door. Tears freely fell from her eyes.

"I'm so sorry, Scrambo. I'm so, so, sorry." The truck's headlights looked sad and her heart ached as she turned and followed Snow.

Why though? Scrambo asked. *I helped. Why are you leaving me?*

"I'm sorry, I'm so sorry," was all she could say. She walked away and glanced into his sad, down-turned headlights.

And they who die shall fill an honored grave, for glory lights the soldier's tomb, and beauty weeps for the brave.

She pulled Charles out of her pocket and considered throwing him as far as she could, but she met his beady little dog eyes and chuckled.

Brandi held the plush out on her outstretched hands and laughed at his mustache, at his eyebrows. He was simply too cute. She burst like a balloon, unable to control her laughter. Snow ran back and clasped a hand over her mouth, so hard that Brandi's philtrum broke on her teeth. She glared at her with bulging eyes.

"Please," was all that she said.

Brandi replaced Charles in her pocket, but still quietly snickered to herself. She followed Snow into the streets for an hour, chortling the entire way. She kept laughing even after forgetting what was so funny.

Snow turned around and screamed words, but Brandi wasn't focused. She just kept laughing.

Chapter 13

Conan reached back for his full tenor, gracing an empty Club Depression with his bright C note. The vibrations tickled the inside of his ears and adrenaline made his heart beat in tempo with Jackie's crushing beat.

Buried in acid rain
I can still hear your footsteps
Splashing on the waves

Rufus toyed with his effects pedals during his extended solo. Conan checked his vibrating phone. His mind played over the worst-case scenarios. Snow had texted him. They'd wait until everyone went to bed and make a break for it. That left hours to kill.

"Hey, you totally changed the lyrics?" Jackie said. "I liked the original ones."

"I might change them again too. Depends on how things are going."

"Old ones were sweet," Marc said, laughing. "But I dug these. *Regenerate, regenerate,* that's sick."

This will probably be our last time together. Right, Dad? I should try to enjoy it. You'd tell me that, but...

"Yeah, whatever," Jackie said. "Nobody gives a shit."

"Don't be like that. No one tells you how to write drums," Marc said. "Let Conan handle lyrics."

"Fuck you. All I said was that I liked the old ones."

"Yo," Rufus laughed, lowering his hands. "Check your hostility, my guy. Club rules, remember?"

Conan stepped to his open notepad and wrote,

Forever I am muted
Yet blamed for your words
Whispered to me.

The others' eyes tickled the hairs on the back of his neck. Undoubtedly, his rapid-fire scribbling was loud enough to draw concern. He scanned his writing and a bowling ball dropped into his stomach.

Sorry, Dad, I know you loved Jackie too, but this is for the best.

"Do you have a problem with me or something?" Conan said, putting his notes down and glaring down his nose at Jackie.

"Yeah," Jackie said. He'd lost his red cap during practice and his hair covered one eye. "All day, you've been a dick. You can give a shit about the show, the tour, and us. You're not into it, bro."

"Jack, that's enough," Marc said. "Conan already said he was sorry. You heard what happened earlier. We're lucky he's even here."

"I never even met my dad. Nobody gives a fuck." Jackie threw his sticks on the ground. "Why am I the one getting black-balled? He can't be that torn if he's going to school and ditching me for chicks."

"Yeah, okay, jealous," Conan said, rolling his eyes. "I've seen the way you check out Brandi. Dude, go for it. Now's your chance. Pack of smokes says she won't even talk to you."

"Whoa, whoa, whoa." Marc lowered his hands down as he stepped between them. "That doesn't sound like you, Conan. Step back, dude."

"Consider yourself lucky you got this band, man," Conan continued. "Without it, you wouldn't have shit. Hold up, I got a bargain for you. I'll start writing lyrics to fit your third-grade reading level, and you shut the fuck up. Deal?"

Rufus put a hand on Conan's shoulder and squeezed.

"Cool it, man."

Jackie and Marc's shouting mixed together, becoming incoherent behind them. A phrase popped into Conan's head like a lightning bolt. He covered his mouth with his hand and lowered his gaze.

"October sign."

"Twenty-two. Seriously, he's about—" Rufus turned his head. "Why did I say that?"

"You said it when you first met Snow. It was weird then, but I get it. Rufus, trust me. What about those dreams you've had? The fires, being eaten, all that weird shit."

"How do you—" Rufus paused, swallowing loudly. He put his hand on his head. "October sign? Twenty-second? It's like some sleeper agent shit. Snow? From Preston. I know her how?"

"I'll explain everything, but Jackie's gotta go. If he sticks around, he'll only get hurt."

Rufus slowly turned from him. His arms went slack as his willpower evaporated.

"Hey, Jackie, we're gonna call it."

"You're seriously taking his side? Hell no, let's run the set again."

"I ain't taking nobody's side. Y'all just giving me a headache. Come on, I'll drive your ass home."

"Fuck that," Jackie said and kicked over his cymbal stand. The China crashed onto the ground, clattering like an aluminum trash can falling down a staircase. Its golden body split and cracked in half.

"I'm sick of this fucker!"

Jackie rushed Conan, but stopped when his face was an inch away. It took Conan everything to keep from fidgeting. He aimed his focus on the cigarette and blood smell of Jackie's breath.

"I've had your back," Jackie said. "For almost ten years now. You've always thought you were better than me. Even when I practiced my dick off. I see what you're doing. Treating me like a little kid who needs to stay out of your way."

Jackie had his fist clenched so tight that Conan expected him to lash out.

Sorry, Jackie, you're not dying on me. Not this time. I'd rather you hate my guts.

"Don't you get it?" Conan said, forcing a straight face. "I *am* better than you."

Jackie's eyes bulged with rage, his nostrils flared, and he shoved Conan aside.

"I'll get you, fucker. You'll see," Jackie said, rubbing his jaw. "Fuck your ride. I'm out."

Marc glanced at Rufus with a slack-jawed expression and let Jackie go.

"I'd do the same to you, if I didn't need your help," Conan said, letting his arms drop to his sides.

"Ight," Rufus said, packing his cigarettes. "This better be good."

"Bro, what?" Marc added. "We're supposed to be stoked. This ain't it. What about our gig?"

"Rufus, for us to pull this off, I'm going to need you to believe me. Things are gonna get weird these next three days."

"Man, you keep saying that." Rufus rubbed his head. "You're talking like some chosen one bullshit here."

"All those dreams, Rufus, burning, dying, they've happened in the past. Well, not the past. Last time we did this, you called it parallel universes."

Rufus groaned, rubbing his head. Conan related, but had gotten used to his own headache. He credited that to his writing.

Rufus started picking up Jackie's mess and sparked up a cigarette. Conan joined him, but his own cigarette tasted stale, like sucking on a campfire log, and the smoke clung to his throat. He coughed his way through it.

"Last time?" Marc asked. "Conan, I'm tripping. Start talking, yo."

"I've seen our future. I ousted Jackie to protect him." He checked the time on his phone. "Here. I'll prove it. Follow me."

"Dude." Marc laughed and followed him out back. "That sounds like some schoolyard, the-floor-is-lava bullshit. Seen the future, dude?"

"Because you won't believe me." He rolled his cigarette between his fingers, crunching the tobacco and then flicking it away. "If I predict something impossible, you will."

The cousins glanced at one another.

"In about five minutes," Conan said, "there's gonna be a million rats coming through here. Enough to turn the streets black. Consider it a sign that we're all gonna be in a lot of trouble. I'mma need you on board after that. Seriously."

His nose wrinkled at the growing stench. Marc scratched his face nervously, but remained silent. The vomit and death scent eventually became overpowering. The first rat appeared. Seconds later, the streets turned black with rodents.

Marc turned and sped inside, peeking out through the window.

Rufus stared at the rats with a frown, pulling at the corner of his mouth. He slowly turned and stepped back into Club Depression. Conan followed, waiting for his response.

Rufus trudged to the stage and noisily shuffled through cardboard boxes and plastic bins. He produced a silver box.

"I knew it. October sign. I didn't want to believe you, but the dreams, everything, all along. My head, three more days. October sign twenty-two. I been thinking about it. I've been thinking about it my entire life. That's the day I die, October 22nd."

He opened his box, revealing two handguns and bullets. Conan took a seat and started writing.

Stay beside me

And bury me headless
Because I don't want to see your suffering.

His power was in his words, at his fingertips. He could change the future. He had traded Jackie, but gained Rufus early on.

"Yo, what is that?" Marc asked as Rufus pulled a small baggie filled with white powder. "I thought you fucking quit."

I was too hard on him, but if it means protecting Snow, I have to make this deal.

"Drastic times call for drastic measures, cuz." Rufus grabbed a mirror and razor from the bottom of the box, then took his prize to the table. The blade repetitively clicked like a drumstick on a snare rim.

Vultures, consumers, carrion comforters
Vomit so violently
In places where sin cannot hide.

"Do you think you need that?" Conan muttered, gazing up from his words. The slashes of ink didn't even appear like his handwriting.

"October sign, mothafucka. You just popped the bubble and gonna ask me some dumb shit like that? Yeah, I need it."

Rufus snorted a massive rail and a small rock stuck in his nose hairs. He retracted into his seat and slammed his boot down like he'd just burned himself.

"Yeah, kinda," Conan said, sighing as Rufus cut himself another line.

"I can't believe you're still holding onto that shit." Marc recoiled. "You've really been lying this whole time?"

"I've only been saving it in case those contracts fell through," he chuckled. "There ain't no other kids here. Calm down. If shit's gonna get crazy, you gonna want me crazy too. So what the fuck's up, future boy? How'd I die last time?"

"Eaten, but I won't let it happen again. Everyone gets out this time. That's why she sent me back, why I remember all this."

Rufus dropped his straw and frowned. He kicked his feet up onto the table.

"Eaten." He cleared his throat and exaggerated a cough. "Ight, what do we gotta do?"

Conan scribbled a couple more lines into his book and looked up at his friends.

The end of the world
Of my mind

Whatever line
Begin the decay.

"Brandi's already working on it. She remembers too. There's a girl, Snow, who needs our help. We keep her safe until Sunday's over and we win."

"We win? Like some kinda fucking game?" Marc threw his hands in the air and started pacing. "Conan, I get it. Your pops, dude, but look—Jackie probably ain't never coming back, and my fucking cousin? He's been clean for years and you got him doing lines now too."

Marc's chest rose and fell sluggishly. He reached into his pocket and his inhaler hissed as he took a puff, shaking his head.

"I looked up to you guys."

"C'mon, Marc," Conan said. "We aren't really role-model material."

Rufus scraped his powder into its baggy. What he'd taken hadn't changed him like Conan had seen in movies, nor how Rufus himself warned him it would affect them. The only change was the twitch of his eyes.

"Sorry, cuz, it's hard to explain. If you realized what it was like in my head, you'd get it."

"No one gets it. You've always been on your own, man. This band, this tour. This was our way out, man. You *preached* it."

"Marc, let me tell you something about that show and tour," Rufus said, walking to his freezer and digging out his vodka. He loudly clattered a pair of Solo cups onto the ground. "Conan, how many times have we done this already?"

"I only remember one other time." He wiped his brow. "Snow said it was thousands."

"Thousands, bruh." The alcohol burned Conan's nostrils as the liquor poured with the same resounding sound you'd hear on a Coke commercial. "We gotta hold that. We've been stuck here forever, trapped. Marcus, we were never gonna make it. That's the truth of it."

"What did you do with my cousin?" Marc said, squeezing his eyes shut. "This is so messed up. What happened?"

"I'm right here, where I'll always be. Like a painting. This town, man, this town's a place for kids' dreams to die. It's fate. Look at me, I worked so hard, hard as I could. I helped y'all and look where that got us. Nowhere." He laughed. "I knew I'd be remembered forever, just didn't recognize how. This, this is it. I'll live forever in all y'all. Hold onto that. But I ain't getting fuckin' eaten either. Not this time."

Conan stood up and snatched the bottle. It was cold enough to sting his hand. Something was different. There'd been no earthquake.

So if that wasn't the reason for the rats running away, then what was?

He took a tasteless shot, winced, and put the cap back on.

"We're gonna need you up later. Brandi and Snow are grabbing us a weapon. Guns won't hurt them."

"That's it. I'm fucking out," Marc said, throwing his hands in the air. "Your crazy ass wants to die because you'll be remembered? More like—you're both fuckin' nuts."

"Any crazier than a sea of rats flooding the town?" Conan said. "For Snow, it's worth it. It means everything."

"Nah," Rufus said, putting his hand up. "Nah, you're good, Marc. Thanks for everything, cuz. Do you need a ride home?"

"I'll take my bike. I got nothing to worry about. If I see Jackie, I'll talk with him. We should—we should still try to play on Saturday, man. Fuck, we worked so hard."

Conan took in a deep breath and overcompensated with a smile.

"Yeah, we will," Rufus said. By the way his eyebrows squeezed together, Conan could tell he was glad Marc was leaving.

"I know what I gotta do. I've seen it now, memories that aren't mine. They're up in that mansion right now, ain't they? That's where it's all going down." Rufus drummed a beat with his fingers on the table. "Conan, I gotta burn that fucking place to the ground. If I don't, that's how I get my ass eaten. I know it. I know if it burns, it won't happen. It's the only way."

***

Five hundred seventy-two...

Five hundred seventy-one...

Five hundred seventy...

Almost back, Rufus's text read.

If he didn't come back soon, Conan would kill him.

Conan stared into the half-empty party-sized bag of Doritos and tapped his foot on the floor. Rufus ran out of powder around 1:30am, immediately leaving for more. Conan had counted from one hundred six times, and lost count of how many squats and pushups he'd done. He never wanted to see a bag of nacho cheese chips again.

His phone clock said 3:32am, and he was going to lose his mind.

Snow had texted him, saying that Brandi couldn't get her truck started, and they were heading to the abandoned K-Mart on foot. They'd be close by now and—

I'm outside.

Conan sprung from his seat and barely remembered to grab his lyric book and pen before taking off. Rufus had his head tilted back and was tapping a straw inside of his nose when Conan hopped into the passenger seat.

"Seriously? I never knew you were on it."

"Never was," Rufus said, snorted, cleared his throat, and snorted again. "Crack was a lot cheaper. Stronger too. I'm living large now. This is my rainy-day fund. And yeah, I need it. Picking up potential murder victims at three in the morning. Yeah, sounds like a rainy day to me."

The girls waited for them in the K-Mart back alley. Snow'd been worried about being followed, and when they drove through the narrow alleyway, Brandi jumped out from the shadows.

Rufus's brakes shrieked to a stop and Brandi burst into a giggle fit while tapping a rhythm on the hood. Snow plodded behind her, her face scrunched and red. The door was open for a short time, but the powerful alley musk enveloped Rufus's Honda.

"Drive, now," Snow said, throwing herself into the back seat. "Around town, wherever, we need to make sure you're not being followed."

"Yes, masta, right away," Rufus scoffed, and glanced in his rearview mirror. "Nice to meet you."

"Hiya, Rufus!" Brandi boomed, enthusiastic and loud enough to carry to the next block.

Conan glared back at her, feeling his own blood drain from his face as he saw Snow's lips pull back.

"You said we could trust her," Snow snapped. "She's been trying to attract as much attention to herself as possible. If we're followed, it's her fault."

"You got the knife?"

"Of course."

"Then she did her part."

"You don't understand. She's insane. She keeps talking to herself and—"

"Snow, we've been through a lot." He glanced down at his scribbles. "We've already lost friends today. In the past, people have died for you, but I've never seen you this upset."

Conan's symptoms had crescendoed. Sweating, nausea, and a thickness building in his chest.

Snow had her hands on the knife, squeezing as tight as possible. He reached back and gripped her hand.

"I get it, you're scared."

"So this is the girl that everyone died a thousand times for?" Rufus laughed. "And, Brandi, you're okay with this?"

"Okay with what?" she said, looking lost.

Rufus chuckled. "Musta hit your goddamn head. Shit, I think we all did. Especially you, Conan. You think this girl gives a damn about you? You're nuts. Just look at her. All she cares about is getting herself out. You really can't tell?"

Snow showed her teeth, but Conan raised his hand.

"Don't worry about it. Right, Brandi?" He smiled. "We love each other. Focus on that. I'll take care of the rest."

Snow glared at him with wide eyes and shook her head.

"This isn't right," she said. "None of this feels right. This—this is going to end badly. I can feel it."

"Yeah, with that attitude," Brandi laughed and held up a small stuffed dog. "Somebody smells like rigatoni."

Snow shook her head in disbelief.

"Even though we messed up, everyone is fighting for you. We're fighting to prove that you've got a way out. Everyone does. That's why we're here. Brandi said it before."

Snow propped her elbow against the window and leaned her head against it.

"Maybe we'll go back again. I know we've made a mistake we can't fix."

"But before you said you couldn't?"

"Yeah," she said, and glanced at the passing streetlights. "Maybe, maybe not. Maybe I just gave up."

I'm still searching for answers
After being trapped by loyalty
Stripped of time
Skinned of destiny

Born onto your knife

Chapter 14

We're being watched, lassie, Charles harrumphed. *Yes. Everything is going according to the commander's plan.*

Brandi chuckled as the screen door clattered shut behind her. Her dad had actually gone to work for a change. Not having to explain Scrambo made her chortle, releasing a smidge of built-up tension in her neck. She slumped onto her old brown couch and breathed in the stale odor of dust and cigarettes, glaring at the dishes piling up in the sink.

"Told you. Nobody cares," she said. "Especially when it's me."

Her cell phone rang, making her twitch so hard that pain shot through her skull. She'd set the jingle to "Billie Jean," which prompted Charles to disco dance on the coffee table. Brandi clapped her hands, consumed by a giggle fit until the song nearly finished.

"Y'ello?" she answered.

"Yeah, see, Cindy," her mother said on the opposite line. "I told you she ain't dead."

Brandi grimaced as Charles fell onto his face. Her mother's nasally voice made her want to kick a hole into the wall.

"School called," her mom said, smacking gum. "Said you weren't there. Cindy wanted me to make sure you didn't get Kylie'd."

"Thanks, Mom," Brandi said. Her gaze wandered to the dirty clothes strewn throughout the hallway.

"No problem, sugartits. Oh, and some hungry-looking pale bitch came by and woke up Daddy first thing this morning. Your friends shouldn't come by the house."

Hubris! Pure hubris, Charles said. *Too sorry to say, love, if River gutted your mother before our eyes, I would not shed a tear. Tragic, too tragic.*

"Hey, don't say that. That would make me really sad."

"Well, it ain't like you're ever home anyway."

"Oh, sorry. I meant sure, Mom. *Annnnd* that I love you."

The line fell silent, and Brandi wiped her nose. She glimpsed her smudged makeup on a mirror magnet attached to her fridge.

"Love you too, baby. There's some spaghet in the fridge. Have fun, but don't get knocked up or your throat slit, yada-yada, kay, baby?"

"Yeah. Okay, Mom. Bye."

Her mom hung up and Brandi took the magnet from the fridge and pitched it into the pile of dishes.

Now, now, Charles said. *In times of expression, we should turn to music. Why not show me your woodwind, dearie?*

Brandi dropped Charles onto the kitchen table and trampled over wet towels and trash bags to get to her room, but her small space remained undisturbed. All she could fit within her confinement was her clean white bed, filled with stuffed animals, an ebony desk, and a giraffe lamp. She dug under her bed and pulled out her flute from middle school. She had time to kill anyway. On her way out, she stopped at her desk and pet her small, droopy-eyed elephant plush, Pokey.

He was quite introverted, though, and kept to himself.

She plodded to her mom's bong sitting by the fridge, ripped herself a bowl of dirt-tasting homegrown weed, and assembled her instrument.

Brandi pressed the cool mouthpiece to her lips and played her favorite: "Sally's Song," by Danny Elfman. The wistful melody bounced off the trailer walls, and Charles got up onto his hind legs and twirled a jig as she dusted off her repertoire. After playing the theme from *Batman,* she popped the leftover spaghetti into the microwave. It was canned sauce, but smelled of garlic and made her stomach rumble.

"Just sayin'." She gave a twirl. "If we gotta trade my parents' lives, it's no big deal. I'm alone, whether they're alive or dead."

I could completely control a person—a person that I found physically attractive. Charles had lost his accent and sounded like he was speaking through a voice changer. *And keep them with me as long as possible, even if it meant just keeping a part of them.*

She glared into Charles's beady eyes. When he said nothing, she slapped her hands down, shaking the kitchen table.

"Spit it out or I'm running you through the garbage disposal."

What happened to Kylie can still happen to you. Charles tilted his head to the side and spoke in his scary voice. *You have to leave this town behind.*

Brandi sucked her teeth. Despite the munchies seconds ago, she'd completely lost her appetite.

"Are you done? I like it better when you're fun. I already pretended like nothing bad happened after Kylie left—not gonna do the same with Snow."

So that's the case! Charles blubbered, his accent returning. *Why not turn your back on them and make yours a life worth living?*

"You're not getting it." Brandi dropped into her seat and blew her hair up with a sigh. "Snow's helpless. Everything's gonna go to hell no matter what. We already saw that. The point is to help. There *has* to be some hope for us somewhere. Even just a little. That's better than abandoning her—like Kylie."

You hope for her, so there's hope for yourself? Well, I hope you're prepared to go down with the ship. Skipper, you've tied yourself to the anchor.

Thump-thump-thump!

Footsteps clattered their way up to her front door. Brandi made two extended lunges, arriving there as her screen-door squeaked on its hinges. She opened up with exaggerated enthusiasm, rubbing her head.

"Yo, what's up?"

The first wintry day of the year nipped at Brandi's arms. River wore a black button-up coat. The bags under her eyes, darker than ever; her glare, threatening as a rattlesnake's.

"Where is my sister?" she said, unamused.

"Snow? Oh, shit, we had a hell of a night. She's insane. All that crazy shit that was on her list before her eighteenth birthday. We were all like *sheeeeeowww* and *fwooom* and *kablaam!* I don't even know how I'm still standing. I'm so hungover." She raised her hand and let her shrill laughter carry throughout the trailer park.

River slammed her palm on the door's threshold. She leaned in closer, and Brandi caught a glimpse of the bloated demon from her past life.

"Shut your lying mouth, whore. Where is she?"

"That's uncalled for. What's with the hostility? I dropped her off before I came home."

"Liar!" she screamed, and old lady Judy next door peered through her blinds.

"Whoa, you like totally got a stick shoved up your ass or something?" Brandi laughed again, holding her gut. "Moms called me and said you swung by this morning, made my lazy-ass dad get up and everything. How'd you even find where I live?"

"Brandi," she hissed. "My sister needs to be returned home *this* evening or I cannot guarantee your safety, nor your family's. I will not ask again." River turned her back. "We can ruin all your lives in an instant. I've no idea the game you're playing, but it will end worse than you could ever imagine. That's a promise."

Deflect her, Miss Taylor! You cannot allow her to realize what Miss Snow means to you.

"You think I give a shit what happens to me or my parents? Snow's her own girl, completely able to make her own decisions. If she didn't go home, then that was her choice. I've got no idea where she went."

"Then you'll find her," River seethed and started down the stairs. She glanced over the trailer. "I don't understand why you hate yourself so much. You could have been worth something."

"But you still can't hate me, can you? Why'd you come and not Misty, huh, Riv?"

River curled her lip.

"I'd have never let you touch me if I'd known this is the filth you roll around in. I should have known when I saw your muddy eyes. You're a pig and nothing more. Next time, it *will* be Misty."

Brandi let her go with the last word. She watched River saunter into her black SUV and drive away.

"She's right though, I'm a ghost," Brandi sighed, walking inside with a chuckle and a glance toward Charles. "If I didn't hate my parents, and myself, it probably wouldn't be so easy to sacrifice it all for Snow."

Our group hootenanny is back on, she texted Rufus and forked down a mouthful of spaghetti. The garlic was pungent enough, but it needed black pepper, which they had none of.

***

"*Annnnd* here you go," Brandi said, handing the bag over to Snow. "Cold cheeseburgers, water, fruit snacks, and I put my DS at the bottom. One charger is for Rufus's phone. It gets shit service in the school, though, so only step outside and use it if it's a total emergency. The other charger's for the Nintendo. Plenty of games too, cuz we probably won't be able to pick you up 'til tomorrow afternoon."

Snow glanced over Mr. Stephend's English class and frowned. Her gym bag loudly ruffled as she dropped it onto the pale green carpet floor.

"You're sure nobody will be here?" Snow asked.

"Even if Mr. Stephend does pop in tomorrow morning—tell him you're with me. He will understand. Believe me, he's like the coolest teacher ever. Oh, don't fall in love with him. Actually, do. Conan would be so pissed, right?"

Brandi rolled her shoulders and flashed a quick smile.

"I better get going."

"Brandi," Snow said as she turned. "Thanks for all your help. I know you're only acting this way because of me. I get it, you're trying to keep your mind occupied. It's a lot. But, truly, thank you. For whatever it's worth. Most people in your situation would want me harmed."

Brandi met Snow's eyes and her breath caught in her lungs.

"I did the first time. Everyone's already pretty messed up. I'm not okay, I don't think. Rufus is on drugs again and Conan is, well, he's Conan. If that's what we gotta give up for *you* to get out? It's okay. Everyone deserves a chance."

Brandi took a slow step toward the door, then scurried away. Her sneakers tapped hard on the concrete, sneaking past the office camera and hopping the chain-link fence by the baseball diamond. As her knees bent, Rufus's Honda coughed to life.

Brandi froze when she turned around.

Behind the school, by the light of the moon, she saw an abhorrent giant. A torso made from a stag's head. Antlers sprouting from its sides made up six gnarled appendages. Its skin was a mottled blue with a decapitated tree-trunk neck. Sprouting from the bloody gap was a sycamore-sized bouquet of orchid flowers that blocked out the stars.

Brandi's own screams played in her head. She shook violently and nearly vomited. Conan gripped her by the arm.

"What's wrong with you? We have to go." She let him drag her away, but gaped backward at the monstrosity through the rear windshield. A tingling in her chest wrapped stiff fingers around her heavy heartbeat.

I don't know why you're upset by his presence, Charles chuckled. *His existence is because of the choices you've made.*

"How can that be from my choices?" Brandi asked.

Blood, the bodies, the shit stink of the parlor. The sound of her own limbs being ripped from their sockets. Snow, pressing the gun to her head.

He's the part of you that you refuse to acknowledge.

"To hell he is." Brandi's insides lurched. "I don't care what kind of medication or therapy I need, that thing's not sticking around."

Rufus and Conan both glared at her with hungry eyes. They spoke, but the sound of their voices was drowned out by her heart beating in her ears.

"See what you've done? I can't even focus."

The audacity, lassie. You're the captain of the ship. You have nothing to blame me for.

The boys had stopped the car and opened the trunk, filling the copper-smelling air with the chemical essence of gasoline. Conan popped his head in and spoke unintelligibly to her, like his words were being said backward.

She hugged herself tight.

You've made your decision, Charles said, popping out from her pocket and dancing on the dashboard. As he twirled, his head floated from his torso, and she watched it spin until she became dizzy.

You did it in your past. You truly thought you'd be able to help and escape with your life? You died in those past lives. You will die here. The deal has been sealed. This is war. You save her, you die.

"How's that fair?" She swatted the floating dog's head. "It started one way, to help this girl. Now what, giants and monsters? What am I doing here? I could have left, I could've been improved. I could have stayed in the past, with Adria and River. Back then, or now. Why is this right? Kylie was hurt, murdered because of me. She was murdered because I spent all of my time with Conan. Murder, murder, murder. Now I've lost my fucking mind and I'll never be with him and I don't even know why I still love him. Not caring is the answer? Why, what was it for? What do I need? To be loved? It's impossible. I'm like River. When you love someone like this, you'll never be loved back. Killing each other and dying is much simpler."

Yes, the floating head said.

"I'll take my life and be done. Done with worrying, done with—"

Her right cheek exploded with pain. She'd been struck so hard that her gaze moved to staring out the window. She rubbed absently at her cheek. When she turned back, she saw the plush laying sideways on the dashboard and Rufus grinning at her from the passenger seat.

"You don't think I know what you're up to, longhair?"

He'd hit her hard enough to coat her tongue with blood. She touched her fingers to her lips and glimpsed down at the wet crimson.

"I saw that shit last night. I was hoping you'd pull yourself together. Guess that ain't happening." Rufus took a seat and grabbed a mirror from his center council. He poured out his white powder and tapped some out of his straw. He leaned in and wetly snorted up the line.

"See this, see what I'm doing? This shit, it's entirely out of my control now. I quit, but couldn't stop thinking about it. I chose this. The pain, remembering all that shit that hasn't happened, but has? That's what this dulls. Pain."

He took another sniff.

"Rufus, I want to strike out at someone who deserves it. I don't want to care if it's right. I just want what's there to burn."

Her face stretched into a snarl.

"Now that sounds more like it. Do that, but get your shit together, or I'mma have to slap you up some more. I ain't going anywhere, longhair, we all knew that all along. Nobody is, nobody but you. And if you think trading away your pain for crazy is a good call—well, then I'mma slap you even harder. This—these drugs—it's a dependency. I won't even feed myself over this shit. I get it. Conan tossed your ass aside for another pretty face. You did everything for him. It isn't fair, it hurts. Get control of it. We need your help. When it's over, you're on the first bus outta here."

Brandi clenched her shaking hands.

"You ready to do your part now, boss?" he asked and took another rail. "You know what you gotta do, right?"

"Distraction fire, and you got the real one," she said, hopping out of his car and leaving Charles behind. The nightmare giant was gone. Rufus walked her over to his trunk and handed her a compact but potent red gas can and a pack of small green propane tanks.

"Shit spreads fast, hit it at two o'clock on the dot and get the fuck outta here. Are you sure you'll be able to get to the club okay?"

"Yeah, yeah, I'm fine now. I am. Thanks." She lunged forward and gave him a hug. "We got this." She grabbed her supplies and started walking. The trek around the black gate bordering the Devereuxs' garden would take at least an hour, but that would put her right on time.

Rufus was right. She wanted her memories gone. The pain. The torture. The sadness. Kylie.

As she walked through the chilled night, she let herself cry. It didn't matter anymore. She'd have to find something else. A different way to deal with the pain. The pain of remembering what they went through.

"Shut up, why cry? There isn't anyone left to feel bad for you." She sniffled and wiped her eyes, taking a deep breath of the garden plot. "Crying? You think there was ever any hope? Remember how smart Rufus was? And he was never gonna get out."

This was Conan's fault. Brandi started her fire and couldn't help but imagine him burning.

"Maybe you're the ghost, Rufus, but for you, we're getting the fuck out of this place. I promise."

The flames spread through the garden almost instantly and reached licking fingers against the propane tanks. As she cleared the fence, the explosion was loud enough to wake the dead in Adria's basement. Seconds later, Conan's explosion matched hers.

She ran as fast as her legs would carry her. Her surroundings blurred and her chest felt like it would collapse. When she couldn't run anymore, she hid under a parked car and prayed.

Chapter 15

Conan's eyes peeled open to harsh sunlight bleeding in through Club Depression's windows. He threw off his scratchy blanket and gave a big stretch, not having slept that well in a while. Sleeping on the stage cramped his back, but thinking about seeing Snow again put a spring in his step. He enthusiastically hopped over to the plastic table in the middle of the hardwood floor.

Things have been crazy since you left me, Dad, but today they're finally getting better.

Brandi glanced up at him. Her eyes were sunken as if she hadn't slept all night. She toyed with a half-eaten bowl of Fruit Loops and clanked her spoon against the side of her bowl. Rufus sat across from her. He crossed his arms and his face tightly scrunched up.

"Morning," Conan said, and passed a smile between the two. His nose wrinkled at the stink of re-burned cigarettes.

"Shut up," Rufus said without opening his eyes.

"What's his problem?" Conan asked, Fruit Loops jingling as he poured himself a bowl.

Brandi raised her hand, as if preparing a rhetorical reply, but shook her head.

"Headache? I don't know. It doesn't even matter," she said, glancing away.

"I'll tell you," Rufus stated, creaking open his bloodshot eyes. "I shoulda made sure they were dead. I should have stuck around and seen them burn. None of them died, I sense it."

Conan glanced from Rufus to Brandi and let out a heavy sigh. He took his hand off the carton of milk, suddenly losing his appetite.

It's your fault, he could imagine his father saying. *They meant everything, and you did this to them.*

"When can we go get Snow?" he asked.

"Well, first we gotta scheme up where the hell we're putting her," Rufus said. He stood up and rummaged through a pile of greasy napkins, pulling out half a cigarette. "Pretty much gotta make her disappear. Gonna have to pin the fires on her, so there's that angle. Make time to practice for tonight too."

Conan popped a mouthful of dry, artificially sweetened loops into his mouth and walked to his bag. He had to step over a shattered vodka bottle along the way. Rufus's glare made him still and Brandi completely ignored him, which was somehow worse. He chewed his nails and pulled out his notebook.

A tranquil hallucination

My cadaver lost at sea.

"I think we should get her now."

"Doesn't make any difference to me," Rufus said, grimacing at his cigarette's repulsive stink. "Still gotta figure out what we're gonna do with her." He pointed his cigarette at Brandi. "And figure out where the hell you're going. No way we're letting you stick around. Gotta get y'all outta my hair for good. Quicker I do, the quicker I can get back to rotting."

Conan turned to Brandi.

"You're going to leave town?"

"I guess." Brandi shrugged. "There's nothing here for me anymore, and since I'm the last one who saw Snow, well, you get it."

"Yeah." Conan let his fingers graze over Jackie's broken cymbal. The cold metal made his fingers stink like pennies. Rufus was changing, and his extra-dry deodorant can hissed as he showered himself, covering up the cigarette with vanilla and citrus.

"I think it's best if me and Snow leave too." Conan said. "I don't think I'll be able to play the show."

Rufus lifted his head back, glaring down at him.

"What, you're gonna run away from everyone who ever cared about you? I told Marc we're playing. You're gonna make me a liar too?"

"It's better this way, isn't it?"

"How the fuck would you know?" Rufus said and threw down his deodorant. The can loudly clanked and busted open, hissing out its contents. "You let this girl manipulate you from the start. You turn your back on everyone for her and can't take care of yourself. What you gonna do, rob liquor stores along the highway, dumbass? You don't even have a car."

"I know, I know," Conan muttered with a small nod. "Yeah, I get it. I fucked up. Everything, both of you. It's— It sucks, and it's my fault, but thank you. Thank you, both of you, for everything, but I have to."

Rufus crossed his arms. He leaned against the stage and shook his head.

"But you got your girl, right?" Brandi said. Her smile actually seemed genuine. "So at least you can be happy. Seriously, I wanted to help her."

"Yeah. Thanks, Brandi, you especially. For you to forgive me and help her, you're really amazing. Always have been."

"I never forgave you," she said, getting up. "Whatever. Let's wrap this up."

As they walked around back, Brandi gave Rufus a playful shove. He answered with a practiced stink eye, but it went right through her and bore into Conan. Conan let her sit shotgun and sat in the back seat, closed his eyes, and began counting backward.

One hundred...

Ninety-nine...

Ninety-eight...

He tried to clear his mind, but his focus was solely on Snow.

His palms grew sweaty, and he found himself chewing his fingernails again. They'd leave town, and they'd be together. What next? Build a life? Have children? It totally depended on her. The more he thought about it, the dryer his mouth became.

"Hey, wake up," Rufus said. "Cause I need to break this down for you. First off, you're a real selfish brat and you always have been. Nothing we gonna do can fix that. Now it's just this chick. Whatever. The point I'm trying to make is that you owe everything to Brandi and—"

"Rufus, you don't have to—" Brandi started.

"Yes, I do." He cut her off. "Conan, she's getting outta here and leaving your ass behind. Thanks to you, she's fucked up in the head and burning down houses. Now, consider yourself damn lucky that she's got some money saved up. Cause if not, I'd be cutting her off my stack. Now, there ain't a lot. I was saving it for tour, but if I keep it, I'll just shove it up my nose, so it's gonna be yours. This piece of shit car too. You hear me? You're gonna take it uptown and then you're gonna drive your sorry ass forever and a half away from here and all the way to Michigan. Ain't nobody gonna find y'all there. I got an auntie who will put your ass to work. Consider it the last thing anyone's gonna do for you. Rest is on you. Hope it was worth it."

Rufus put the car in park outside the school. He stepped out and slammed his door so hard that the windows rattled. Conan followed, gazing up at birds chirping in a nearby tree.

"Say thank you, motherfucker."

"Thank you, Rufus. Seriously."

"You're coming in too, Rufus?" Brandi asked.

"Damn right I am. Gotta grab my phone and get another thank you. If she just all, whatever, shit, I dunno what I might do."

They shared a laugh but fell silent as they hopped the fence. Peralta was a different place on an October Saturday, inhabited by ghosts. They only had an office camera to worry about. Conan was sure it didn't even work. As they rounded the corner to Mr. Stephend's class, his stomach turned fluttery.

Brandi pulled out the key he'd given her as his teacher's assistant and the locking mechanism clicked.

We've done it, Dad. Conan's heart beat fast. *Next, get the hell out of town.*

The door opened, and Conan's heart stopped. He pushed Brandi aside. The entire room spun around him, making him dizzy, going faster and faster. He ran to the teacher's desk and threw the chair out from under it.

"Where is she?!" he screamed.

Brandi's unfocused gaze stared through him. She folded her arms over her stomach and bent over slightly. Rufus sneered, looking Conan up and down in disgust.

"Don't you fucking look at me like that," Conan growled and stomped toward him. "What did you do? You got something to say?"

"Yeah, man, what I was telling you all along. She ain't give a shit about you. She peaced. Now she gonna blame—"

Conan struck him with a right cross, busting his lip and turning Rufus wild. He hit Conan back much harder, making him stumble backward. Rufus hit him again, dropping him to the floor, and then picked him up by his shirt, grimaced, and dropped him. Conan stood up and rage blurred his vision. He could still smell her here, that sweet, unforgettable scent.

"Where'd she go? Where is she?! A note, anything?" He flipped over the teacher's desk and the resounding *boom!* made everything else sound like a whisper. "Why? Snow, why?"

"Conan, you need to calm down, please," Brandi pleaded. "We'll find her."

Conan reached to his waist and pulled out Rufus's Beretta. He clicked the safety off and pointed it at Brandi. Her eyes grew wide, and he quickly put the cold barrel to his own skull.

"Why's he got a gun?" Brandi asked, shaking.

"I gave it to him last night. You were being the crazy one then, remember?"

"Conan, put it down, please," she pleaded.

"Why? Why should I? It doesn't matter. This is the only way out. It's the only thing that makes sense anymore. Quitting. I didn't see it. How many songs did I write about failing her? Thousands, fucking thousands. I can't take it anymore. I can't help her. Brandi, I made a promise."

Brandi scanned the classroom. Her eyes sunk into her skull, as if she stared into an abyss. The last place on earth, a hole in humanity, their coffin. An ache grew in the back of Conan's throat, but he couldn't swallow.

"No," she said, shaking her head. "Please, god, no." She covered her mouth.

"What?" Conan said. "You're stalling. What is it? Tell me."

"Start looking for a camera."

"A camera?" Conan said with Rufus in unison.

Brandi walked past him, lightly shoving him aside despite the loaded weapon. She yanked out the drawers of Mr. Stephend's desk and began rummaging through the cubby holes. Rufus scowled at Conan as he pulled the clock off the wall. Conan lowered the gun and loudly clicked the safety back on. He walked to the whiteboard and grabbed a marker.

A tranquil hallucination
My cadaver lost at sea
It calms me to a relief
But won't release me from your disease.

"Brandi," Rufus said, by the bookshelf next to the teacher's desk. "It's here."

Conan scurried behind her and peered over her shoulder at the WI-FI camera, blinking a blue light up at them.

"How'd you know?" Rufus asked. "What's it mean?"

Conan's mind was a mess of panic. Adrenaline still pumped in his veins from pointing the gun to his head. Something about the way Brandi's shoulders trembled made a sourness bubble in his esophagus.

"I—I—" Her trembling became worse. "I really fucked up," she said, shaking her head. "No, no, no. How'd I never see it? NO!" she exploded, ripping the camera off the wall and stomping it.

"You fucking piece of shit, you rotten, disgusting... I'll kill you! I'll fucking kill you!"

Conan put his hands on her shoulders and she swatted them away, stomping the camera until she'd separated each individual piece—then she stomped more, crunching and scraping the machine into unrecognizable bits.

"Janna, one year ahead of us. Then Kylie. I guess I was next on your fucking list, huh? Was that the plan all along?"

"Mr. S?" Conan didn't believe it.

"Yeah. Mr. Fucking S," Brandi turned and snapped at him. "Go ahead, say I was an idiot for never seeing it. Him and Kylie were obviously fucking. Now who knows where she ended up. And Janna? They're probably in a ditch behind his house right now."

Fire pumped into Conan's veins. He gritted his teeth.

"You did this to her. You said it would be safe here. Brandi, if he—"

"Shut the fuck up, Conan!" Brandi screamed. "Not everyone is out to get you. Stop blaming others when you do nothing yourself. Get your shit together, especially if you think you're gonna take care of her. Shit doesn't always work out, asshole."

She barely even paid him a glance as she walked out the door.

"Yo, yo, yo." Rufus blocked her path. "What if you're wrong?"

"I'm not, I know I'm not. He wanted me in this life, it's fucking obvious, and in the past lives, the ones I didn't survive, he already got me. It's all over my skin, fucking crawling over me. He needs to pay."

"If he did anything to Snow, if he fucking touched her—" Conan added.

"But what if you're wrong?" Rufus repeated, sniffed, and wiped his nose. "High as fuck on cocaine, and I'm still the one talking sense into you nutjobs. Goddamn."

"You just burnt down a fucking mansion because you were scared of a dragon-bitch eating you and you don't believe *this*?" Brandi said, trying to shove her way past him.

Conan reached for his gun again. Blood rushed to his ears, building pressure from his clenched jaw.

"That was different—the visions. I got nothing on this one. What if she left and y'all castrate an innocent mothafucka? Then—"

"An innocent man with a camera in his classroom, for god knows what? He was waiting for *me* to post up here. Snow was supposed to be me, Rufus."

"The fires weren't much different from this, Rufus," Conan said. "What do you need then, proof?"

Rufus sucked his teeth twice.

"Yeah. I can use some proof."

"Fine. Then we'll get you some." Conan threw his arms down. "You always wanted to start a fire. How about breaking and entering?"

Rufus groaned.

"How do I feel about all this shit? Man, I just know when the taxman comes callin' it's gonna be me who answers for all y'all dumbasses."

My commitment
Martyrs those around me
I'm afraid to scrape my palms
Reliant on their tears

Chapter 16

"You guys cannot be serious," Marc said in a too-quiet voice, rubbing his forearms.

Brandi ashed her cigarette, choosing to move herself to the outskirts of Club Depression, not even offering a shrug.

"Of course they aren't serious," Jackie said, twirling his drumstick until it blurred. "Rufus wouldn't have had us come if we weren't playing. Come on, enough of your *lore.* Let's run the set."

"We aren't joking," Brandi said, tired.

"Tell them, Rufus," Conan said, pacing the room. "We're wasting time."

Rufus rubbed his brow. He connected the tips of his fingers and pressed them against his nose.

"I brought you here to tell you in person," Rufus said. "It's not happening. Sorry for leading you both on."

"Seriously?" Jackie said and kicked his bass drum. "What's Conan holding over your head? All this bullshit for a chick he barely met?"

"I'm out," Conan said. "I'm gonna kill this fucker myself."

"Chill," Brandi said, snapping her fingers emphatically and offering to share her cigarette. "I want it done too, but you owe them."

Marc's amplifier buzzed as he unplugged his cable and put his bass on his stand. He ran his hand through his dense hair and a sharp breeze seeped in through the open windows. He peered off the back porch and crossed his arms.

"More confusing than anything," he said. "What's your angle, Brandi? Conan left you for this girl, and now you want to help her?"

She paused before reacting, and still only offered him a forced smile.

"It goes deeper than that, but yeah. If we don't, nobody's gonna."

Marc clucked a laugh and shook his head. "Guess I should have known."

"Yeah," Brandi said. She walked to her bag and dug out an open bag of M&M's. Not even peanuts coated in creamy milk chocolate helped her mood. She took her phone out and read Conan's newest text.

I can't stop thinking about getting him. We have to go soon.

She plopped down next to her recently liberated elephant, Pokey, and quickly tapped her response.

It's okay. I know we will get her back.

"You clowns are gonna ruin the most important night of our lives." Jackie's drum throne squealed as he stood atop it. "I get it. If you're for real and this chick is in the dude's cellar, then call the fucking police. It's not on you."

Conan offered the remaining cigarette to Brandi, but she shook her head, burying her face in the elephant, still scented with baby shampoo.

"Sorry, Jackie, you just don't understand," Conan said, and dropped his cigarette into the garden planter full of butts.

"It's personal," Brandi said, glimpsing the deep lines of her face in the reflection of Pokey's eyes. "For what he's done, and for the lies. I'd do it myself, even if Snow wasn't involved."

"And every second is another wasted," Conan said.

Brandi watched Jackie's veins strain against his skin. She just wished he'd finish whining and leave them to be miserable without him.

"Maybe I'm a ghost, destined to haunt this town forever," she said, lifting her elephant up.

"Why're you quoting that stupid song still? He broke up with you. It sucks ass anyways."

Jackie threw his sticks down.

"You know what, I regret every second I've spent hanging out with you losers. Hey, Rufus, fuck you for leading me on my whole life. You made me think I was gonna be somebody."

Rufus had avoided eye contact until then.

"Hey, don't take it out on him. Blame me," Conan said, putting his phone in his pocket and letting his arms go limp.

Brandi's phone vibrated, and she checked his text.

I'm sorry. You deserve more, but she's the only hope we have left.

"I was hoping," Conan said, "that whenever I was a dick before that—you'd peace out. Rufus wanted us to come clean."

Conan's written and spoken words both made her empty. She stepped to Rufus's half-full vodka bottle and poured herself a shot.

"Snow's number one priority for me," Conan said. "Sorry, but touring, none of that matters. I didn't want you to get involved 'cause I knew you'd want to help. I didn't want you to get hurt."

Jackie stood up and picked his backpack up from behind him. He slung it over his shoulder and leapt off the stage, his landing echoing resonance throughout the club.

"That's it then?" He glanced around and laughed. "Fucking really? It's because I'm real? You're so full of shit." He shook his head. "What if she's already dead?"

"Yeah. You're right, Jackie," Brandi said, as a cloud passed by the sun. "I hope she is."

Her words made the others' necks bend. Conan curled his shoulders toward her, caving in his chest.

"If she is, it's my fault, and I deserve the same. None of that would change how much I'll enjoy blowing Stephend's brains out, so right now, I really don't give a shit."

She moved to Rufus's silver case. He left it unlocked, and sweat and odorous metal puffed up when she opened it. She plucked the baggie of cocaine rocks out and dropped it onto the counter. She took his gray gun and checked to make sure the safety was on.

"Holy shit," Marc whispered as she passed.

"Give me a ride," Brandi said to Rufus, who was heading for his coke.

"So that's it then?" Jackie said, raising his hands and dropping them. "After all those empty gigs, after dodging jail throughout high school, after all these years? The promises? This rich magical bitch shows up, and it all goes to hell just like that? That's not real life, man. It's not."

Brandi ignored him completely, shuffling behind Rufus.

"Fine," Jackie said. "Fine, fuck all of you. I'll go."

Brandi blinked absently as Jackie threw his middle finger into Rufus's face.

"Fuck you, Rufus. I coulda done something else with my life. Fuck you."

"Hey, man, I tried."

It was too late. Jackie didn't hear a word and slammed the door behind him. The echoing boom acted as a catalyst and Conan went to grab his bag. He tossed out his lyric book and loaded a roll of duct tape, a pair of pliers, and a pack of nine-millimeter bullets. He eyed the gun in Brandi's hand and she handed it over to him.

"Go with him," Rufus said to Marc, who'd been poking the inside of his cheek with his tongue. "Go," Rufus repeated. "I don't want you to be an accessory to murder. And tell your momma you love her."

***

Hey Mr. S, I really need someone to talk to right now.

The rest of the text she sent were the streets she was staying on. She'd lost track of time from when she sent the text and grew exhausted from waiting on the abandoned city block. She lay on the sidewalk, and considered getting up and getting her blood flowing, but didn't find the motivation.

You can't blame yourself. No matter what, Conan's text read.

His checking in reminded her of simpler times. When he was all that mattered to her. That's how she got Kylie taken away. The memories sent her spiraling down even further inside her mind.

She highlighted the text and deleted it.

Headlights appeared across the street. She immediately recognized Mr. Stephend's ivory Palisade. He stopped before her and wearily shook his head. His green eyes met her gaze, and a smirk appeared in the corner of his mouth.

"You're seriously still out here?" he said, scratching the back of his head. "I really have rules against this kind of stuff with students, but hop in."

She slumped into the heated seat, glaring down at her hands and letting the warmth seep into her fatigued bones. She cleared her throat and took in a shallow breath.

"I told Conan I was running away. He screwed around on me."

Mr. Stephend's peppermint air freshener dangled from his rearview mirror. It still carried the scent like it was brand new. He waited until Brandi offered him an overly bright smile before putting the car into gear.

"It's high school bullshit, you really shouldn't let it get to you, Brandi."

"It's a mess," she said, and buried her face in her hands. "I'm sorry. Last night, I used your classroom to hide a friend. I don't know where she went. I think she ran away too."

I'm such an idiot. She hit herself in the head. *If he's been by the classroom today, then it's over.*

"Okay, okay, I get it. You're having a rough day. Come on, we'll swing by my place and have a cup of coffee. We can talk about it, then I'll take you home."

"I'm not going home. I told my parents I'm leaving. They said good riddance."

He pulled into his driveway and his hand moved like a snake, brushing against her knee and up to her thigh. Her chest grew heavy. She wished she could leap out of her skin.

"We will figure it out. Come in. It's freezing out here."

Brandi followed Stephend inside and her heartbeat crawled into her throat. Noir movie jazz played from a stereo deeper within. Pizzicato cello and an eerie sax melody. Woodland critters covered the dining room table, mice with fun hats, brooms, and baked bread decorated every inch of the entryway. Just as Brandi turned a confused look to Mr. Stephend, a skinny blonde with wispy hair, giant blue eyes, and a gap-toothed smile sauntered in from the jazz room.

"Oh?" she said, hurrying to Brandi. "Hello, miss. I'm sorry, I didn't know we were having company?"

"Brandi, this is my wife, Shandra. Sorry, Mousey, Brandi texted me hours ago. She's an exceptional student of mine and she's going through a hard time. I told her we would talk it out."

"Well, I'm all ears," Mrs. S said, but with a disappointed glower. "First, I need to talk to you alone. Brandi, please make yourself at home. Coffee, cream?"

"Yeah, uh, cream please. Anything with sugar."

She flashed her an impatient grin before dragging Mr. S away, already bickering at him. The jazz's volume turned up to cover their argument, and the track changed to a drum-centric piano and clarinet track.

Brandi glanced around the room again. The toasty atmosphere made her hug herself. It smelled like cinnamon and sugar. A beautiful home with a wonderful homemaker. *She* was the intruder. Brandi's chest somehow felt heavy and empty at once.

Rufus was right. She'd been wrong.

The camera? It could have been for anything. Mr. S got in trouble for stopping two students fighting. Maybe that was to prove otherwise. She felt like an idiot. She glimpsed herself in one of the display cases full of rodents, and despite her makeup, it looked like the vitality had completely drained from her features.

Brandi started to text.

The game's off. Snow ran away.

When she hit send, her phone network jammed. She tried to send it again. Nothing but a sudden chirping coming from the opposite side of the wall.

The sound increased the closer she got. Whistles, buzzes, and that continuous chirping.

When Brandi turned the corner, she saw a wall full of modems and routers, wires covering every inch, and different-colored flashes, each one sounding even more upset by her cellphone.

Her heart skipped a beat.

I'm going to die here.

"Jonesy says you're having boy trouble," Mrs. Stephend said. Something about her tone was off. "An older woman like myself could teach you about men's needs."

"Huh—what?" Brandi asked.

When she turned around, Mrs. Stephend tackled her. The wind exploded from Brandi's lungs, taking most of the fight out of her. She scuffled, but Mrs. Stephend was ropey and much stronger. Mr. Stephend appeared, and as Brandi kicked and scratched his wife, he zip-tied her hands behind her back.

"No! NO!" Brandi screamed as they dragged her down the hall. Her fight-or-flight senses pumped her full of adrenaline and she kicked drywall and bit and scratched whatever she could. Her struggle quickly left her exhausted.

Electronic buttons beeped, and the couple hoisted her into a padded room. The door slammed shut behind them and Brandi was stuck glaring at a greasy bondage table. She screamed so loud that it hurt her ears. Then Mr. Stephend kicked her in the mouth.

"Fuck!" he said. "She bit me."

Brandi lay on the floor, too scared to move. One of her front teeth loosely jiggled.

Do I deserve this? Did Kylie suffer like this before she died?

"Go cover it up. Burn yourself on the stove, and be more careful next time," Mrs. Stephend said and rolled her eyes.

Brandi glared up at the woman. She noticed and licked her lips the same way Brandi's father would after eyeing a medium-rare ribeye steak.

"Don't look so scared. It doesn't sell as well as sad does." Her boney fingertips glided over Brandi's cheek, her thumb grazed her lips. "Jonesy says you're a smart girl. If you are, my advice is to try to enjoy it. He said you were friends with Kylie? That's nice. She almost lasted a month. She *was* a good girl. Really, we've never been so lucky. You brought us the last one too? We seriously shoulda cut you in. Too bad. No problem, though, just don't struggle."

She slammed the door shut and a heavy sounding electronic latch clicked into place.

"Snow is...? Snow was here, and she's...?" Brandi fell from the table and hit her shoulder. The splitting pain rolled her eyes into the back of her head.

The air tasted stale but caught like barbs in her throat.

Like breathing in a crypt, sharing the oxygen with the dead souls that occupied it. Her own grave. She'd failed Snow, and she was going to die here. By the time anyone figured it out, it would be too late.

Her pulse went from slamming in her chest to a steady beat, and finally, as her eyes glazed over, it slowed to a near halt.

Conan, Kylie, Snow, I'm so sorry. I hope I don't end up a ghost. This is the worst place I'd want to haunt.

Time moved differently in her prison. Brandi thought about Scrambo and what the Devereuxs could've done to him. Rengifo didn't make it to this universe, but Charles did; she was at least glad she'd left him behind. Then there was Pokey, waiting for her. She'd do anything to have him.

I'm going to die alone.

The mechanical door clicked. Brandi refused to pick herself off the floor. Mr. Stephend appeared in her line of sight with a tripod and camera. He was completely naked except for a chicken mask over his face. Brandi discerned the sloshing of water, and Mrs. Stephend stepped in, also naked but for a gas mask hanging from her neck. She set down a yellow bucket and slapped a wet rag onto the bondage table.

"Making us work so hard this week," she said, bending over Brandi. "That's fine. You're more of a passion project anyway. We've been waiting for you for a couple of years now. Sit."

Brandi's eyes shifted up to her, and she wiggled her loose tooth as a reminder of what would happen if she didn't listen.

"Good, don't fight," Mrs. Stephend chuckled and grabbed the rag. She started working on Brandi's makeup as Mr. S set up the camera behind them.

"God, all this makeup, I'll never understand it. You cake it on until you look like someone else, or worse, older. I get it. You want to attract grown men? You don't need all this."

The water she used to clean under her eyes was scented vaguely with bleach.

"The real trick's no makeup at all. How old is she, Jonesy?"

"She's almost eighteen, I think."

"Fuck you," Brandi said, unable to hold back. "Kids loved you. I wanted to be a teacher because of you. We thought we could trust you."

"Brandi," he said, and sighed, shaking his head. He approached her and crouched down. His lips and eyes were the only recognizable things through his rubber mask. "You can talk to me. You can tell me anything you want. Just wait until the camera is on."

"Where's Snow? Where is she?"

He slapped her with the back of his hand, lifted his mask, and spat in her face. Brandi froze completely still, processing what had just happened. Mr. Stephend chuckled and turned back to his camera. An electronic reeling sound started up.

"I'm telling you," Mrs. Stephend said. "Take all this makeup off and you look fourteen. That's what older men really want. It's what they pay for, at least. Doesn't matter what—" She paused.

"Jones, someone's in the other room."

Mr. Stephend put his hands on his hips: the same stance he used in class when he was disappointed, but perverted by his flaccid member. "It's soundproof. You couldn't—"

"Go check, now." She paused and waited.

Mr. Stephend gave her butt a playful slap and shook his head. He left the door open on his way out and Brandi screamed.

"Help! Help me!"

Mrs. Stephend punched her in the throat and yanked her hair back.

"You're lucky our clients have requests, sweetie, or you wouldn't have a tongue. Don't worry, though. Things are about to get really exciting, I promise."

Chapter 17

Conan's sweating hands trembled. Low-volume jazz music played from a stereo in the kitchen, accompanied by a percussion of broken glass crunching beneath his and Rufus's feet. Rufus adjusted his ski mask and nodded toward the doorway. Someone would have heard the window break.

Dad, you started this... But tonight, no matter what, it's on me.

The kitchen was warm. An aroma of Italian sausage wafted through the air. Conan glanced at the oven timer ticking down from eighteen minutes to seventeen. Rufus pressed a finger to his lips, gesturing to the hallway behind him and the sound of padded footsteps.

Conan's eye twitched as a naked man wearing a chicken mask turned the corner and raised his hands.

"Oh shit," he said, frozen solid. "I don't keep cash in the house. If—"

"Shut up," Conan growled. "You move and it's your fucking kneecap."

Rufus rounded the corner, gun ready. The chicken man backed into the wall—knocking down a picture. Its corner hit the ground, and a fractured crack spider-webbed over a portrait of Mr. Stephend and the Peralta girls volleyball team.

"Where are they?" Conan asked, shoving the gun against the chicken man's head.

"Who? Wait, is that what this is, some vigilante justice bullshit? Are you kidding me—"

Conan slammed the gun down onto his beak. Cartilage squashed beneath the grip and knocked the chicken mask sideways. He fell to his knees and groaned as Conan ripped the mask off.

A breath hitched in his lungs. Conan thought he wanted to hit him again, but hesitated. The first did nothing for him.

Find her. Find her. Find her.

He shoved his gun into Stephend's mouth and stared vacantly at scratches and a fresh burn on Stephend's arm. He paused slightly as Rufus measured and ripped a long strip of duct tape.

"Where are they?" Conan repeated.

A hushed scream came from the doorway. Conan glanced up and saw a naked woman quickly turn and flee. She bumped into a long table full of porcelain animals and sent a deer and fox shattering to the ground. Rufus leapt over Mr. Stephend and chased after her.

Conan spun around and gripped the roll of tape. He finished binding Stephend in the fashion that Rufus showed him.

There was a lot of scuffling, like someone throwing a bag of potatoes around. A wave of exhaustion hit Conan. He wasn't sure if he should help or stay guard. There were no gunshots. He wasn't sure what it meant.

He leaned to glimpse down the dark hallway, keeping his gun against the back of Stephend's head, and counted backward from one hundred.

Eighty-eight...

Eighty-seven...

Eighty-six...

Rufus appeared in the hallway with the naked woman slung over his shoulder. Her arms and legs had been zip-tied, and he held a cattle prod in his southpaw.

"Dude," he said, slamming the woman onto the couch. "I'm officially losing my fucking cool over here. They got spiked dildos, meat hooks, and iron brands and shit."

"You didn't find them?"

Rufus shook his head, glancing at a cut on his elbow.

"You're never gonna find her either," Mr. Stephend said with a smile.

"You're really trying to get shot?" Conan said and stomped Stephend's head into the tile.

How did I let this happen? Is it my fault? What about that piece of shit who crashed into you, Dad? These monsters? Everyone's just this fucking terrible? Where is she?

Mrs. Stephend squirmed, her voice muffled by duct tape. Conan walked to her and ripped it off her face, leaving a red streak.

"Please," she begged. "I don't know what you want, but do whatever you want to me. Just let my husband go."

"He's already snitched himself out, lady," Conan said. "Where are they?"

She leaned toward her husband, showing her gap-toothed sneer. Her sweaty and naked body glistened, perfuming the confinement with a strong bacteria odor, and making Conan's stomach roll.

"You idiot, why spout off? Keep your mouth shut."

Conan raised his gun and pointed it at Mrs. Stephend. His heart was a void, but he knew he wouldn't pull the trigger.

"I'm tired of asking," he said. "Tell me where she is or I'm going to paint the walls with her fucking brains."

"Kill the stupid bitch, then," Mr. Stephend laughed. "Or fuck her, whatever you want. She's the really evil one. My mouse, over there. If it wasn't for her, no one would have gotten hurt. You'd be doing the world a favor."

"You didn't have a problem with *evil* when you were fucking those little girls' slits. You little bitch." She spat, but the bodily fluid only ran down her chin.

"This is too much, man. Over our heads kinda shit. I got a horrible feeling." Rufus's watery eyes showed as he shook his head.

Beep! Beep! Beep!

Eighteen minutes had already passed, and they had nothing to show for it. Conan fought off thoughts of failure as he walked over and cleared the oven panel.

"Help! Help!" Mrs. Stephend screamed.

Rufus rolled his eyes and stretched a fresh piece of duct tape over her mouth. When she couldn't scream anymore, she changed to sensual moans and wrapped her legs around him, grinding herself against him. Rufus wrestled to pry her off of him.

"She's cracked out, man," Rufus shouted, wiping himself down as if she carried a terrible disease.

Mr. Stephend tried to stand, but Conan soccer-kicked him in the head. His neck lulled to one side and the English teacher went motionless. Conan scanned the front yard. It looked like a middle of nowhere suburbia. Green lawns were neatly cut to perfection, entirely peaceful.

"We have to find them and get the fuck out," Conan said.

"You're not finding shit," Stephend cried, then groaned. "You'll never get them back. It's over." He kicked his feet like he was throwing a fit and rubbed his skull against the tile.

Conan's mind imagined Brandi and Snow both dead, and the portal of desolation inside him tore into a chasm.

Find her.

Conan dragged a chair from under the kitchen table. Its legs screeched in protest as he whipped it around.

"Grab him," Conan said.

They both took an arm and dropped Stephend into the chair. Conan grabbed the duct tape and bound him to it, running through most of the roll. As he did, Mr. Stephend laughed and shit himself. A yellow and brown slurry poured out from the back of his chair. Rufus gagged and spat up in the sink.

"*Hahaha*, hey, Mousey, looks like Daddy's little blue pill's kickin' in!" he shouted into the hall and squirmed, rubbing himself in his own excrement as his member turned erect.

Conan grabbed a dish towel and tossed it over him. He went to the counter and pulled the biggest knife out of a butcher block set.

"HA! Let me guess, chop my balls off? I'd like to see you try. You don't got the stones."

"You won't have to find out. Tell me where they are."

Rufus checked on Mrs. Stephend, who'd fallen on the floor and moved like a slug. When he went to collect her, she renewed her earlier struggle.

"I know you," Stephend said, tilting his head. His ear was already swelling to cauliflower proportions. "You're Conan, that kid who never does his own homework and acts too big for school. Brandi's boyfriend? Did she put you up to this?" He chuckled. "She had to have. This is right where I expected you, making dumbass decisions. Next stop, jail, your whole life wasted."

Conan gripped the knife so hard that his gloves squeaked against the rubber. He lifted the blade so that it would reflect the glare into Stephend's eyes.

"Tell me where she is." He tried to sound brave, but his mouth was gummy with an excess of saliva and the words came out jumbled.

"The closet in the hallway." He lifted his head, aiming his bloody nostrils at him. "But If you want the code, let my wife go."

"Not happening."

"Well, then I guess you're screwed. Too bad you won't be able to ask your girlfriend about it."

Rufus came back into the kitchen and saw the knife in Conan's hand. He did a double take toward Mr. Stephend.

"He says there's a code to get into the closet. That's where she is."

Rufus rolled his eyes again. He grabbed another dish towel and opened the oven. Heat, powerful basil, white wine, and ricotta flavors stirred with Stephend's shit. Rufus grabbed the bubbling lasagna and flung it into Mr. Stephend's lap.

"*AHHHHHHHH KYHAAAAAA! AH! AH!*"

Rufus gagged him with the dishtowel and checked out the window.

"Man, nobody really don't give a shit about nothing no more, huh? A cheese grater's next." He pulled out the gag. "What's the code?"

"5135679—5135679. Hospital, please plea—" He gagged him again and motioned for Conan to go.

There are times
I think I'll be okay
But it's a lie
Inside my mind
I ignore the signs.

He rushed through the hallway and found the keypad. His heart caught in his throat. An exhausting voice nagged inside his head.

Failure. Failure. You're a failure. You're too late.

He punched in the code.

The dungeon smelled stale, like bleach and Ms. Stephend's sweat. Brandi stared at him from behind a heavy metal table. She was alone.

So it was all for nothing.

Despite his ski mask, she hugged him tight. He hugged her back, and every beat of her heart against his chest made him sink deeper and deeper.

"You came back," she said, her voice cracking.

"Yeah." He forced a smile. "Did they hurt you?"

Brandi shook her head. "Nothing serious."

"Snow?"

Brandi's eyes lit up, but she shook her head. Having no makeup on her face made her seem younger, more vulnerable. He turned and stomped his way through the hallway. On his way back to the kitchen, he smacked down a glass raccoon holding a cookie jar. He rounded the corner and stomped through the lasagna mess.

"The dark-haired girl? Where is she?" he asked and yanked the gag from Stephend's mouth.

"I—I don't know who you're talking about."

"Where is she?!" Conan shouted and punched him in his swollen ear.

Stephend's eyes rolled to the back of his head. Fresh blood coated the knuckles of Conan's glove.

I know you're worthless, Dad. If you've been watching over me, you haven't done shit. But please, please, please, make her be okay.

Conan grabbed the knife from atop the counter. He held it up to Stephend's neck, then lowered it to his manhood. Thinking about what the future held stabbed pain into his chest.

"You have one more chance."

Stephend looked at him like he hadn't understood a single word. The burns on his crotch looked severe enough to be infected without proper treatment. The stink was hard to ignore, like iron and leather.

Conan gripped a cup of water and splashed it onto Mr. Stephend's face.

"Boat—boatshed, outskirts of town."

Conan tossed the cup into the sink.

"Help me grab the wife. Come on," he said.

We were supposed to leave town. We were supposed to... Shut up--shut up. Nobody cares what you think right now. You're stupid. If you've got no good ideas, then you have to stop.

Rufus was right. Mrs. Stephend definitely smoked *something* before they showed up. Her pupils were dilated, and when he picked her up, body odor clung to him like putrid cologne. She continued to moan and gyrate as they dragged her into the padded room and placed her on the cold metal table. Conan tied her legs down.

"What are you doing?" Rufus asked.

"Nothing she wouldn't."

"Yeah, but—"

"Hold the door if you don't want to help, Rufus," Brandi said. "There's no keypad on the inside. Trust me, if I told you what was going on, you'd have already killed her."

Rufus sighed and strapped her arms down. It wasn't until she was completely bound that her muffled groans turned panicked.

"What if nobody finds her?" Rufus asked.

"That's exactly what she deserves," Conan said, and yanked off his ski mask.

He refused to say more and slammed the door shut behind them. The keypad made a mechanical whirring and latched itself locked.

"Pull the car around back. We're taking him with us."

Rufus's shoulders slumped, and he trudged out the back door. Conan imagined the police showing up and gunning everyone down before they could leave.

Some questions are better left unanswered, huh, Pops? Guess you're right. I shouldn't have hope. There's no going back now.

He grabbed a broom and swept up the mess in the kitchen. Brandi stood with her arms crossed, watching him, then looking at the groaning Mr. Stephend.

"You will call the cops, right?" she asked. "You're not gonna let her die in there for real, are you?"

Conan paused but didn't look up. "If they aren't already on their way, yeah."

He glanced down at the pen and notepad on the fridge. A small grocery list: butter, carrots, brown sugar, written on a possum and fox notepad. He grabbed the pen but hesitated.

"I can't believe these monsters have cute shit all over the place."

"Yeah," Brandi agreed. "Monsters are just people too, I guess."

He glanced over at her, wishing he was someone else, and anywhere else but here.

"I'm scared of what I'll write."

"No matter what happens, Conan," Brandi said and smiled. "Thanks."

He nodded, lifted the pen, and wrote.

The pulse that blights my chest
Is in disagreement with my inhibitions
Another miscarriage of my desires
Segregated across my curling spine

He stared at the words and ripped the note off the wall.

Rufus came inside and shook his head as Conan and Brandi cut Stephend free.

"Should we hose him down, or at least put pants on his muddy fuckin' ass?"

"Broken windows, screams, cops already probably on the way." Conan shrugged. "There's no time. I'll grab his legs."

Through their silent drive, Conan sat next to Mr. Stephend.

They'd at least put a towel on the seat, but he still stank like hell. By the time they drove past the city limit, a stench bred on Conan's tongue, a disgusting tang crawling down his throat. Whenever Stephend drifted, Conan would slap him with a gloved hand.

"Hey," Conan said. "Wake up."

Stephend stirred, as if waking from a fever. He glanced at the road and spit onto his own lap.

"Take Parkway here. Ride it all the way up, few—few miles. It's there," he said. "My legacy."

Conan bit his lip. A mile later, they saw the shed.

It didn't look grim, or rusted like in horror movies, but just a normal tin building. The only thing odd was a pack of stray dogs surrounding the perimeter. One particularly mangy bastard barked at the Honda, and Rufus hopped out and chased it away.

Conan refused to think about what the dogs could mean. He ran to the shed and pointed his gun at the padlock.

"What are you doing?" Brandi asked.

"Brandi, I have—" He covered his face as his heart wrenched itself. "I have to."

"I meant—shooting it only works in movies."

"Here," Rufus said, walking to his trunk.

He pulled out a sledgehammer and presented it to Conan. When Conan went to take it, Rufus clinched it tightly, giving him a worried frown before letting him take it.

Conan closed his eyes and imagined himself in a box. He slowly counted down from ten, calming himself.

One last dance of
Our lips colliding into each other
Harmonious by definition
Your third eye saw through me.

It took him two swings, and the second one shot electricity through the nerves in his elbow. The lock clattered onto the hard soil below.

Conan pushed open the door.

Decayed fruit hit him full blast. Flies buzzed over every inch of the flat space. Mrs. Stephend's bacterial sweat times a thousand. Rotting meat. Death. He turned dizzy. A desolate space of shifted soil, two garbage bags full of clothes, a blue bicycle, a pair of shovels, and a wheelbarrow.

Brandi wordlessly followed in behind him.

Without thinking, and only letting his hands and legs drive him, Conan grabbed the nearest shovel. He picked a spot that looked recently disturbed and started digging. His chest grew heavy as he thought he sucked in honey and lilies instead of decay.

He imagined himself playing a show, going away from his thoughts.

Brandi grabbed the second shovel and helped. Minutes passed, and they uncovered a body. They'd killed her recently, completely naked, pale, a ghost. Her arms and legs were tied behind her. A bag had been zip-tied over her head. Her lips stretched backward, covering half her face in an expression of painful suffocation. She had red hair.

Conan picked another spot.

As they worked, he sank into the wet ground. He lifted his leg and a clump of hair stuck to his shoe. He readjusted himself, but nowhere seemed firm. They uncovered a large black bag, and Conan's heart drummed in his head. He fought his thoughts off, not allowing any to intrude.

She isn't here. She's not here. She's not here. She's not. Don't worry. She's not here. She abandoned you.

He unzipped the bag.

Volatile decomposition nearly made him pass out. Brandi took a step back and vomited. Her shoes were black with corpse grime and she let out a frustrated whimper as she kicked the gore off of her sneaker.

Whoever had been in the bag had liquefied. They weren't recognizably human any longer.

Conan couldn't hold it in and vomited sour bile onto the muddied floor. He took a step back, closed his eyes, and again, he imagined himself climbing a box and counted backward from ten.

"Conan," Brandi said from behind him. She was on her hands and knees, sifting through the rotten swamp.

Brandi pulled the bag from her face and let out an anguished cry.

Snow didn't appear harmed, or even disturbed. By some miracle of god, she seemed peaceful. Conan ran his fingers over her face, leaving a streak of grime.

"No," Brandi whimpered. "No, no, no."

When Snow didn't open her eyes, the portal of emptiness within consumed everything. Conan stood, and his mental fog turned blinding. He exited the shed and passed by Rufus on the way out.

The October air was thick and sweet—putrid. It could have been from the corpse crud buried in the back of his nose. He sparked a cigarette, washing away the aroma. Air would never taste crisp again.

He walked to the car and puffed smoke at Mr. Stephend. The murderer winced and coughed, looking like a pathetic, naked worm.

"Get out," Conan said.

"I'm sorry. I have a problem," Stephend whimpered. "I have a problem. I need professional help. I can get better."

Conan lifted the gun out of his belt and clicked the safety off.

"Yo, yo, yo," Rufus said, shaking his hands. "You're not a—"

Conan pulled the trigger.

The back of Stephend's head blew to pieces, painting the ground with his brains. Conan put the safety back on and placed the Beretta atop Rufus's car. He took a long drag of his cigarette and listened to the buzzing flies.

A tranquil hallucination
My cadaver lost at sea
It calms me to a relief
But won't release your disease

There are times
I think I'll be okay
But it's a lie
Inside my mind
I ignore the signs
And your toll on me
Which means nothing.

Chapter 18

Club Depression's babbling crowd grew into a chaotic hum.

"When are they playing, Brandi?" a teenage boy Brandi didn't recognize asked her in passing. She answered with a shrug, carrying the cashbox backstage. She placed the money next to Rufus's silver case and eavesdropped on the boys.

"So, this is our final form then?" Marc chuckled. "Ditching agents on Saturday night so we can play a secret Sunday afternoon gig for no one but the hangover crowd and whatever kids got caught up in the text chain?"

Brandi gave Pokey a pat on the head and glanced at Conan, wondering how he'd react to Marc's pep talk. He stood near motionless, his eyes red from not sleeping and his notebook clenched at his side. Jackie was behind him, arms crossed and glaring.

I can't see myself living in the future, Conan's latest text read. *But today, I'll fake it for them.*

It would be their last show together, and she wasn't even excited to watch. She wanted out, but couldn't even dig up motivation to text him back, let alone think about tomorrow.

She locked Rufus's stuff in his locker and followed the boys to the stage. Patrons filled Club Depression from wall to wall. It appeared more solid than a Saturday night gig, but with the benefits of a warm afternoon sun pouring in through the windows. Brandi glanced out the back door and considered leaving—then and there forever. Instead, she pulled out her phone and replied.

Maybe there's still hope. Not for everyone and everything, but we have to let that go and try again. Don't we? We can only help so much, and can't let every terrible thing beat us down. Right?

A need to avert herself from the crowd paired with the fragrance of cigarettes pouring in from the patio made her crave her own. Feedback kicked in as Rufus struck an open chord. The patio crowd forced its way inside, and as Brandi admired faces familiar and new, she saw River Devereux leaning against the far wall.

Maybe I'm a fucking ghost! Conan screamed at the top of his lungs.
Lost and dying sucked to the bone
To reach you, to be with you, it's just another omen
Maybe I'm the fucking villain

Brandi mouthed the lyrics as she walked along the mosh pit's outskirts. A high school girl who Brandi forgot the name of recognized her and screamed in her face. Brandi gave her an overly bright smile, but couldn't understand her shouts over the music.

If River expected her, she pretended like she didn't and nodded her head in tempo with the song. Brandi crossed her arms and let the song finish before beckoning her outside. River's expression remained unchanged, but she led the way.

The theater exploded into cheers, but was cut off by Jackie's drum solo—leading into the next song. Brandi closed the outside door behind them and the music became muffled by the walls. Despite loving their show, Brandi found herself exhausted. She sagged against the railing, meeting River's sunken glare, and sparked a cigarette.

"You look terrible," Brandi said. She inhaled, but the tobacco flavors reminded her of boatshed corpse grime. No amount of brushing her teeth could get the taste of that abyss off her tongue. She offered River a pull of her cigarette, but she declined.

"Spirits inside you are probably bouncing around like popcorn, huh?" Brandi said. "Today's the day, right?"

"I suppose I shouldn't be surprised," River said, exasperated. "It's really gotten to where I cannot care anymore. When you burned my home to the ground, I had given up hope in whatever plans my mother had for us. Nothing aligned."

One of the regular kids' mother, Rosa, was outside of the club with her taco cart. The meat sizzled, and warm spices of cumin and oregano wafted through the air. She turned and waved at Brandi.

"That was all Snow. I had nothing to do with it."

"Nobody died," River said, ignoring her. "Except for Weasel."

"That's terrible. I'm so sorry."

"Needless to say, Misty was devastated. We were keeping your truck until then. Yesterday, she ripped it to pieces."

Brandi ran her fingers through her hair, wincing as she yanked on a tangle, and lowered her head.

"I didn't come here to make you feel poorly," River said. She came away from the railing and a luminescent green nimbus passed behind the whites of her eyes. "By now, my guess is that Snow's very far away from us. I came to you today because no matter what's done, something monstrous, something terrible, is going to happen tonight. I wanted to ask if you'd take me away from here." River placed a hand over her heart, as if to pledge her honesty.

Maybe I'm a ghost to them? Conan, Rufus, they'll be out of my life soon. If I'm selfish, I can still live this life—with her, I could do anything.

"River, you don't love me," she said, shaking her head. "You just don't have me, so you want me. That's how all you rich kids are. If you could buy me, it would totally defeat the purpose. You only want what you can't have, whether that's because of your mother or me."

"Peculiar and enticing," River said. She reached a hand out, and Brandi placed the lipstick-stained cigarette into her outstretched fingers. River took an inhale, and the smoke she exhaled made the same cloud shape as whatever had passed through her stare moments ago.

"The spirits grow restless, both those within me, and the ones beneath the earth. My time's running short. This desire, which, yes, we both know that's all it is, is all that's left anchoring me here."

Maybe we're all ghosts? Every single one of us. Always have been. It's depressing, but not a surprise. We try to change fate, but streams only flow in one direction.

River gave Brandi her cigarette back. Prominent dark circles had appeared around her burned ocean eyes.

"Your drummer friend in there, he came to us and told us everything. I know that you've been keeping her safe, and I know it was you who started the fire."

And maybe we're all still going to die.

"Then stop talking to me and go to the proper authorities."

"That is not how my mother operates."

The sizzling meat ceased, and Rosa scraped it into one of her heated trays. A couple passing by stopped for tacos. The club rumbled behind them, and after talking with Rosa for a moment, the couple took their food inside.

"My earlier offer still stands," River said. She reached a hand up and cupped Brandi's chin. Her fingers were rigid as stone, and Brandi swatted them away.

"So does my reply. It would never work, River."

River's shoulders dropped, and after swallowing, she gave her lip a chew.

"Brandi, there are worse things than death, physical or emotional. Where's my sister?"

The band turned silent and Conan shouted something that made them cheer. Brandi took a drag from her cigarette, coating her teeth with flavors of tar, considered quitting for good, and passed it to River.

"What do you think?" Brandi asked. "Is dying worse than being depressed? Which would you rather? Go on the rest of your life as you are, fucking popcorn popping inside of you, making you into an even crazier bitch than you've ever been, or end it all?"

River lifted her chin, glaring as Brandi pushed off the rail. She chewed the inside of her cheek and her stomach did a flip.

She walked over to Rosa. Food had been tasteless, but she needed to stall.

"Two chicken, two beef please," she said and took out a five-dollar bill.

Rosa hurriedly put together the tacos, exactly how Brandi liked them: lime, chile, onion, cilantro, and radish slices. The food was neatly organized, and she drizzled *verde* on top of the chicken and *roja* on the beef, completing her lovely portrait. As Rosa handed her the plate, she glanced at River.

"Any trouble, *mija*?"

Brandi's fingers pressed against her parted lips, but she shoved her free hand into her sweater pocket, smiled, and shook her head.

"Not any more than usual. Thanks for asking." She nodded and Brandi took half a taco down in one bite. Serrano chile combined with whatever sweetness Rosa had mixed in her sauces nearly made Brandi transcend to heaven.

"Best tacos in town, seriously," she said, bringing the plate over to River and offering her one.

"How? It's from a cart," River asked, and actually smiled.

"Are you kidding me? Making tacos fancy ruins them. Try one, the chicken's not spicy."

"I can't. I can't eat," she said, pressing a hand into her abdomen. "Because of what she's done to me. It would just come back up."

Brandi's ears turned hot. A brisk lightheadedness had come over her.

"I guess that answers my question, then. So you'll continue with Adria's bullshit? You can run away yourself. You know that, right?"

"I'm scared." River chuckled, but sounded as if she were holding back tears. "I've never been alone."

"Yeah. That makes sense," she said and glanced down at her plate, still beautiful, made with love. She'd had no appetite, but took another bite. Rosa's cooking was delicious, and if it ended up being her last meal, she wanted to finish it.

"So if you won't help me escape—please, tell me where my sister is."

The music inside thumped, and the crowd jumped in tempo with the drumbeat. The walls shook behind them. Brandi had lost track of time. The boys' set could only go so long.

"I don't think you want to see her," Brandi said, setting her plate down and inhaling a massive oxygen intake. For a moment, she'd forgotten about breathing entirely.

"It's not a matter of what I want, Brandi. It never has been. It's a matter of *your* life. Please, don't be stupid. Despite your antagonism, I truly don't want to see you hurt."

"She's dead."

A gust of wind blew strong enough to sway the nearby trees. Brandi covered her plate and Rosa chased down a pair of sliced radishes, shaking her head as she tossed them into her trash bag.

"Where is she?"

"In a boatshed outside of town. We already called the police."

River's open hand shot out and gripped Brandi by the throat. She squeezed hard enough to constrict her windpipe and then released.

"Liar. Stop *lying!* Where is she?!"

Rosa glanced over her shoulder, but Brandi dismissed her with a wave and a shake of her head.

"She's gone, River."

River flared her nostrils, and a bead of sweat broke on her brow.

"Shut up. Ever since I've looked at your face, everything's made me sick. Shut up, shut up. I'll hurt you, Brandi. I'll hurt you worse than you've ever known. Tell me the truth."

"I'm sorry."

"*Liar,* she could have stopped anyone." River's entire body tensed up, as if to hide her arms trembling. "You don't know what she is capable of."

Maybe it eats away at some people. Maybe others don't get that luxury. They just break.

"She could have turned back time. I know." Brandi's words made River twitch. "But she didn't. Not this time."

River struck her with the back of her hand hard enough to drop her to the concrete. Brandi touched fingers to her cheek, and they came away bloody from deep, burning scratches. River lifted her by the hair. Brandi saw flashes of her past and felt the ghost of her limbs being torn away.

"One last chance." Her eyes were infectious, cloudy, and her breath stank like rot.

Brandi saw Rosa hurrying inside.

Maybe I don't want to give up? Maybe I want to try again?

Big Ben was watching the front door. He'd be by in seconds. A car door slammed across the street, and Brandi saw Misty, dressed in slacks and a button-up coat, accompanied by both her long-haired and short-haired goons.

Big Ben bounded down the Club Depression stairs with a single leap. River glanced over and freed Brandi.

"We *goth* a problem here?" Ben lisped. He cringed at Misty's approaching goons.

Without warning, River strutted forward and punched Ben in the stomach. He looked like he weighed over three of her put together, but her single blow dropped him to one knee.

Someone shouted inside and the music came to an abrupt halt. Showgoers poured out and brought the stink of reefer and body odor with them.

Marc appeared at Ben's side and Rufus at Brandi's.

"Conan's grabbing the guns," Rufus said. "Should I call the cops?"

A punk with a pink mullet was having a one-sided argument with an incredibly bored Misty Devereux. She waved her hand, and her goons took the man down. As they stomped him, more showgoers ran to his aid, and a brawl broke out. Brandi's phone vibrated.

Where is the knife? I need the knife! Conan's text read. She vacantly stared at the cracked screen and shoved her phone back into her pocket.

Rufus went to help and River knelt down next to Brandi. Her skin had taken a dingy hue to it and her voice had lost its luster, becoming gravel.

"Do you want to die, Brandi? You and all of your friends? They're pouring out of me, leaking from my mind and orifices. I won't be able to control it much longer. They want to see your blood. Snow's the only one who can stop them. She can help both of us. Where is she?"

"I know," Brandi said. A tear ran down her cheek and burned the fresh scratches. "Things could have been different for *everyone.* I failed her. Just because she gave us a second chance, doesn't—didn't guarantee anything. We went back. She counted on me to help her. I failed her. River, she's gone."

"No." River shook her head, spittle fell down her chin. "No, no, no."

Voices raised behind them, a cacophony of cheers, heckling, and primitive grunts. The Devereuxs' goons were being overwhelmed by sheer numbers. Misty stood on the outskirts of the rumble, her arms crossed and drumming her fingers.

"ENOUGH!"

The shriek that erupted from River's lungs was entirely inhuman. It drove a nail into Brandi's eardrums.

The showgoers stopped their advances and gazed at River with slack jaws. Brandi glimpsed Conan appearing with Jackie on the back patio. His hand had been on the hilt of his gun, but he replaced his shirt and moved behind her.

Brandi's body felt too heavy to move, and every muscle whined in protest as she turned to face River.

"Snow turned back time," Brandi rasped, her body trembling. "She said she'd done it thousands of times, maybe more, she'd lost count. Every single time, she ended up dead. She sent me back with the memories, hoping I could help. I made it worse. We brought a monster down because of her, but I think—I think she gave up."

It doesn't matter. It doesn't matter because I failed. We're all going to die, again.

River's eyes remained clenched shut tight. The occasional orb of light passed behind her eyelids. She twitched at every one of Brandi's spoken words.

Misty massaged her temples. "What are we doing?" she asked with a scowl.

River opened her eyes, and they glowed like two lanterns.

"Nothing you're willing to," River said and cackled. She hunched over, burying her face in her hands. "Snow's gone."

Misty turned stiff, her jaw line became hard as she glared down at Brandi.

"Don't you remember? All those times she died?" River laughed like it was the funniest joke in the world.

Misty stepped away. Parts of the crowd were dispersing now that the major fight had finished, but Rufus, Marc, and Big Ben still argued with the bodyguards.

"River, you're unwell. We need to get you back. Mother'll know what to do."

"I won't!" River screamed, clenching her face. Light bled from the cracks in her fingers.

"I remember, Brandi. You betrayed us once before. But another time, another time." Her glowing eye peered from behind her parted fingers. Brandi's instincts told her to run, but her legs wouldn't budge. "We were together, and we were happy. I remember, I do."

"River, I—" Misty said, but River turned on her.

"If you want to do something for me, then go kill Mother. I'm so irritated, irritated with your *helping,* Misty. Why can't you do anything for yourself?"

"I—I—"

"Do it! Kill her!"

Misty hung her head.

"I can't do that."

River raised a finger and pointed at Rufus, Marc, and Big Ben.

"Those three, her friends," she said. "Bring them with us."

Misty scratched the back of her head, apparently glad to have orders. It was the first time Brandi really noticed how she carried herself. She'd elected to only wear formal makeup, just like Brandi, not overdone, and with her dyed hair pulled back in a neat bun.

Maybe she's a ghost too? A ghost of her sister's potential.

"You heard her, I guess. Into the truck and nobody gets hurt."

"Fuck that." Rufus laughed, and as the long-haired goon approached him, he swung his leg in a horizontal arc. Rufus's foot connected with the man's head, making a solid *thump* and knocking him out cold.

Marc and Ben surrounded the short-haired goon. The pink-mullet punk, along with another skinhead, crept up behind him.

"Miss Devereux, can't I just shoot them?" he growled.

"What part of keep your mouth shut didn't you understand?" Misty said, and threw River a frustrated glance. "We should leave."

"Don't go anywhere," River said, leaning down next to Brandi, breathing her death breath onto her. The same stink of the corpse sludge glued onto the sneakers Brandi had to burn.

River approached the group and walked past the two punk rockers, addressing her goon.

"Your orders were to never be questioned."

"Yeah. Sorry, but this is kind of—"

River's nails flashed, and the man gave a choked gasp. A bead of red peeled out from his neck. Panic flashed across his eyes and crimson spurted from the paper-line wound, painting the nearby sidewalk. He gurgled and collapsed to his knees, placing his hands down into his life's blood.

A scream broke out and the crowd turned hysterical. The skinhead ran at River with a knife in his hand. She raised her claws and her black fingernails shot outward, piercing the man in the eye and bursting out the back of his skull. She lifted her victim five feet into the air and flung him at the fleeing crowd. The pink-mullet punk turned to run, and she extended her index finger, stretching her nail half a block and piercing him through the heart.

Conan was at Brandi's side, lifting her up.

"We have to run, now," he said. Jackie stood with him, gaping at the carnage.

"If we run, they'll kill you," she said. "River remembers. Not everything, but enough."

Conan winced. "The knife? What did Snow do with the knife?"

"River, you idiot!" Misty shouted. "Do you have any idea how badly you've fucked up? This is over our heads."

Brandi pressed a finger to Conan's lips and shushed him.

"Don't bring it up again," she said.

Maybe this shame, maybe it's just a part of me.

"River! We will go with you. Don't hurt anyone else."

Whatever happens, happens. All we can do is accept it.

The entire crowd had dispersed. Rosa's taco cart had been flipped over, grease spilled around it like a body outline. The smell of wasted food, Rosa's livelihood, made Brandi's heart sink.

"Those two are coming as well," River said, pointing her bloody fingertip at Conan and Jackie. "Bring your guns." She smiled, showing blackened teeth.

"We'll go. Nobody fight her, all right? Just get in the truck," Brandi said, lowering her hands and taking a step back. For the first time since meeting Snow Devereux, her breath came easy. "Please, just let me grab my elephant."

Chapter 19

Adria Devereux sat in her office's only chair. She rubbed her brow as her brown-haired assistant popped open an emerald bottle. Ruby wine glugged from its neck and filled her glass to the brim. Conan glanced up from the indiscernible black and gray acrylic rug to her fireplace and bookshelf-covered walls. He wondered why someone would need so many books, yet alone how they'd find time to read them all.

"Chaos wins the day," Adria sighed, and took a long slug off her wine. "My own daughter. How was I so oblivious?"

Conan nodded toward Adria, and a tightness left his chest. He'd been blind too. Snow had told him so many times that he'd lost count—there was nothing he could do.

A chance, Dad? I get it now. You were trying to show me. It's not like you wanted to die. It really doesn't matter what the future holds. Huh?

He glanced at his friends and tapped his fingers on his lips. Rufus, Jackie, Marc, Ben, and Brandi.

They all deserve so much more than what I brought into their lives. The death. Whatever chance they'd had, I stole away.

The dread he'd grown so accustomed to churned within. It took his focus away from his friends and put it solely on the woody stench of the office, catching in the back of his throat. His gaze drifted to River and the way she lulled. How she explored with her eyes. It reminded him of Snow.

Our future doesn't exist
Like a movie
But you died in the first scene
And I'm not worthy of being a memory.

"Enough of your sulking," Misty Devereux said. "You need to wake up. River needs you."

Adria readjusted her blindfold, leaned back in her chair, and finished her glass in two gulps.

"Soon. Not like there's a rush anyway." She loudly smacked her lips. "Can you not see? I'm grieving your sister."

"You're not grieving her. You're grieving your ritual. Help River, now."

River spun on her heel and faced her family as if in trouble. Misty ignored her and snapped her fingers.

"She's not herself anymore. Why are you procrastinating?"

River moped away, walking past Conan and the others. She glanced out the door's window and into the corridor.

"Such an old school," Conan heard River whisper. "This office has no windows. There's only one exit, and the door opens inward. How strange." She smiled and Conan saw her eyes roll into the back of her head.

Jackie slunk toward River, but her bodyguard caught him in a bear hug.

"Hey, man, c'mon, let me go," he said, wildly scuffing his feet against the floor. "Screw these bitches. Why do we gotta stick around for this family feud bullshit?"

The goon offered him nothing, roughly shoving him to the front of the group. He wouldn't meet Conan's stare and quickly retreated to Marc's side.

If you die I live
Spending my time running away
Barely a ghost
In the black eyes of those who pity me.

"Because you didn't keep your mouth shut, Jackie," Brandi hissed behind him, and Jackie's cheeks turned bright red.

"What's that mean?" Rufus asked, yellow crusting the sides of his maddened stare. He'd gotten the least sleep of all of them the past four days and his eyes looked to be vibrating in their sockets.

"Jackie snitched us out," Brandi said.

Rufus flared his nose. He blinked rapidly and barreled toward Jackie with a scream. Conan's limbs fidgeted, but before they escalated to blows, he placed himself between his best friends.

I understand why he did what he did. It's my fault. Just like how this is Adria's. Right, Dad? It's all right, but she still deserves to pay. Right?

"We never asked you for anything," Misty continued berating her mother. "Please, just help her. You can't just sit here and get wasted. She needs you. We're running out of time."

Adria didn't even appear to be listening, resting her chin on her fist and holding her glass out for a refill.

I am a gutter
To crowd your bodies in
A waking breath
Strangled by the hands of fate.

"Aren't you supposed to be the strongest?" Conan asked. Somehow his voice affected everyone and turned the office so quiet that he could hear Misty's quivering breaths.

"Only one exit, and it opens inward," River said, still peering out the window.

"Snow turned back time," Conan said. "Why can't you? You're her mother. Can't you bring her back?"

"Of course not," Adria said with a dismissive wave. "I wasn't even aware. She truly was one of a kind. And such potential, wasted."

"Yeah," Conan said and loudly clicked his foot onto the floor. "And you were gonna sacrifice her for what? To live through that?" He pointed at River, still staring out the door. "You—Adria, you deserve to suffer."

"Look at my daughter!" Adria's scream bounced off the walls and caused a stir in the hallways outside. Her seat squeaked as she leaned toward Conan. "I am suffering, boy. Rejoice, *ha*, rejoice in knowing that you've ruined everything. My daughters, her life, all of our lives. Rejoice, boy! *That* is still my life. She is my treasure. *Regardless* of her becoming *worthless*. Rejoice then, she was supposed to ascend."

Misty rolled her eyes and unbuttoned her coat. She leaned against the nearest bookshelf and pulled out a cigarette. Conan licked his lips at the sight of it, nearly tasting the smoke himself. She sparked it and pressed the butt to her lips. He tried to focus on that instead of River jumping up and down.

"Put that out," Adria snapped, sniffing the air. "How dare you, girl, you miserable—"

"Fuck off," Misty replied, taking a long drag.

"Mother," River interrupted, leaping to the center of the room. "Snow is dead."

"I know, lovely, I know. It's truly a tragedy, I—"

"No," River repeated, chuckling. "She's *dead*."

Punished by humanity
Cradled in an angel's arms

Perverting our sanctity
I promise
Another devil will follow.

"Did you get it?" Conan asked Brandi with a calm breath, lifting his head up and meeting her eyes.

"Yeah, but remember what Snow said?"

"Yeah. I remember." He cleared his throat. "But she's the only thing Adria cares about."

"Snow wouldn't want that. River doesn't deserve it either."

He watched Brandi pull the zipper of her jacket down so that the head of her stuffed elephant stuck out the top. She retreated her hand through her sleeve and fumbled around within it. When her arm filled her sleeve again, she stealthily passed him the killing blade.

"Brandi, don't worry. This isn't the end. Not here. Not in this fucking town."

River let out an exasperated groan, flexing her practiced soprano to end on a high-pitched cry. She slunk over to Misty and buried her head in her chest. Misty tossed her lit cigarette onto the ground and clenched her sister tight. Conan forced his gaze away from River's exposed throat and shook his head at the wasted tobacco.

"They hurt, Misty. They're hurting me so bad. Little claws, little teeth, cutting me from the inside. Shadows behind my eyelids. I can't be myself. They're whispering. Blood. Out—want out, to hurt you. They want blood—everyone's blood and to put it inside of me."

"Well?" Misty said, stroking River's head and looking up at her mother, still sipping wine. "What are you going to do?"

"A lifetime of work, down the drain," Adria moaned. "Fine. It will be painful and messy. I'll need your help as well. At least you did well bringing so many vessels. We're going to have to split her entities up. It'll kill these degenerates. A couple may get lucky, but we need to begin, I suppose. The sun is setting."

"Yo, fuck that," Jackie said, and tried to power his way through the bodyguard. The goon's open palm crunched against Jackie's face and he tumbled onto the floor. Jackie picked himself up and renewed his assault.

"You're scared?" Misty asked, letting go of River and leaning toward Jackie. "You should have come to us sooner."

"I helped you. I told you where she was," Jackie grunted through his pain.

"You sold your friends out, moron, and for all the wrong reasons too. You're exactly where you belong."

I've accepted the man who I've become
And that's no man at all
If they stitch my eyelids shut
It's so you can see the world.

"River, before anything, there's something Snow wanted me to tell you. For your ears only. Did you know we were in love? Everyone's in this mess because of me."

Misty remained distracted by Jackie's bargaining. The guard looked exhausted, and Adria was more preoccupied by her wine and groping for her cheese plate. Conan rolled his shoulders. He took in a cleansing breath of the burning cigarette and walked to River.

Misty whipped around.

"You're seriously eating at a time like this? This—you—you're the problem. I can't stand you. If you spent more time just being our mother instead of grooming us for *your* future, she would still be here. You selfish bitch. I hate you."

River was close enough for Conan to lean in and whisper. He smelled her and winced. Her odor overpowered everything, bringing him back to the shed with Snow. He wished he didn't leave her there.

But the past is the past. Right, Dad?

"Snow loved you. She thought you were the most amazing person in the world. She'd do anything for you. There's only one thing she wished you could have done differently. If you did, all of your lives would have been different."

"What—what's that?" River asked.

"She wanted you to say no, just once in your miserable life—"

I know this isn't what you'd want. But you're gone.

"If you just told your mother no, once in your fucking life, you could have all lived."

"Conan, don't!" Brandi shouted

River smiled as Conan plunged the blade into her heart. It stuck as if driven into a solid piece of wood. She took a step back, gasped, and fell backward. Her skull cracked on the floor and she lay with her eyes glaring up at the ceiling. Conan glanced up from her and smirked at the Devereuxs.

Misty glared at her sister's body. Her jaw fell open.

"Go, now!" Conan said.

Big Ben and Rufus took point. The single guard turned to Adria's assistant.

"I need backup!" he shouted, using himself as a gate to block the only exit.

"That's the blade. He stabbed her with the killing blade!" Misty shouted, covering Adria's face with spittle. "He killed her. You let him kill River!"

Misty was shaking Adria wildly by the shoulders. Conan kept the smile on his face, but couldn't help but feel a tug at his heart. The matriarch yanked at her long raven hair and, though she wore a blindfold, Conan knew by her twisted expression that she was fighting back tears.

She would have hated the violence, and so would you. But you're not here and neither is she. Guess there's nowhere for me to go. There never has been. I'm as selfish as ever. It's who I am.

"Kill them," Adria said.

Her brown-haired servant woman produced a long wooden flute from her sleeve and played a single drawn-out note.

A clattering like every door in Preston Academy opening at once echoed down the hall. Conan's mind raced back to the past—the army of student zombies that Adria had under her control.

Without her, I really don't care. Sorry, everyone.

Conan reached down and gripped the ritual blade's hilt. It slipped from River's lifeless body as easily as any other meat. He went to Misty's still burning cigarette and picked it up off the floor. The filter was bitter on his lips and the nicotine steadied his pulse.

The door pressed against the grunting bodyguard's back. Arms belonging to Preston students groped at him through the cracks. Big Ben pressed him against the gateway, attempting to wrestle his gun away.

"Guess I screwed up," Conan said, partially to his friends and partially to himself. "That didn't make me feel better at all."

"Back off, back off," Rufus said and pulled out his own gun. "Folks, shit's about to get real messy."

The zombies didn't listen and Brandi matched him, pulling out her gun and pointing it at Adria's assistant.

"Call them off. Now! There's no need for any more death."

A pair of student zombies had crept in through the crack in the door. Adria's bodyguard was stuck between them and Marc, Big Ben, and Rufus. The large man's square head distorted in frustration, still unable to bring his gun down.

One hundred...

Ninety-nine...

Ninety-eight...

Adria and Misty screamed back and forth. Conan tuned them out. He glanced down at his shaking hands, then to the blocked exit.

Ninety-seven...

Ninety-six...

Ninety-five...

Crack!

The guard's gun went off and Jackie stumbled backward. He hit the carpet and his red cap fell off his head. A maroon pool stained the rug beneath him and he clenched at his chest. Crimson tongues thick as branches crept over his shirt. He groaned and his hand came away dripping. When he looked beneath himself, the blood puddle had taken the shape of a round ghost.

"Oh fuck," he said.

Eighty-six...

Eighty-five...

Eighty-four...

Conan's whole body went into a spasm. He gripped the knife tight and glared at Adria. Misty still held her by the collar, shaking her wildly.

Seventy-nine...

Seventy-eight— No, there just isn't enough time.

"Why couldn't you have just been our mother?" Misty said, verging on tears. "This is your fault. They died because of you. Listen to me, listen!"

It would be too much to get between them. He needed to help the others get out. The Preston students didn't have weapons, but were countless. Marc and Ben disappeared behind a wave of them. The office was growing smaller and smaller. Twenty or more had already crammed inside. Brandi turned Rufus's Beretta on the crowd and dropped three students in the doorway with three well-aimed shots. Conan smelled blood, shit, and death that wasn't there. His skull swam with crushing memories of the past.

It's happening again. Dad, you'd be disappointed. Snow, she warned me; she fucking warned me, and I still chose this.

"This is who I am? I'm just as bad as Adria. No, I'm worse."

"Let us out, just let us out!" Rufus shouted, waving his hands in the air. "Please!"

Brandi snatched away his gun and started firing off potshots. She screamed something and pointed at Conan. A buzzing in the back of his head blocked her out. He slapped his ear, but the ringing only magnified. He replaced the knife in its makeshift cover and grabbed Jackie under the arms, dragging him behind Adria's desk.

Black uniforms engulfed the exit—the office would suffocate under the crowd. That realization constricted the smoke filling up Conan's lungs. He choked on a cough and threw Misty's cigarette away.

He glimpsed Big Ben, fighting the bodyguard for his gun with one hand and pulling Marc to his feet with the other. A deafening shot burst through the ceiling, spilling down debris. Brandi and Rufus had exchanged their guns for a pair of long black lamps, swinging them like baseball bats. Rufus had snot running down his lips and his eyes bulged out of his head. It didn't stop him from cracking open a young man's skull. Brandi's expression remained fierce, determined.

Every one of them is here because of me. If they die, it's my fault.

Misty lifted Adria by her neck, shaking her, screaming at her. The matriarch looked completely defeated, accepting her fate, whatever it meant. With River gone, she had no more reason to live.

I can relate. We are the same, the two of us.

He dropped next to Jackie, exhaling, completely drained. Even the students, who crawled atop each other like a horde of spiders, died because she ordered them to. His friends were here because he told them so. To help, to die. Knowing it would soon be over brought Conan a strange relief.

If you stay beside me, then I'll be all right
If I die, it's because I could've been anything
A smoking barrel
A noose too tight
A mask of fate
You think you're alone
But time takes its toll
Forever.

"Bro," Jackie rasped. "What the fuck happened to us? We were brothers. Why'd you have to fuck everything up?"

Conan did his best to prop him against the desk. The office had grown sticky and hot. Jackie's hair stuck to his forehead as if soaked.

"There's no excuse. When she showed up, I became this. I couldn't let go. I couldn't—"

"Fuck that," Jackie coughed, his teeth stained red. "It is what it is. You gotta get out of here, man." He coughed again, accompanied by a crackling wet exhale. Conan felt Jackie's body shake and watched as his eyes glazed over.

He was gone.

See, Dad, you abandoned me and I became a monster, just like that, just like her. There's no redemption—no saving the day. I don't even know why I'm here. A monster doesn't deserve to be. Yet, here we are, Adria. Whatever's happened has happened. It doesn't matter, right, Jackie? All that matters now is getting out, but I can't even see straight anymore.

Our future doesn't exist
Like a movie
But you died in the first scene
And I'm not worthy of being a memory
After accepting this suffering
Punished by humanity
Cradled in an angel's arms
Perverting our sanctity
I promise
Another devil will follow

Chapter 20

"Fucking give me that!" Rufus shouted.

He threw his lamp pole down with both hands. The ringing metal clattered over the groaning Preston High zombies. Brandi saw Conan give a half-hearted shrug in reply to the ritual blade being snatched away.

Rufus jumped in place, getting his blood pumping. He stage dived into the mosh pit of student bodies, slashing at anything and everyone he could.

A heavy, dull pain cascaded through Brandi. She glanced at Pokey, safely tucked into her sweater. She wished she were as strong as Rufus, but drowned the thought in her mental fog.

Maybe she died and there was nothing we could do? Maybe I failed her, Pokey, but maybe, despite all of that—we can't give up.

She turned to Adria's assistant, who'd been cowering against the farthest bookshelf.

"Please, there must be a way out," Brandi pleaded. She licked her dry lips and clasped Adria's assistant's hands in her own. "You think you mean anything to them now? Fighting is the only option. Everyone here, everyone you know, will disappear. We have to trust each other. Get our back and we get yours. Adria offered me your job once already. If we go, you go. I've seen this all in the past. It hurts, but it's the way things are."

Adria's servant's dull eyes hadn't a single bit of electricity in them. Brandi glanced down at Pokey. She wanted to reassure him he'd be safe, that she'd get him out, but watching the sea of black uniforms pushing their way through the corridor, hand over fist on top of each other, she guessed they would all suffocate beneath them.

A sound like peeling duct tape backward went off behind her. Brandi turned around and saw Misty's jaw elongating to the length of an alligator's.

Crunch-snap!

Misty bit Adria's head off and her pharynx swelled whilst she noisily gulped her mother down.

Adria's servant fell to her hands and knees, greedily sucking in large breaths of air and rubbing her throat as if she'd been drowning.

Brandi turned around, gazing into the servant's eyes—full of tears, staring at the scene behind Brandi. Rufus walked backward in retreat. All the Preston students had stopped their advances. They surveyed the office with the scared eyes of children.

CRUNCH!

"You have to know a secret passageway, or another way out of here," Brandi said, trying to ignore Misty's chewing.

CRUNCH!

No one moved, staring at the horrific scene of cannibalism and matricide, faces constricting in horror, frozen.

"Rufus," Brandi said, quiet as she could. "We need to kill her."

"Yeah," he said, lowering his gaze. "You're right. No matter what it costs."

Marc and Big Ben swam out from the crowd of bodies, their clothes torn and their bodies bruised, but Brandi allowed herself a sigh of relief after seeing them alive.

CRUNCH!

Misty had finished her grisly meal. She wiped her lips and glanced around herself, wearing a grin that stretched her facial proportions to their limits. Her neck ground into place as if controlled by clicking gears and other mechanisms. Her eyes locked onto Adria's assistant.

The brown-haired woman pressed up against the bookshelf, knocking down a row of leather tomes. She erupted into a scream—cut short by Misty lunging through the air and smashing her mother's lackey chin-first into the floor.

Don't be scared, Pokey, we got this. I promised I'd get you out.

The Preston students clawed at each other, clogging the exit in a black-uniformed mass. Blood leaked from their assimilation and painted the border of the doorway threshold. The office door swung back and forth like a laughing maw, crushing student limbs and breaking fingers in its doorjamb.

Brandi put a hand over her mouth, smelling everything she had in her last life, but congested and boiling in the compact space. The students in the back line didn't even try their luck. Instead they glared on as Misty gurgled down handfuls of flesh. They puked their guts out, curling into fetal positions, or crying in each other's arms. One boy repeatedly slammed his face into Adria's ebony desk, keeping a dull tempo throughout the carnage.

Rufus gave Brandi a quick nod and crept around the perimeter.

"Don't even think about it!" Misty screamed. She shot up to her feet, and her elongated face snapped back into its human shape.

She lifted her servant's masticated head from the carpet and Brandi clenched her eyes tightly shut, secretly hoping that her entire life had just been one horrible, drawn-out dream.

"Unless you're really in a hurry to be my dessert, guitar boy? How many times have we had this fight? How many times have you ended up inside of me? Some things never change."

Rufus gulped loudly and glared down at the floor. He clenched his head in his hands and began shaking. Brandi reached for him, but no words would come out of her aching throat.

Misty rolled her eyes, and her stare landed on the mass of students blocking the exit. She lifted her painted fingernails up and all the students stopped dead. The boy slamming his head onto the desk froze halfway and remained stagnant. A girl curled on the floor wet herself.

Brandi's heart slammed in her chest.

"The rest of you, where I can see you," Misty said calmly and sighed. Her sapphire eyes turned gray and dull.

"Now!" she barked, turning to Conan sitting next to Jackie's dead body.

Brandi hugged Pokey tight to her chest as Conan took his place by her side. Marc and Ben went to stand beside Rufus.

Dizziness tried to take Brandi. She nearly collapsed.

Maybe she's only grieving, and maybe there's no way to redeem her? This can't be the end.

Misty's eyes had lost all their light now, taking on the bleached appearance of cataracts. She rotated her servant's severed head and wildly bit into her face, sucking out both eyes like a depraved beast. She discarded the mangled skull over her shoulder like trash, and her eyes regained their color.

"Misty, you're going through a lot right now. I need you to listen to me."

"Oh?" Misty said, grinning and showing gore-encrusted teeth. She wiped her hands on her button-up and laughed as she looked over herself. "Please, Brandi, tell me more about what *I'm* going through."

Brandi stroked Pokey's head. Fatigue had made the tips of her fingers numb. She looked from Misty to the others. Marc had backed himself up to the wall and his lip quivered.

"I'm sorry, there's no way I could know that."

"No, there isn't," she laughed.

Misty's eyes glazed over and fell upon Rufus, then Big Ben. Both readied themselves for a fight, as if it were all they'd known.

We're ghosts for sure, but they're doing everything they can. Even now. It doesn't matter how much we hate our lives, or how badly I just want this over. We're ghosts, but I'm not gonna let her kill me. Not like this. Not searching for a scapegoat. I'll fight for them like they fought for me.

"Misty, it doesn't have to be like this, it—"

"So tell me how it's going to be then, Brandi?" She laughed, genuinely amused.

"Fucking—god dammit, Misty, fine. Do whatever you want with me, all right? *Anything* you want, but let them go."

Misty licked her fingers and grimaced at River beside her, then to Rufus, Big Ben, Conan, and Marc. Brandi swallowed loudly, sweating but chilled at the same time.

"Just them?" Misty asked.

Brandi's breath caught in her lungs—a violent shiver passed through her body.

"There's no shame, guys," she said, but didn't look away from Misty. "Get out of here if you can."

"You really are talented," Misty said, and nodded. "Fine. if that's what you want."

Misty lifted one hand and the Preston students' trance was lifted. Their screams renewed, louder than ever. The group stuck in the door became completely backed up. Brandi recognized a pink-haired boy from the past. He picked up the broken lamp and started driving it into the blockage. First it was silent, but then his pole stuck into them with wet stabbing noises. Brandi's stomach did a flip and stayed upside down, making her slouch. Misty winked at her, and the earth shook.

The pink-haired boy dropped his lamp pole and clenched his throat. He coughed violently, sputtering onto the floor. He met Brandi's stare and shot through the air, slamming into the balled-up Preston students.

The air was sucked from the room. Brandi fell onto her knees and sour stomach acid shot from her esophagus and out of her lips. Her heartbeat slowed to a near stop as Conan collapsed next to her. His face turned blue.

The remaining Preston students levitated into the air and smashed into the ball accumulating in the doorway. Bones snapped, broke, split. Misty twisted her fingers as if holding a globe in her hands. She clapped them together and the biggest water balloon in the world popped, splattering every inch of the walls with red blood. Hot fluid painted Brandi's face and splattered her entire body. A flood like an above-ground swimming pool tearing and pouring thick red gushed down the hallway, smashing into the wall and dispersing down the north and south corridors.

Maybe if I was a ghost, I'd never have to be here.

A human shape stood at the end of the long hall. Brandi recognized the pink-haired boy, despite him being entirely blood-soaked. He patted his body down, assessing the damage, and chuckled in disbelief. He turned on his heels and ran, his maniacal laughter echoing the whole way.

"Holy fucking shit!" Misty shouted. "This was Mom's power? Really? And she fucking wasted it all on politics? She really was gross. This feels *good*."

Stale metallic air inflated Brandi's lungs. Despite the acrid taste, it was like refreshing heaven. She heaved in gasp after gasp and spat blood out in puddles. Even after the flood dispersed, her hands remained submerged in half an inch of sticky red.

"All righty, go," Misty said, raising her hands. "G-T-F-O, you merry band of fucking losers. Get up, Brandi. I've got something to show you."

Brandi picked herself up off the floor. She put a hand atop Pokey and coughed. The white elephant's face had been painted with blood, but he was still intact.

I couldn't help Kylie or Snow, but I'll get you out. I can. Remember, I promised.

The others stood to their feet, gathering around her.

"Go," Brandi said and coughed, placing her hands on her knees. "Please, don't come back. Go. Learn from my mistakes. Just because you *can* come back doesn't mean you should. Just accept it. Leave me."

Marc was already backing toward the door; his eyes moved from Misty and flickered to Brandi. Seeing him leave brought an unexpected relief to her aching muscles. Conan, Ben, and Rufus didn't budge.

"Get out of here, you idiots," Brandi said, standing straight. "And don't do anything stupid. I'm so tired, so tired of doing stupid shit. Just go, get out. It's over. Please, let me do this."

Marc was at the threshold now, shaking, his eyes bouncing to the others. None of them moved.

"Stop being stupid," Misty groaned. "None of you are heroes. Brandi's the closest thing you've got. How about you let *her* walk with fire, and you get out like *she* wants? If not, I'm just gonna kill you."

"Wait," Brandi said and unzipped her jacket.

Her red hands stained the sides of Pokey's fur, but he looked grateful nonetheless. She couldn't help but smile back at her oldest friend's cute, aloof, stuffed-animal demeanor.

"Take him with you. I promised him he wouldn't be left behind," she said, giving him to Conan. "Get him washed and take really good care of him. Please, don't forget. Really, that's all I need."

Conan nodded as she spoke, but didn't appear to be listening. He stared boredly down at the white and red elephant, and as Pokey left her hands, a weight lifted from her shoulders.

No, it has always been there. Maybe that's why I loved him, maybe that's what he saw in Snow. A fucking ghost.

Conan took her elephant, turned, walked past Marc and through the exit. His shoes lightly splashed in the blood. Marc took it as an invitation to run full-sprint, his footfalls sounding like rain in the wet. He passed Conan and turned down the hall.

"Please?" Brandi asked, verging on tears. She looked at Rufus and Big Ben, still unmoving.

Rufus placed a hand on Ben's shoulder and led him to the doorway.

"Hey, Brandi," Misty said, wiping a crescent beneath her eye. "You're the expert. How's my makeup look?" She laughed and waved Brandi over to River's corpse. Her eyes were still open, but painted red from the explosion.

"Come over here," Misty chuckled, giddily. "I'm going to bring her back."

Brandi shook her head. Her sweats and chills from earlier returned, making it impossible to appear casual.

"No, Misty, I don't think that's a good idea."

"*Pfff,* of fucking course you don't. You're a square." She raised her eyebrows. "Remember the way she looked at you? God damn, to have somebody admire me like that. Love at first sight. You ruined her—you know that, right? You alone got to her. It's okay though, you're mine to do whatever I want with. You said so yourself. I'm going to give you to her as a trophy. Kiss her."

"Misty, you have to accept that she's gone. Some people break, some die, and some leave forever. It's devastating, but you have to move on. You can."

"I didn't fucking stutter. Get on your hands and knees, now."

A heavy lead brick fell into Brandi's stomach, but she did as she was told. She pressed her lips to River's and Misty pressed her hand onto her back. Heat exchanged from her palm and left through Brandi's lips.

A palate fouler than hell crept into the back of Brandi's throat. Misty's palm moved up to Brandi's neck and then to the top of her head, pressing her into River hard.

Misty's hand gripped her hair and yanked back, tingling nerves ripped through Brandi's scalp and shot through her entire body.

A familiar scream sounded through the air. One of the guys had come back for her.

The surviving Devereux sister let her go and Brandi had to catch herself from falling atop River's corpse.

Brandi turned back in time to see Rufus driving the knife point through Misty's palm. Misty hissed through her teeth and, with her free hand, smacked Rufus and gripped her shoulder in one fluid motion. She ripped her own arm off, tearing like peeling the skin off a large fibrous orange, and flung it away.

Brandi didn't hear where Misty's arm landed, but when she checked behind her, there was only a landscape of red camouflage.

Rufus screamed as Misty latched her powerful jaws onto his face. He managed to get both his feet under her and spring her off of him, but not without massive damage. He'd lost his bottom lip and half of his cheek. Sour bile once more churned Brandi's stomach. She turned away, renewing her scavenger hunt.

"Some people just refuse to change," Misty laughed, and spat onto Rufus.

Brandi searched at a frantic pace. She glanced backward—Misty had tripled in size. A powerful tail stuck out from her backside and smashed into Rufus's back. He fell limp and Misty slithered next to him, biting him in half with two snaps of her powerful jaws. His legs spasmed and twitched wildly, bouncing off the floor and speckling the walls with dark droplets.

Maybe there is no altering fate.

Brandi forced herself to look away. Despite the tears burning her eyes, she had to find it—and there it was, in Jackie's lap. Her breath caught in her lungs. She pulled the blade out and armed herself.

The school walls creaked as if being ripped to pieces. The foundation beneath shook like a volcano was about to erupt beneath them. Brandi used the office desk to keep balance and closed her eyes.

River seized on the floor, cobalt light pouring from her eyes and mouth like searchlights. Her limbs began to stretch and tear, breaking and reshaping into long pale worms, reforming her fingers into bulbous gray tubers.

Misty reverted back to her human shape, her clothes in tatters hanging from her body.

"YES! COME ON, BABY SISTER! GET UP! GET UP!"

She placed her hands atop River's skull, pulling her scalp backward. Her raven-black hair multiplied, growing down the length of her back. Brandi's knees buckled. Every part of her was shaking, but her instincts kicked into gear.

Fight or flight. What's she done to her? Fight or flight? Flight! Flight!

Brandi turned and ran for the exit, ignoring Misty's chorus of raucous laughter and the thousands of tortured screams exploding from River. The magnitude of the earthquake doubled. She lost her footing and fell hard onto her shoulder. She stumbled to her feet and winced at the open elevator shaft. A burst of hot sulfur shot up from the cavity, but she was beyond gagging or considering what it could mean.

She was only focused on running.

Her heartbeat thumped like a piston. She made her way to the stairs and down one floor, wincing at the shriek of spirits, like creaking metal. The closer she got to the ground level, the more prominent they became. She saw spectral skulls, animal and human, made up of blue and orange gas, shooting through the floor and ceiling like flames. Their faces all gazed at her, undressing her down to the skin with pained, empty sockets. Frozen fingers crept down her spine, and a stench of death clung to her blood-soaked clothes.

Brandi reached the first floor and burst through the doorway, completely lost, but nearly out. She had to be. She paused at a classroom window to catch her breath and couldn't help but chuckle at her unrecognizable reflection.

After spending so much time on her appearance throughout high school, perfecting her look and practicing her steady hand, this would be how it ended—a mud cake of foundation mixed with blood clogging her pores.

She rounded the corner and saw a blockage in the hallway.

The pink-haired boy was hunched over the corpse of another student. Brandi shook her head, unable to feel any sympathy, but she couldn't leave him behind either.

"Hey," she said, reaching out.

The boy slowly turned around, and his face followed. It had nearly sloshed off his bones. He held the throat of the dead girl lying before him in his small hands. He growled and gnashed his teeth like a dog and picked himself up off the floor.

"You're fucking kidding me." Brandi swallowed, and the accumulated blood scraped down her throat and fell into her stomach.

She made a B-line for the exit, but the boy's head shot from his torso like a mortar. His teeth latched into her knife-holding arm and his spine wrapped around her limb, digging burrs into the tissue. She screamed and fell sideways, trying to pry the monster's head away.

More were coming, groaning and snapping their jaws. Too many to count, their faces elongating into long alligator snouts.

"Fuck no. Not like this, not like this."

She took the knife from herself and carefully pressed it into the monster's forehead. As it broke an inch of flesh, the tombstone jaws released her. She gasped with relief, but winced at the stench that poured from the wound.

She turned on her heels, leapt through the nearest window, and burst into a garden bush. Spider webs caught on her skin and hair. She didn't look back. Branches slashed open her arms, but she barreled through.

Something wasn't right. The town's air was off, stinking like raw sewage and oil smoke. She made it into the streets. An ominous purple and red fog had overtaken the sky. The stars were still visible behind it, but too bright, too close to the planet.

Tires screeched and Brandi's gaze bolted to two cars spinning around in the middle of the street. There were no headlights, and one crashed into the school next to her. A beanpole of a man shot out from it and scurried to the other car.

"I'm so sorry!" he called out. "My car just died out of nowhere. Are you okay? Hey, are you okay?"

One of Misty's malformed gator zombies leapt out of the driver's seat and bit into the man's face. He screamed and collapsed onto the ground before going still. The monster howled up at the sky and Brandi could hear more, thousands, paired with screams coming from every direction.

Her heartbeat had slowed to a grinding halt. She thought she may pass out.

So, you really still cannot accept that you're all alone? asked the sky.

"What– You? Seriously?" Brandi gasped, staring upward.

Well, then you better hide.

She slowly backed into the bushes. A mass of pale white flesh fell from the heavens and crashed into the asphalt.

River's flesh had turned gray and bruised purple with rotten blood. Her legs were bent backward like a grasshopper's and her swollen arms had burst like blooming plants, tendrils waved like petals, and long bloody black claws protruded from the would-be buds, scratching against the concrete. The cobalt of her eyes still glowed like two lanterns, illuminating the space in front of her like signal beacons. She raised her neck back and her jaw unlatched, stretching her lips backward and exploding into a screech.

"BRANDI-LYNN!" she shrieked, and leapt through the air.

Brandi glanced back up at the sky. It didn't matter if she was alone or not. There wasn't time to be afraid.

All that mattered now was fighting for her life.

Chapter 21

Stark loneliness
Angel lies, a polarizing tragedy
A part of me
Blood stains cornering your mouth
Haunted ground
Eyes like flowers
Dream, torture, memory, denial, ghost, peace
I won't call it art, I won't scare myself
Poetry, shackles, your memory, destruction
I'll carry—

"She died alone, cold and alone," Conan said. His vision blurred, as if staring up and out of a lake. His legs were stiff and body heavy, not unlike after sleeping uncomfortably. "But a future without you...a future without you—"

His cheek lit up with pain and a flat slap rang through his ears. Fire was the first thing he noticed, or rather the aroma of smoke, and after a moment he recognized the bleachers and hardwood floors of Peralta High School's gymnasium.

Brandi snapped her fingers in front of his face. She had pulled her hair back and her neck and clothes were stained brownish-red. A gun and girdle were strapped to her side, and she held a steaming Styrofoam coffee cup in her hand.

"Finally awake?" she asked.

Conan glanced around.

Brandi's elephant rested in his lap. Big Ben, Marc, Kimberly, and some other kids from school were there; adults as well. A hoarse-voiced woman with a puffy jacket flailed her arms, arguing with an older bearded man in army fatigues. A table loaded with various-sized guns and boxes of bullets had been sprawled out in front of them. Conan grimaced, scratching his itching palm—there were not many.

But my friends are okay, Dad. It's unbelievable. I dragged them all down with me, but here they are. I've got an opportunity, a real one, to apologize. Do I deserve it? After what I've done?

"Yeah, I— Where's Rufus?"

"Dead, like everyone else. Hey, you're back, seriously? Done with the mumbling? It feels like it's been forever. You're lucky Big Ben dragged you here—no one else wanted to bring your ass along."

"Oh."

I don't deserve any of them, do I, Dad? I owe them more than I'd ever be able to pay back.

Conan glanced in his lap and chuckled at the expressionless elephant. He ran his hands through its fur, snagging on the spots of dried blood. A blush crossed his face, and a prickling crept over his neck.

"What's so funny?"

"I forgot to wash him. I'm sorry."

"Yeah, well, you didn't let go of him either. So, whatever."

The gym doors burst open and a man and woman, both dressed in camouflage, entered the gym. Two women, a young man, and a child followed close behind. The soldier woman took a stretched triangle position, leaning her gun and torso out the door and firing a pair of controlled bursts into the night. Conan didn't even flinch at the volatile decibels, but watched the children clench hands over their ears.

"Target neutralized!" she shouted and slammed the door behind her.

"That's enough, Giacomo!" a man with broken glasses said. He ran up to the old bearded man. "There's not enough food for everyone. We need to wait this out."

"*Cállate y siéntate!*" the old man barked and pointed toward the barrel fire by the basketball hoop.

Brandi rolled her eyes. She took a seat and buried her face in her arms.

"Please tell me you have a cigarette," she said.

Guilt broke me
Fantasy consumed me
I'll never be okay
I'll never be the same
I became a killer
And can't even blame you.

"Brandi," he said. "Really, I'm sorry. For not washing your elephant, for everything. I've been a horrible piece of shit to you and everyone else. Will you ever forgive me?"

I'll make it up to them. I promise.

Brandi sipped her coffee, and Conan noticed the killing knife in a duct tape sheath slung onto her hip. He felt the throb of his heart crawl up into his throat.

"Conan, you've been shell-shocked for a while, but it's like—Misty set off some real apocalyptic shit. I'm kind of stuck on that. Sorry, I'm not really in a forgiving mood."

Dad, I get it. I can see it clearly now. I'll make this right.

"Please, forgive me. I got you and everyone else in this mess. It would seriously mean a lot to me."

Brandi glanced down at him and then to Pokey. She handed her steaming cup of coffee to him and snatched the elephant away. She pressed him to her lips, clenching the stuffed animal tight. Conan took a sip of the coffee, wincing at the overly sweet chocolate creamer.

"Conan, it's my fault just as much as it is yours," she said. "River's out there. Misty brought her back. If she busts in here, it's because she wants *me,* Conan. Eventually, no matter what, she's gonna find me, and god knows what she'll do when she does."

Conan glanced back down at the knife. His eyes stayed glued to it, losing himself in the indiscernible markings. He drifted away.

She haunts me
Soft jaded skeleton
Stealing the autumn
I scare myself
Seeing your body.
I call it art
I'm so scared.

"Conan?" Brandi asked.

Reality flushed back, and he took another swig of coffee, smelling the nutty roast rather than tasting it.

"If I kill Misty Devereux, will it end?" he asked.

Brandi's jaw stayed open until she leaned back against the bleachers and whistled out a sigh.

"Fuck if I know." She paused and then sat back up. "Adria's assistant played the flute to turn those kids mindless, but when Misty killed her mother, the original spell broke. So, maybe?"

"Give me the knife."

"What's happened to us?" she laughed. "We used to talk about going to the beach. Now it's killing people."

"I've already killed. I— Everything's different, everything. My mom's out there, Brandi, but I don't know. This is all that matters."

"Now that Snow's gone, right?"

Brandi rested her head on his shoulder. The argument below was getting heated. The bent-glasses man's voice grated on Conan's ears. Big Ben stood from his seat beside Marc and went to help the old man, but even he moved sluggishly. The sugar and caffeine accumulating in Conan's stomach made it grow tight.

"I think she knew," Conan said. "I think this has happened before."

"Yeah. I think so too."

"She lived this life, experiencing the worst fate of any of us. This one especially. I can't imagine what else she's been through, but this time, she accepted it. She chose to let it happen like this. She accepted it was unfair, got sick of her fate and her reality. We can't give up, Brandi."

"I never gave up," she said. "That's on you."

She'd been there almost the entire time, despite him deserving nothing of her. He needed to help her; he needed to help her so badly that it hurt.

I can't stop the agony
Same as I couldn't stop you
Buried in your feathers
How am I?
Who am I?
What would I be?
Not a heartbeat
Not a brushstroke
A manifesto.

"Conan?" Brandi asked.

He laughed.

"It hurts, daydreaming about what could've been. You know? Like, what if I remembered this moment—when she first approached me?"

Brandi's knee bounced, her toe tapping a rhythm onto the bleacher wood.

"Yeah, well, shoulda, woulda, coulda, Conana-banana. Rufus, Kylie, my parents, you, everyone. Horrible shit happens constantly. Girls go missing, innocent people get murdered, animals are abused and butchered for no apparent reason. It hurts. The more you contemplate, the more you suffer. Let it get to you, and it'll consume everything. It'll ruin your whole fucking life. We just have to accept that there's horror in this world *everywhere*. We have to be the outcast. We have to uncover goodness, no matter how deeply it's buried. It's there too, and no matter what, we gotta."

"That's it, then?"

"That's it."

"You're right."

Brandi nodded her head and zipped her elephant up in her jacket. The metal teeth made a strained clicking as the stuffed animal bulged her stomach. She pulled the plush up from the snout and his beady eyes poked out. Conan smiled and petted the elephant's head.

"You never forgave me."

Brandi leaned in, as if she wanted to kiss him, and his heartbeat skipped. She paused and grinned. "I won't either, not unless you pull this off. Do that and I'll let you make it up to me. A nice *fucking* restaurant too. Somewhere I can get dressed up for. Not burgers and fries, you broke fucker."

She unbuckled the knife, and the tightly stretched leather creaked loose.

"You'll want a gun too."

"Yeah," he nodded. "You'll stay here right, where it's safe?"

"Nope. Not a chance. If you're gonna get close to Preston High, you're gonna need someone to distract River. You'll never make it otherwise. Don't worry, I know a girl."

"Shit."

"Totally." She rolled her eyes. "Stupid, right? And this whole thing started with us breaking up."

Without Snow, what would my life be? Thinking about it was like taking a shovel and scooping out his insides. It hurt too much to consider—remembering Brandi, Rufus, Jackie, his mother, and his father.

"I get it. And it's ending with us splitting up."

"I can count on you, right?"

"For once, yeah. I promise."

Brandi led him down the steps and he felt himself involuntarily relax. His breathing slowed as he remembered how many times they'd walked down these same bleachers together. He stared at the surrounding families and absorbed their anxiety in waves.

"Wait here," Brandi said, letting his hand go. "I'll talk to Giacomo."

He watched her go and surveyed the room. He sniffed burning wood smoke and tasted the unmistakable artificial flavoring of chicken cup-of-noodles on his tongue. The man with the broken glasses sat with his arms crossed next to a young mother, filling up two ramen cups with water from a kettle hanging over the barrel fire.

Conan's skin crawled.

Dad, they're here because of me. My choices, and I'll never have what they have because of it.

The mother put a cup down next to an overly excited young girl. She sat next to the man, whispering into his ear and kissing him on the cheek. The man appeared seconds from breaking down. He took in a large gasp of air and sat up straight.

Mom's gone now too, Dad. Sorry.

"God, I hope she got out," he said out loud.

Could you see all along?

Poisoning me?

Would you apologize?

Would you disappear?

Again?

Are you satisfied?

You gave up

You disappeared

Would you—

He slapped himself. He needed to keep his cool. If he was going to fade away, he'd have to wait until the end.

Brandi clapped her hands in front of the old man, appearing to have a tough time with convincing him. Big Ben went to her side and offered his help. Giacomo gravely shook his head and pointed to Ben—then to the children at the table. Ben placed his hands on the table and glanced backward. He pointed at Conan, then to Brandi, and lastly to himself. Giacomo briskly shoved his assault rifle into Brandi's open arms. He wagged a finger at her before letting his weapon go and grabbing a backpack. Bullets jingled as he swept boxes into the sack and looped it around her free arm.

Big Ben glanced back at Conan. He nodded solemnly and then threw up the peace sign. The old man handed Ben a pair of magazines, and Ben walked off toward the exit, stepping outside with the soldier woman from earlier.

Brandi's newly gained supplies made a metallic clatter when she dropped the sack in front of Conan. She looked away as she unbuckled her pistol strap. She appeared taller, stronger than he ever remembered, and his chest swelled with inspiring breaths from just being near her.

"So, good news and bad news," she said, and offered her holster. "Big Ben traded his services for this rifle, but only on the terms that I get it. Giacomo loaded you up with nine-millimeter bullets, though."

"Ben just offered himself up like that, for real? What's that dude's deal?"

"He'd have helped Giacomo anyway." She raised her free hand and let it fall. "Honestly, Ben's one-of-a-kind. Seriously, he's genuinely one of the few legit good people in this fucking world."

"You too though," Conan said, adjusting the girdle so it would fit around his ribs.

"Yeah. Whoopity-doo. Whatever. Odds are, we're all dead either way."

"No," Conan said, sternly shaking his head. "I'm tired of making promises I can't keep. Not this time. If I die, it's gonna be after I drive this knife into her heart."

"You haven't even seen her. You really don't know what you're up against."

"How many mistakes have I made these four days? *All* of these four days? Thousands? Millions? I'm gonna make myself useful this time. For you."

She blew a raspberry and clicked the tip of her shoe onto the wood flooring.

"What we're dealing with are monsters, Conan. Animals made from brute force, abuse, and grief. Misty wants to rip and tear and destroy in a really desperate fucking act out."

"Yeah. Sounds like the playing field is even. Except we have each other."

"If that were true," Brandi chuckled, "we'd have never gotten into this mess."

"I fucked that up badly." Conan smiled. "You're flying solo now anyway, where you should have been all along. You're too good for a scumball like me."

"Well." She choked back a sob. "I'm over it," she said, despite the tear running down her cheek.

Conan gripped her in the tightest embrace he could.

"So this is the end."

"Yeah," she agreed, gulping loudly.

"I'll go first," he said, and loaded his pockets full of two clips and slung the jingling green bag over his shoulder, feeling the weight of it on his back.

He nodded toward the old man on his way out to the western exit and watched Brandi move toward the eastern one. Before leaving, he glanced at the family in the corner one last time. He clenched his teeth and kicked the heavy metal door as hard as he could. The metal clang resounded throughout the gym, but he didn't look back again.

See you soon, Pops.

The school itself was eerily quiet. On the far eastern end he could hear gunfire, but besides that it was only the ominous sky, looking terribly polluted, warning him to keep away.

A song about whatever happens, happens

I won't fear the future.

Even if it's without you.

I can't bring you back.

I'll look forward to making it up to another.

He rushed out the front gate and into the parking lot. Bodies lay strewn out, covering the painted lines, their domes split open and leaking fluid. A dog-shaped humanoid with a gaping jaw ran across the sidewalk. A *BOOM-CRACK!* detonated through the air, followed by a ringing hum. The creature's head turned into mist and dropped its neckless body, dragging across the street.

"One point for the doomsday preppers, I guess," Conan said and hugged the wall, leaving the school with his gun at-the-ready. "If only they knew I'm to blame."

Reaching Preston on foot wouldn't normally take long, but he avoided the main roads and stuck to the back streets. There was an irregular beat to his heart, but he buried any fears as deep as he could. The air was thick and hot. He could smell fires nearby, and when he reached the crossroads of Tournament Ct. and Sunburst Lane, he had to kick himself. His heart wanted to go home and see his mother, but nearby shouting brought him back to reality.

He pressed himself up against the nearest wall and watched a group of four—two men and two women—running from a monster. The monster's head fired from its neck and wrapped its spine around the slowest man's neck, dropping him to the street and chewing on his face. Another humanoid zombie stopped to gorge itself.

There was no point in helping. He didn't want to draw any attention to himself and needed to save his resources. Besides, he'd gotten used to the sounds of lips smacking flesh; however, the monsters blocked his progress. He took in a deep, controlled breath and completely ignored the breaking bones.

One hundred...

Ninety-nine...

Ninety-eight...

Patience was his power.

Ninety-six...

Ninety-five...

Ninety-four...

THUMP-THUMP!

Something massive had interrupted his counting, landing near the feasting monsters. He bent his knees and fear entered his heart.

If it weren't for the sapphire eyes, he'd not have recognized River. She'd been transformed into a nightmare. Her hair had grown down her back and her legs had become springboards. Most disgusting of all were her arms, peeled like bananas and with gore-drenched, razor-clawed vectors scraping against the sidewalk. River sniffed the air. Conan clenched his gun, aiming his shaking hands and forcing his eyes open.

A pair of distant gunshots echoed nearby. River's mouth stretched open like tearing pizza dough. She howled into the sky and shot into the air. The group of monsters that had been feeding answered her howl back and followed in her trail.

Conan waited, then forced his legs to move. He aimed his gun down the street with shaking hands, then fled. He'd wasted too much time already, but at least he knew River hadn't found Brandi yet. This needed to end before she did.

He glanced up at Preston High atop its hill and a woman's shriek pierced through the air. He thought of his mother once more.

Ninety-three...

Ninety-two...

Ninety-one...

He cleared his mind and burst into a full sprint, ignoring nearby howls, only focusing on what was in front of him.

I'm sorry I ended up being this, Dad. I get it. That's why you never wanted to help me.

"But if you're up there listening," he said between gasps, catching his breath, "just fucking abandon me. Help Brandi. If anyone deserves it, it's her."

Inside my mind
Is a black place
Not a dark place
It's like a script covered in marker
A second skin
Covering an eye lens

Chapter 22

"Sorry, Ben," Brandi said out loud and hurried to the street corner. Her legs had grown restless. All she'd wanted after splitting with Conan was to run. Ben clung to her like glue the minute she stepped outside the heavy gymnasium doors. It had taken her a lot more small talk than she had originally planned before Ben had gotten distracted enough for her to slip away.

"Brandi?!" Big Ben's panicked shouting came from inside the school perimeter.

"It's just me and you now, Pokey."

She checked her earplugs before twisting around. She dropped to her knee and fired a muffled burst at a charging quadruped, liquefying its face.

"And I gotta say, it's kinda great."

She bit her lip and started toward the street corner. Liberation fueled her spirit. Her heartbeat spun into a frenzy. The town had become something unrecognizable. All the streetlights had died. The purple moonlight had a gaseous presence, combining with a thin, damp orange dust caking on the asphalt and sidewalks.

Sweat dripped off her brow as she glanced down at Pokey, counting herself lucky that her jacket hugged him so snugly. The thought crossed her mind, and she immediately got on herself for getting distracted.

Another pair of Misty's zombies burst out of an alley. They turned toward Brandi and one screamed a howl into the sky. The second charged, luminescent foam spraying from its mouth.

Brandi took aim on reflex. Her first burst dropped the charging beast dead. The second shot was a hit, but her rifle clicked empty, and the surviving beast gave its wound a quick lick before it charged. Breath snagged in her throat. She fought back a cough and hurriedly clicked and locked the clip into place, grateful that Giacomo had made her practice a hundred times. Without a flinch, she switched the lever and dropped the beast with a semi-auto shot.

"Not like saving bullets is gonna matter," she said with a heavy sigh. She paused, distracted again, thinking about River, what everything meant to her. "Bullets aren't gonna do shit anyway."

Her nose twitched as a thick, putrid stink filled her nostrils. It was familiar, sickening, offal. The corpse grime in the shed?

No.

River's rotting visage, latching onto her lips and dumping foul vomit down her throat.

THUMP-THUMP!

Thumping like a giant rabbit.

THUMP-THUMP!

Dover Street in front of her was open—plenty of alleyways to turn down. Her heartbeat sped into rapid-fire. She raised her shoulders and turned around.

"Maybe I'm a ghost, Pokey, and we'll haunt this town forever."

THUMP-THUMP!

River had found her. Her malformed arms split open and held her hulking torso upright, tall as a ladder and with fresh blood dripping from her gore-drenched maw. Her search-beam eyes landed on Brandi and her maroon lips slowly peeled back, unleashing a scream powerful enough to rip through Brandi's earplugs and drill into her brain. The rancid stench that she'd pinned down earlier clung to her skin and crawled down her throat with cruel nostalgia.

Pokey, I really fucking hope this is the right call, buddy.

"Hey, Riv, I—I'm sorry. I was gonna do my makeup, really doll myself up for this, *buuuut* was shit outta luck, so I went all natural."

River paced toward her. Light from her eyes scanned the perimeter, waiting.

She's seeing if it's a trap. Which means...

Brandi risked a shaky breath.

"You're still in there, huh? You're listening? Good, I really, really need to talk to you. I want to help. I promise."

River's glowing orbs turned wall-eyed. They extended and retracted like telescopes. She took another step forward and belched. Brandi wet her lips and nodded. She slung her heavy weapon over her shoulder and held her hands up in surrender.

"A second chance—another one. Things would be different for us, I mean that. I'm sorry—but I mean—I'm still willing to try. If you are? We'd have to convince Misty, but me and you could at least be happy."

River snapped her jaws hard enough to crack a tooth and snorted. Even from this distance, heat seeped from her heavy breaths.

Is it actually working? Brandi flinched.

"I'm willing to try. I am really—to be with you. For real. Right now, in this life."

River's growl rumbled through her entire body.

Brandi slowly gazed up. Behind River, in the alleyway, a dead man sat next to a yellow dirt bike.

It's old enough to have a manual choke. Oh shit, please, keys be there, please, please.

"Seriously, River, I mean it. I'll do anything to bring you back. Do you know of a way?"

River barked and snapped her jaws, pelting the street with thick saliva. Brandi met her eyes and planted the balls of her feet.

"It doesn't matter to me, really. Even when I was little, I've always loved monsters."

River reared back and screamed into the air. Brandi saw her opening and ran. River launched herself. Brandi ducked, sliding into the alley, scraping her palms raw. A gust of wind chased River's momentum, yanking Brandi's hair sideways. River dug her razor claws into the street and kicked up sparks in deceleration.

Maybe I'm a ghost. There was never anything to say. Some things end in violence. There's nothing we can do. No matter what. Some people just can't learn. It's hard to fix yourself and grow, but that doesn't matter. You have to. No matter what.

Brandi hopped onto the Yamaha and snickered. The keys were in the ignition.

"Well, looks like somebody's watching over us after all."

The light from River's eyes appeared, and Brandi fired up the bike with two pumps of the gas. She whipped the rear tire around in a one-eighty and the exhaust snap-crackled, bouncing off the walls like malevolent laughter. She inhaled sweet carbon monoxide, tasting it like ice cold water, and yanked hard on the throttle.

As soon as the tires hit the street, she flew through the gears as quick as they'd carry her. With an open mile in front of her, she put broken-down cars, cadavers, and street signs between them in seconds.

"BRANDI-LYNN!" River screamed, sounding far away but much closer than she'd prefer.

Brandi glanced down every alleyway, trying to make her mind up when to turn. A haze covered her judgment. Too much adrenaline pumped through her veins—taking her focus completely away. She reached a signal with barely enough time to notice a beast waiting in ambush.

River's thumping drew nearer, reverberating like small quakes.

Brandi slammed her boot down, yanked on the brake, and pivoted her bike into a sliding stop, burning her shoe's bottom and shooting heat into her soles. She steadied herself, then blasted through the nearest alleyway—past the next street—down another alley, and back on the main streets.

Maybe I'm a ghost. It is my fault, after all, but no point in guilt trippin' now. If I do, it'll consume me.

She paused, stopping to check the street signs and catch her breath. She read Torrance Place, heard a growl, and lifted her rifle with barely any time to block a creature's leaping claws. Its razor teeth bit into her rifle and she fell backward and off the motorcycle. Flames shot into her skidding back as she bit off the tip of her tongue.

The monster's head tilted and its neck stretched like a snake, coiling back and striking at her. She swayed side to side, rolling the monster onto its back and mounting him with her rifle's barrel aimed down into its gullet. It bit down on the barrel just as she pulled the trigger, blasting amethyst brains down a storm drain.

She coughed and cringed, fighting through the pain and lifting her bike up. This time, she had to kick the throttle over three times before it fired. She couldn't hear River, but the hairs on the back of her neck stood on edge. The exhaust sputtered and popped, climbing back to speed as she made it to Filmore Avenue.

Almost there, she thought and allowed herself a glance backward.

"Hey!" a girl shouted.

Brandi looked forward and saw three prepsters in the street, and with barely time to avoid them. Instinct kicked in and she pushed the bars down, dumping the bike so the pedal took the brunt force. Her shoulder hit hard enough to shake her teeth, and she bounced herself onto her back.

"Holy shit!" a boy called. "Are you okay?"

Brandi groaned as she forced herself upright.

They were all her age. One young man armed himself with a golf club, another had a square-shaped head and a gun gripped with sweaty palms. Lastly, a red-headed girl stood between them, hugging a wooden baseball bat.

Brandi recognized them from around town, but couldn't lay her finger on where. She started toward her bike, but the gun-toting boy beat her to it.

"I got it," she said, and her clipped tongue throbbed so hard that her eyes rolled backward.

The boy stood her bike up and waved her off.

"You were totally flying. It's dangerous out here. You don't know what the hell you're gonna run into."

Brandi sucked on her teeth and squinted her eyes, hesitantly assessing herself.

"Thank you," she whispered, grateful to see herself still in one piece. She gripped the handlebars. "You gotta get the hell out of here. Now."

"No, wait," the guy said, smiling like a moron. "Hold your horses. You're with us now. We'll protect you, okay? Don't be scared."

Brandi's eyes twitched. Her tongue hurt so badly that she couldn't even spit at him.

"Let her go, Brock," the golf club boy said. "She doesn't want our help."

"Let go," Brandi growled through clenched teeth. "Get to Peralta High School. They'll help you."

"Come with us. Why are you trying to run?"

Brandi swore she heard something land a block away. She punched the blockhead in his smiling face, but wasn't strong enough to knock him down. He let go of the bike regardless, gripping his nose.

Thump-thump!

"What the fuck's your problem? I'm trying to help you."

"Run," Brandi said, kicking the motor over. "Get out of here *now.* You're already fucked."

THUMP!

River was behind Brandi.

She could sense it.

Brandi glared into the redhead's emerald eyes and could see a monster's crimson snarl in their reflection. The redhead dropped her baseball bat. Her eyes became the size of golf balls and her grimace widened into a gaping scream.

Brandi stared forward, burned rubber, and turned all her attention onto her muffler's spewing fumes. The girl screamed again, and one of the young men's voices joined in.

Brandi skidded to a stop and turned backward. The square-headed boy, Brock, had been impaled by River's claws. She dragged him by the leg, gripping onto his ankle with her Venus flytrap appendage. She ripped open his belly, spilling steaming guts into the street.

River lifted him by his entrails and flung him aside.

The others had split up and ran in different directions. The young man was heading toward Peralta. Brandi hoped he'd make it. She glared up at the red and purple sky as it swirled, curling like the lips of grinning faces, taunting her.

Okay, fine, I'll help. But if this starts looking bad, fuck River and fuck them. I'm getting out of here.

"Pokey, this really fucking sucks."

Just as the thought crossed Brandi's mind, River leapt into the air, nearly landing on the young girl. She let out a demonic chuckle and one of her vectors wrapped itself around the girl's ankle. The redhead screamed through her clenched teeth, frantically clawing at the sidewalk, leaving a trail of bloody fingernails behind her.

Fuck, fuck, fuck! Just cause we're better on our own, Pokey, doesn't mean I shouldn't help. Right? Right?!

Brandi babied the Yamaha's gas until she got within firing distance. She forced her eyes open and barely took aim before firing into River's pale back. A deep red dotted line appeared on her spine and leaked globs of thick blood.

"Can you still sing soprano, bitch?!" Brandi shouted.

River's jaw sloshed downward, splitting her skin and revealing curling teeth behind bruising flesh. Fumes bellowed from her like fire smoke.

"Let her go. You want me, right?"

River tilted her bloating head and lifted the redhead so that she glared into her eyes. The young lady's chest rose and fell like a machine.

River pulled her arm back like a lever, and the girl screamed for a split second before her face slammed into the asphalt.

Brandi's legs twitched. She wanted to run, but froze.

River lifted her again and the girl spat out a pair of splintered teeth. Her lips had both burst, but her green eyes vacantly stared forward.

River slung the girl once more, followed by slapping hamburger meat and a spray of ruby blood.

"Stop!" Brandi shouted.

River grinned. She lifted her victim—her face had become one swollen blue and black mess. She'd become entirely unrecognizable, except for her chest, pumping like a piston or a frightened rodent's heartbeat.

"I'd say this isn't like you," Brandi spat and lifted her gun. "But deep down inside, you were always a cruel bitch."

Brandi put the poor girl out of her misery with a single shot. River's jowls lowered in a disappointed frown. She tossed her victim away and let out a powerful roar. Vile miasma permeated, making Brandi's head swim.

"You wanna know something else?" Brandi spat, and booted her kickstand. "I woulda only got with you for your money!"

Fighting through the dizziness, she opened the throttle, and the bike popped into action.

Thump-thump-thump-thump!

River was gaining on her a little with each massive bound. Brandi's heart slammed in her chest. She tasted blood and her shoulder throbbed with a horrible, life-ruining pain. A pressure landed around her waist, pressing Pokey hard into her breast. Her bike flew out from under her and bounced off a lightpost. The motor still ran and the exhaust spat out black fumes.

"Fuck, Pokey," she hissed. "I knew it was gonna get us caught. I'm sorry."

River had her tentacles around her. She turned Brandi around and roared into her face. Sour green mucus covered her all over and clung to her scalp.

"All that talk," River said, her voice buried beneath a hundred voices of irate older men and women. "Now you're with me. You think that I will kill you fast or slow, Brandi-Lynn?"

"You didn't think I talked all that shit without knowing that I might get caught? Kill me, eat shit. You bitch."

"I won't. I'll take you and keep you like a pet in a cage." Her grip grew tighter around Brandi's hips. Pokey squished flat against her and her assault rifle dug into her ribs.

"I'll dress you every day. When I let you wear clothes, that is. On some occasions, maybe I'll even let you sleep indoors. Not when it rains, never when it rains."

River's leverage pulled the trigger of Brandi's assault rifle, firing a burst into her own malformed skull. Half of her features were blown to pieces, pelting Brandi with chunks of gore and bone. River let her go and erupted in a scream.

Brandi had lost her earplugs in the chaos, and all noise was replaced with a deafening ringing.

She only knew the motorcycle hadn't died through feeling its reverberating. She picked it up off the ground and allowed herself just a brief glance back at River's melting body.

Black spines shot tiny fingers from her wounded face, rapidly fixing itself. Her cobalt searchlight eyes shined onto Brandi. She moved forward, fighting for every thin breath. She felt the ground beneath her shaking, *thump-thump, thump-thump,* but didn't glance back again.

She drove, losing focus, her vision blurring. Her hearing returned with skewering pain. River's heaving gasps were just inches away.

She whiffed something rotten, not River's breath, but stinky, like eggs.

"Almost there, Pokey. Finally almost fucking there."

She passed the cross streets of Karling Drive and Applewood Lane and turned hard. She heard River go rolling past her and scraping the street to catch up. Brandi drove to the end of the truck yard and turned around.

"I changed my mind. This was really stupid."

Brandi regretfully ditched the bike and slid her way under the nearest eighteen-wheeler. She aimed her rifle and held her breath. As soon as she saw River's pale flesh, she fired a burst over her head and into the case of propane tanks.

Maybe I'm a ghost, and if I shut up and accept that, I can do anything.

The semi she hid under lifted onto one side from the detonation's force. It landed back down and the suspension creaked.

Brandi closed her eyes and covered her face. The heat was too intense. The air was sucked from her lungs. Her eyebrows felt like they'd been burnt off, but the rest of her skin was protected by her jacket and the semi-truck.

The fire outside roared and crackled. Brandi's vision settled on the dancing flames. She crawled out from the truck and reached a hand over her heart, but settled on Pokey's head instead.

They made it.

Intense heat made it feel like she was trapped in a brick stove. Every direction she looked, there was nothing but wall-to-wall flames. She saw no escape, marching her way to the center of Pat's Superior Propane and smelling rain. Then, sulfur.

She glared at where the stench poured from and watched a pile of gray vomit boil and pop.

A silver claw emerged from the goo, and next a shriveled arm. Inch by inch, River pulled herself out from the fluids, naked and shivering. Her burnt ocean eyes met Brandi's.

Brandi lifted her rifle and unloaded, blowing River's face to pieces, shooting her arms off, and burying bullets into her chest. Brandi's teeth rattled from the recoil, dripping blood from her mangled tongue to the back of her throat. River's form took shape quicker than she could destroy it. Finally she was out of ammo and glared at River down the sights of her empty gun.

River's face contorted until she looked like a mock resemblance of her older self.

"I've tried," she gurgled. "I tried enticing you with everything I had. But monsters never die, Brandi. The longer you stay alive, the more you risk being eaten. You could've left, Brandi. Turned your back, ran away. You can't count on anyone, they can't count on you. It was a mistake to try. Never again, Brandi-Lynn."

"Shut up," Brandi said. "I'm sick of you. I've been sick of you for so fucking long now."

"Then be sick forever," she hissed. "I've finally decided what's best for you, Brandi-Lynn. I can't say goodbye to you. So we'll be together after I eat you. Together. You, me, the gods, forever."

Chapter 23

Preston Academy's halls were colored like rust and sticky to the touch. Conan's gaze darted from classroom windows to unrecognizable territories. He remained alert despite zero resistance, finding the powdery orange residue tainting everything he passed.

It doesn't matter if I survive this. As long as I try. Right, Dad?

He kept his gun at the ready, leading with the barrel every time he turned into a corridor. He hadn't any idea where he was going. After walking a ways, hot torrents of air bellowed out from the halls.

He followed their direction.

The odor was vomit, and the deeper into Preston's bowels he traveled, the more damp the copper specks became, clinging to his sleeves and weighing down the air. Whenever he found himself lost, he'd wait for another gust, and the sound of a woman's sigh.

He made his way into the theater and found Misty Devereux coiled atop the stage.

She'd taken the shape of a gargantuan snake, so long that her corkscrewed bulk stacked atop itself and filled the entire hall. She rested atop the summit of her porous, scaly mass. Her eyes were closed, and she inhaled a massive breath, as if snoring, and lifted her entirety before yawning a long breathy sigh.

Her scales lifted like flaps and showed clusters of holes tightly weaved under her protective layering. Orange particles puffed from the many orifices, tickling Conan's tongue with the foul nectar of rotting fruit.

Bury your heart in mine
I promise, the world won't stop
But you may rest without failure
It's our only duty to accept this.
Eternal and forever.

Adrenaline pumped in tempo with his beating heart. Conan took a quiet step toward her, closing the distance. His hand went down to the blade at his side, grazing its leather hilt with his knuckles, making sure it was still there. Misty stirred, and he hesitated.

"Do you remember me?" he asked.

Misty's eyes wetly peeled open, and she exhaled—tightened her coils, shrinking herself to his eye level. The remnants of her tattered blouse were all that remained of her clothes, covering her breast as she leaned in close.

"Do you mean this life or another?" she asked.

"A different one," Conan said, nodding. "I'm sorry for being so vague."

"Yes," she said, and her snake body moved rapidly, like a speeding train, and when her scales opened to show the pitted skin beneath, Conan cringed.

"Well, in *this* place, on *this* day? I believe you've come here to kill me." She rolled her eyes and plopped her chin on her open palm, gazing down at him in boredom.

"It doesn't have to be like that," Conan said, and coughed into his fist. "I'm trying to find another way. Snow never wanted violence. She never wanted any of you hurt, not even your mother."

Misty laughed, a suppressed chortle that bellied out from deep inside her massive body, as if she was kept buried within the beast, and used her own image as a mouthpiece.

"That's funny. Is that why she liked you, because you're funny?"

"No," Conan said, shaking his head.

Misty slithered behind him. She made a sudden movement, then lunged at him from his blind side. Her scales rattled like metal chains—he raised his hands and flinched backward.

"The more I think about it," Conan said. He waited to be sure Misty wouldn't strike. "I'm not even sure if she loved me."

"Oh? I know *that* feeling," Misty said, gating him in with her encircling body. She lay atop herself, placing both her hands down like pillows and resting her chin on them.

"She may have," Conan said. "When this first started, or perhaps she was even just trying to use me back then. There's no way to tell. She'd done this an impossible amount of times. It had to have changed her. But one thing that didn't change was how much she loved you."

"What are you lying about now?" Misty hissed, rising up like a cobra.

Her eyes showed all the violence that Brandi and Snow had both tried to pull him away from.

"Brandi-Lynn, she put you up to this, correct? What are you even doing here? Why didn't you run? What's the point? What are you trying to convince me of?"

"She did not," he replied, and made strong eye contact. "Every time I make a decision, everyone thinks Brandi put me up to it. I guess I really have always been dense. No. It's only me."

Biting his lip had an effect on her. She stretched out her entire body, curling more than a human vertebra would allow and purring like a cat. Her elongated form spread out like a cushion, and she stretched herself out, propping her head up on her arm.

"Snow wouldn't have used you," Misty said, with a grin tugging at the corner of her mouth. "She wanted out, and it's your fault whatever's happened has happened, because she loved you. Don't sell yourself short."

"Thank you," Conan said, and lowered his head.

"Hahahaha!" Misty laughed and rolled onto her back. Her voice had lost its earlier suppression, and she hit high notes with her giggling as if singing. She placed her hand over her eyes.

"You think that matters? Didn't you hear me? She's dead because *you* took her away and *failed* her. It's your fault Snow and River died." She glared at him between her parted fingers. "It's your fault."

Her body expanded and exhaled like a giant lung. The snake-circle around him bellowed orange spores, dyeing his clothes gold. The rotten honey and plum mulch overloaded his senses. He burst out into a coughing fit—so violent his ribs ached. His vision blurred, and he nearly collapsed, but he fought to keep standing.

"Your mother," he said. "She drew up all your fates. Snow was going to die. River was going to become her *if* she didn't plan on stealing River's body entirely. Then there's you. The fuck up. To help River's appearance—to be a distraction. One day, you'd have to die for her too."

Misty constricted, wrapping Conan in a binding and crushing the air from his lungs.

"Tsk, tsk, tsk," she hissed, arching her back and serpentine tail so that she was looking at him upside down. She caressed his cheek with long fingernails, leaving thin, irritated scratches on his skin.

"Snow sure did like to talk to you about us, didn't she? It's annoying. Between her and River? After falling in love, they would have left me behind. You're exactly like Brandi. You refuse to admit this is all your fault. I don't have that problem. I only have suffering, enough to share."

"You killed your mother," Conan choked out. "You chose now to do it, but you had chances. I get it. You needed to be pushed into becoming a killer."

Misty loosened her grip and glanced at her nails as if they'd been freshly manicured.

Conan inhaled a wheezing gasp, but the spore-filled air was too thick, and his nasal became clogged. He'd been barely able to suck any oxygen at all.

"If you killed her sooner," he whispered, "everyone would have survived."

Misty lifted his chin and sucked her teeth at him. He fought the urge to run—to seek any kind of escape. The world grew dark; dust had caked the inside of his mouth and numbed him, too much had built up and his breaths all became wheezes. Darkness surrounded him.

To breathe life into the both of us
I lost my grandeur on the way
But I'll be your remedy
Only if we never forget each other.

Misty leaned in and open-mouth kissed him. She inhaled, and it felt like an industrial vacuum was trying to suck him into herself. As she came away, he gasped painfully, but was able to breathe again.

He pressed his fingers to his mouth, doing a double take to Misty's lips.

"Now I kinda get it. At first I thought it was because you're handsome. It's not, though. Far from it. There really is something about you. You're right too. I could have ended her much sooner. But I didn't. All that remains is to share my feelings of hate, my suffering, because you made her give up."

Conan hadn't noticed that he'd been leaning against Misty's chest. She had cradled him with her snake body. He checked to be sure he still had his blade and pressed his palm against his heart.

"It's hard, Misty, I know, but accept that it's over. She's gone. You can move on by yourself. It doesn't mean that it will stop the hurt, but it's all there is."

"Why talk in riddles? Why here?" Misty said, running her fingers through both sides of her hair.

"She could have turned back time, gone back and begun anew. Again and again. You didn't know her power. She'd done it already a hundred, maybe thousands of times."

"Of course I know that, moron. She was *my* sister." Misty frowned. "I'm still waiting for her to flip the switch here—if she didn't already leave us behind. The only way for our malice to end is her escaping from it. She was created to be thrown away and she must defeat her destiny. You said it. Snow was one in a million; River was her favorite, and much like yourself, I never stood a chance."

We are tragedy in tandem
And have allowed ourselves
To be ingested by anguish.

"You knew? The entire time?"

"Of course. Memories mix and slowly return as the days pass. If she escaped—if she did—if *you* only helped her—"

"Misty, if you know that," he said, gliding his fingernails over her scales, clicking against each one like a jingling coin. "Then we've been here before. Think about how we can fix this. No one thought you were capable. Now look at your position. Move away from your family. They were never good for you. Obsession isn't good, not for either of us."

"The only thing I hated more than doing what my mother said is when other people try to tell me what to do. Am I just a brainless fucking idiot? It's like you don't think at all. You can't fix everything. Some things are just too broken."

As Misty's grating tone sent cold water down his spine, Conan watched her lips purse. She glared at him and fondled her tattered clothes. He closed in, and she raised her eyebrows, as if to threaten him.

Conan stopped in his tracks, and she lowered her gaze, either trying to look appealing, menacing, or both. Her hand glided over her navel and she caressed her own cheek with a blushing grin.

As soon as she blinked, Conan yanked the knife from its duct tape scabbard and plummeted its tip into the side of her armor—dragging it as far down her flesh as he could. Rusty spores burst into his face, burning like flames.

Misty screamed a primitive roar. The black death spread rapidly from her wound, and she opened her mouth, stretching it to alligator proportions. Her teeth became flat like blades and she snapped like two blocks of wood clapping against each other, severing the base of her tail.

Conan did what his brain screamed. He charged. Before he was close enough, one of the spore-spraying apertures burst and shot out a small replica of Misty. His reflexes were quick, and he moved the dagger into a position where it defensively stabbed the clone's throat. As he did, another Misty clone shot out from her decaying corpse and bit into his shoulder.

It shook back and forth like a dog and sawed through his arm. He stabbed it once between the eyes, dropping it dead with a wet plop.

"That fucking knife. When did you—" Misty hissed, pulling herself out of the giant mass of dying snake flesh. Her waist was completely severed, and from her wide hips a new, thinner tail sprouted, making her look like a Medusa.

Misty cried out, and a third clone shot out from the mass of blackened scales. This one aimed at Conan's hand and bit it off at the wrist. It swallowed the killing blade down, dying in the process. Conan only had time to wince. He reached down with his left hand and Misty lunged at him, taking him down to the ground. She wrapped her gorgon tail around him and squeezed, lifting her chin so his bulging eyes stared into hers.

"Still fighting. That's what she saw in you, whatever this weird angst is, and that stupid thin mustache. Gazing beyond that, I see a young man who's yet to give up. No matter how tortured you find yourself. That's it then. Snowy wouldn't want me to kill you. She wouldn't. Yes, good. I'll keep you. I'll keep you forever. We'll make a daughter of my own. How's that sound? Like a life worth living, just as you suggested."

Hey, Dad, I get it now. You really can't help everyone, right? Troubled people will drag you down and put your life at risk beside theirs. Right?

"No," he choked out. "I already told you, nothing you do is going to make it any better. There isn't a special place or time. Not fate, not destiny. They'll move on without us. That's what she taught me. Friends, family, lovers, everyone."

Misty loosened her grip on him, but he still couldn't breathe. The spores had once more caked themselves deep in his throat. He couldn't speak; he was choking, dying. He looked up at her, panicked, clutching his throat. Despite that, his mind went clear.

Dad, Snow, looks like I failed. Sorry, but at least I'll be able to see you soon.

Misty lifted his chin and kissed him. She tasted like her sister, like honey and lilies, like running away, like the past.

Even after she'd sucked the mass clinging to his lungs, she held him there. He couldn't help but see Snow in her eyes.

"There's nothing we can do about it," he said. "If we dwell on eternity, eternity will consume us. When it's over, we have to accept it. It may never stop hurting, but we have to—we have to accept it. They're gone forever. That's it. No coming back, no second chances. Accept it and do better. Whatever that means wherever; however, that is. Spend time together and love every moment. They'll all leave us. Sometimes, in ways more horrible than we could've ever imagined. Hold onto their memories without regret or pain. Look at what pain's done for us. Let's let them go, together."

Misty moved her tail away and glanced down at Conan's severed hand. Her breath was hot against his lips.

She smiled, and as a tear fell from her eye, Conan's heart skipped a beat.

The few times he'd really seen Misty, she came off as nothing but seductive. Staring into her rich blue eyes now, was like watching the reflection of moonlight in a deep blue sea. He couldn't understand why he had never noticed before. Resentment crept above all his mixed emotions. Despite what he had preached, he regretted never speaking with her until now.

"I don't want to go alone," she whispered into his lips. Her words were small, but as supple as a perfect falsetto. Miniscule in volume, but carrying the weight of a falling mountain. It made his stomach flutter, and the past rushed up like flames from the pits of hell.

The way she spoke reminded him of the beginning, before Snow, back to his very first love.

Music.

Conan reached down and picked up the ritual blade with his decaying hand. Sticky to the touch, he replaced it in its scabbard.

"Will you stay with me?" she asked.

"I will," he said. He reached into his back pocket and chuckled, pulling out a battered package of American Spirit cigarettes. "I kept one hidden from Brandi. Just in case I'd have the chance for it."

He lit it, and as he inhaled the stale smoke, odorous like a re-burn, clogged by the rotten plum of the terracotta spores, and distracted by the honey and lilies still glued on his lips. He passed the cigarette to Misty. She took a small inhale, but her tantalizing glare never left him.

"Would you kiss me?" she asked, pulling the cigarette away from her lips. "Just one time, and mean it, please. The same way... Like you would kiss her?"

Conan nearly collapsed onto her. He pressed his lips to hers and drank her in. He kissed her again and again, biting her lip gently and tickling the tip of her tongue with his own. She clenched his back tightly, cutting into his flesh with her razor nails, embracing him deeper. Conan removed the killing blade and gently pressed it into the back of her heart.

We are tragedy in tandem
And have allowed ourselves
To be ingested by anguish.

You can break my ribs
To breathe life into the both of us

I lost my grandeur on the way
But I'll be your remedy
Only if we never forget each other.

Our hearts cease to beat in unison
And we finally stop grieving
We were not built to walk amongst the living
I consent to becoming your memorial.

Bury your heart in mine
I promise, the world won't stop
Bury your heart in mine
It's our duty to accept this.
Bury your heart in mine
So you may rest without failure
Eternal and forever.

***

"BRANDI-LYNN!" River screamed, her outstretched arm melting like candle wax, dripping into the puddles of herself. *"HELP ME!"* she cried as her legs became too liquefied for standing.

Her searchlight eyes shot out golden light, then flames, exploding out of her orifices like snakes of electricity. River collapsed into a smoldering pile of gunk, black fumes dumped from the gore, filling the propane shop with the frightful stench of a campfire.

The purple sky above twisted and turned. Thunder crackled and rolling lightning crept within the dark clouds. Twirling maelstroms opened in the storm's heart, consuming themselves and exploding into dawn's first light.

A gust of cold, almost freezing wind cut into Brandi and chilled her to the bone. The cherry sunrise doused the roaring flames from the propane plant, and River's remains had completely disappeared.

I'm alive—I'm actually alive?

Brandi lifted Pokey out of her jacket and dusted him off. She glanced at the clumps of dried blood on his sides and sniffed back tears.

"He did it, Pokey," she said with a smile. Brandi zipped him back into her jacket and walked over to her charred dirt bike. It didn't start on the first click, or the second. She winced and gave it a hopeful third try, shaking her head and chuckling as it fired up.

"You really are my good luck charm." She laughed and left the debris behind herself.

The streets were barren and quiet, too quiet.

Through the early morning mist, she didn't see a single survivor, nor any monsters. Corpses strewn about the streets had disappeared. The only remnant left behind were abandoned vehicles. The town had become hollow, a ghost. After realizing that she would not find any other survivors, she rode up Bakery Hill and smelled the sweet flowers on the morning breeze.

Snow's scent.

"Should we look for him, Pokey?" she said and pulled her blood-stained ivory elephant free. "I don't think—I don't think we should."

As she said the words, the sunrise of the fifth day broke the horizon and burning yellow light gave way to blue skies.

Finally, the blue sky said in its ever-present condescending tone and yawned. *You've come to terms with being alone?*

"Yeah," Brandi said. "With crying too. Whatever, I've accepted it. That's the only way I'll ever love again anyway. I'll cry. I'll cry for them all today, but I'll never shed a tear for them, for this town, for Kylie, Snow, or Conan. Never again."

My, oh my. How cold of you, girl.

"You didn't let me finish," Brandi said. "I still have to face tomorrow. This won't be my last struggle. That's guaranteed. Despite keeping my head low, others might still need my help. That being said, not another tear. I won't. But I swear, I'll be goddamned, goddamned if I ever forget *any* of them. For the rest of my life, I promise."

Goodbye, Brandi-Lynn, the sky said, actually sounding sad to see her turn away.

"Goodbye—and hey." Brandi dusted her hands off and buried them in her pockets. "That goes for you too. I don't care where you're heading next, or who you're going to bother with that shitty attitude. Remember me too. Okay?"

end

Acknowledgments

I would like to thank my wife, Alyssa Brandt, for her unwavering support, patience, and encouragement throughout this journey. Without her, this book would not exist.

I am also deeply grateful to my managing editor, Scarlett R. Algee, for discovering my work, believing in this story, and guiding it to publication. Her insight and dedication have been invaluable.

About the Author

Ryan Brandt writes psychological horror in which fractured identities, unstable realities, and dreamlike violence blur the boundaries between the inner mind and the waking world. His short work has appeared in *Bleed Error Magazine*, *Dark Void*, the *Rise* anthology, *W is for Witchcraft (A to Z of Horror)*, and on *The NoSleep Podcast*. Influenced by David Lynch and other architects of the uncanny, Brandt crafts visceral, hallucinatory narratives where reality bends, bodies shift, and terror becomes a mirror of one's self.

www.ingramcontent.com/pod-product-compliance
Lightning Source LLC
LaVergne TN
LVHW091138080826
845145LV00008B/2197

* 9 7 8 1 6 8 5 1 0 1 7 8 7 *